Run!

Hold On! Season 3

PETER DARLEY

RUN!—HOLD ON! SEASON 3

Copyright©2015

PETER DARLEY

www.peterdarley.com

Cover Design by Peter Darley and Harris Channing.

Other Titles in the Series:

For Patricia

Your love, kindness, and unwavering support, against overwhelming odds, trials and tribulations, enabled me to bring the completed trilogy to my readers, while all the time teaching me the true meaning of the words—Hold On!

Prologue

Dr. Frederick DeSouza gingerly entered a neon-lit laboratory, nervously passing the monitor screens. He stepped through a door at the far end in anticipation of what would be revealed within the next hour.

It was a unique moment in his career as a neuro-biological scientist, a career that, hitherto, had come to an end. He'd amassed his fortune and settled comfortably into a life of retirement. That was, until the day he received a visit from Andrew Wilmot, the director of an anti-terrorist, Homeland Security division known as SDT, asking him to come out of retirement.

But what had been expected of him had been an astonishing demand. His specialist skill as a memory revisionist had never been called upon before to *undo* a revision.

The irony struck him as he considered the circumstances. Almost four years earlier, he'd been asked by his late associate, Senator Garrison Treadwell, to revise the memories and personality of a particularly volatile warrior named Brandon Drake. It had been an operation to make the young soldier more manageable, while maintaining his inherent skills, intellect, and extraordinary talents.

However, the experiment led to the creation of a persona who had divided the American people. Drake became a hero; a selfless rescuer of the innocent—women and children alike—as he committed himself to thwarting

1

corruption in government, and tyrants wherever he found them. He'd also leveled a media attack against Treadwell.

Accompanied by his lover, Belinda Reese, a woman whose life he'd saved during a terrorist attack instigated at Treadwell's behest, Drake became a fugitive. He'd abandoned his post with the Eighty-Second Airborne Division and chosen the path of a loner.

Now, the world believed he was dead, blown to smithereens in a cataclysmic explosion. But it wasn't so. He'd survived by virtue of incredibly sophisticated armor and hardware.

Six weeks had passed since the explosion. DeSouza had been instructed to suppress all of Drake's memories since his last revision and restore him to his original persona—a malevolent combatant known as *The Scorpion*. Persistently, he questioned why Wilmot would have wanted him to do such a thing, but he didn't voice it. Faith in the system, a touch of hubris and, in a moment of honesty, his payment for services rendered, had silenced him.

Nevertheless, a touch of guilt gnawed at him. He had no idea what he was about to awaken, and the thought of the possibilities chilled him.

He turned the corner and entered a room with a hospital-style bed in the corner. Brandon Drake lay comatose upon it. His wounds from the crash had required the six weeks of induced oblivion to heal. DeSouza was aware that when Drake came around again, he wouldn't be aware of the crash, or of the four years preceding it. It struck him that he'd been instrumental in the destiny of a

2

man to whom he had never even spoken. An amnesia-stricken, unconscious soul is all he'd ever known.

He watched as Drake's eyeballs moved rapidly beneath his eyelids, indicating the dream state. "Where are you, my boy?" he murmured. "What do you remember?"

One

Yesterday

FOB Thorne, Helmand Province, Afghanistan

September 4th, 2012

Sergeant Brandon Drake dragged a senseless, blindfolded Afghan prisoner into a hangar through a crowd of twelve soldiers. The captive's wrists bound behind him made any possibility of effective resistance impossible.

The hangar conveyed the aura of dereliction, permeated by the aroma of desert musk. Six years had passed since US forces had occupied Thorne, an obscure, military, forward operating base. Its original usage had endured for twelve months, between 2005 and 2006, having been set up as a temporary back-up to accommodate a high number of troops. They'd returned to it only for this one, clandestine operation.

The corners of Drake's mouth widened slightly as he gloated with the knowledge that only he knew the true nature of the mission.

Without warning, he struck his prisoner in the stomach. The captive instantly crumpled to the floor in agony, gasping for air. Drake unbound the man's wrists and spun him around. He grasped a length of rope from the floor and hurled it across an overhanging rafter. After loosening the prisoner's bindings, he bound his wrists in front of him and pulled the rope taut, causing the Afghan's arms to reach up toward the beam. He continued to stretch the rope until his prey's feet almost left the ground. The prisoner cried out with the pain of his arms becoming dislocated from their shoulder sockets.

"All right, Drake. That's enough!"

Drake turned to see his commanding officer, Colonel Darren Woodroffe, standing at the front of the gathering. Amidst the small parade of tan, gray, and green camouflage combat uniforms was a palpable air of unease.

Drake focused his cold, predatory gaze onto the colonel's. Confidence filled his heart. He knew Woodroffe feared him. The colonel's twin black eyes were Drake's handiwork, an offense for which he'd already spent two days in the hole. However, the fact that he'd been summoned away from his confinement so quickly demonstrated the power he now had, unbeknownst to any other.

"We followed the trail to where they were holed up in Lashkar Gar, but they'd moved on," Drake said. "This asshole was the only one left, so he's the only one who can tell us where the hell they are, *sir*." The last word came out with sarcastic, condescending contempt.

Woodroffe came closer to him with a look that showed his determination to maintain his authority. "You're going back to the hole as soon we return to Bragg, Drake. So unless you want your confinement period doubled, I suggest you show respect for a commanding officer. Are we clear?"

"Oh, yes, *sir*."

Woodroffe was about to respond when he was cut off by a shrill female voice coming from the rear of the hangar. He turned abruptly as Private Rachel Martoni entered. Of slight build, and a mere five feet, five inches tall, her golden blonde hair was barely visible from beneath her helmet.

"Colonel," she said, and saluted.

"Yes, Private. What is it?"

"A message came through from Bragg. General Grant wants an update on the operation."

Woodroffe brushed his moustache with his fingers and looked down pensively. Finally, he turned back to Drake and gestured to the captive. "Get what you can out of that clown." With that, he turned and exited the hangar.

Drake's eyes became maniacal, and he could see the men in the room shuddering. Seven of the soldiers, including Private Martoni, followed Woodroffe outside.

Sergeant David Spicer stepped forward from among the remaining troops. A striking, dark-haired soldier of twenty-six, his clean, wholesome features epitomized the motto of the Eighty-Second Airborne Division—*All American*. Undoubtedly fearful, he dared to walk through his reservations. "Hey, come on, Scorp," he said, invoking Drake's nickname—The Scorpion. "Let's not do something hasty. Wait until Woodroffe gets back."

Drake laughed cruelly. "You heard the man. I'm supposed to get out of him what he knows. That's why we're here, Spicer." Prowling around his colleague as a cat would stalk a mouse, he savored Spicer's fears. "Or, would you like us to continue our poker game?"

"S-Scorp, I'm already in over my head. I still owe you five hundred, bro."

Drake positioned his nose a millimeter away from Spicer's. "I'm not your 'bro', Spicer. We had a deal. You were gonna pay me as soon as I got out of the hole." He paused, intimidating David, relishing every moment. "Well, I'm out of the hole."

"Y-yeah, but Scorp, you were released prematurely. I didn't have time to get the money together."

"That's not my problem." Drake removed his helmet to reveal his short-cropped hair. His chiseled features seemed granite-like as he ground his teeth causing his jaw muscles to become more prominent.

David trembled. Drake held his gaze for a moment, and then simply walked out onto the grounds of the small base.

Drake's attention fell upon the unit's two Black Hawk helicopters. *Soon, I'll be out.*

The one-hundred-ten degree heat was oppressive, and the dusk wasn't doing anything to cool it down. His combat uniform and armor added to the intensity of the desert temperature.

He looked around to ensure he was alone, lit a cigarette, and made his way along the side of the hangar. He quickly found a secluded gap between the adjacent living quarters and the sergeant's mess, and concealed himself in the shadows.

He reached into his pocket and took out a sophisticated-looking cell phone. After flicking it open, he selected his contact. It was answered after one ring. "It's me," he said.

"Where are you, Drake?" a stern voice said through the receiver. "I was expecting your call two hours ago."

"We ran into a problem. The hideout in Lashkar Gar was abandoned. We captured one remaining member of al Fajr. Are you sure Slamer wasn't sellin' you a line of shit?"

"Not a chance."

"In that case, they cleared out between the time he planted the evidence and the time we arrived. They were on to us."

"Find out what you can from this captured operative, Drake. The president is pulling you boys out of Afghanistan. I need to give him a reason not to."

Drake contemplated the particulars between drags of his cigarette. Al Fajr—*The Dawn*—was nothing. They were a virtually-inactive, fragmented, al Qaeda-Taliban hybrid. However, manufactured evidence that they were planning a strike against the US, and the likelihood of a retaliation following the current operation, was certain to extend the war. It would profit his benefactor's covert arms dealings considerably, and subsequently, himself. "I'll get you what you want," he said darkly.

"Getting you out of the hole was just a sample of what I can do for you, Drake. There's billions of dollars on the line here, and you'll get your cut. Just do this job for me, and I'll take you out of the army. You'll be wealthy beyond your wildest dreams working for me."

Drake screwed up his lips with a combination of ambition and extreme irritation. "All right. But don't think for a minute that you own me, Treadwell. Nobody does."

"Right now, I'm your only lifeline, Drake. Don't screw it up. Now destroy the phone."

"What?"

"It's an experimental sat-scrambler. You can't afford to be discovered with it. Now, destroy the damn thing!" The call ended.

Drake stared at the phone and stubbed out his cigarette in the sand.

Stepping out of the shadows, he froze in his tracks. Private Rachel Martoni was standing with her attention focused squarely in his direction. Subtly, he palmed the sat-scrambler phone away from her field of vision.

"Who . . . who were you talking to, sir?" she said.

"You don't ask me questions. I'm your superior, and *you* answer to *me*." He made his way toward her and towered over her in order to enhance her sense of discomfort. He stroked the tip of his forefinger under her chin, causing her to shudder visibly. "You've got nothing I can't take if I want to, Private."

"I'm not going to sleep with you again, sir."

"Oh, no? You already know all it would take is for me to spread it around that you like girls, and your life would become a living hell." He could see the fear in her eyes, enhanced by her labored breathing.

"That's not true, and you know it. I'm as straight as you are."

He chuckled. "You know that. I know that. But *they* don't know that."

"What difference does it make? 'Don't ask don't tell' is history."

He laughed mockingly. "Are you really that naïve? You honestly think you can change the mindset of an entire battalion overnight?"

9

She eased herself back, clearly desperate to get away from him. "You really are the most despicable person I've ever known, Sergeant Drake. *Sir*."

For an instant, he was impressed by her courage. Knowing she'd slept with him only because she was afraid of him thrilled him enormously. "It's all part of my charm." Slowly, he moved past her, and she hurried out of his way toward the barracks.

Once she was out of sight, he dropped the sat-scrambler phone onto the rocky ground and crushed it with his right heel.

Drake returned to the hangar, instantly silencing the conversations within. He noticed twenty-eight-year-old Sergeant Barry Stockton interrogating the prisoner. The captive's blindfold had been removed, and his shirt was torn open.

"What've you found out?" Drake said.

"We've got his name," Stockton replied.

"You've got his name? You've got his *name*? What is it? Please tell me. The suspense is killin' me, Stockton."

"Haamid Nabi."

Drake forcefully pushed his way through the remaining soldiers. Each man moved to the side to make way for him, heightening his sense of power. Each soldier held Drake's rank or lower, but it made no difference. He had fear on his side and was the only one among them who knew the truth about the mission. The unorthodox nature of the operation, the obscure base, and their separation from all other defense units, created an aura of confusion among them. They acted on obedience to orders, never questioning.

For seven years, the army had been his prison. A string of criminal offenses had led a district court judge to offer him a choice at the age of nineteen: the state penitentiary—or the army. Since that time, his hatred of authority had never wavered.

Regardless, he'd found solace on the battlefield. He was aware his fellow soldiers viewed the matter very differently. He knew they'd been comfortable back in Bragg, only to be summoned to action again. Their lives were a constant cycle of battle, anxiety, drill, and a return to normalcy, which was always rudely interrupted by another call to battle.

But to Drake, war was his playground—an opportunity to vent the one emotion that drove him: *rage*.

Now, he was more powerful than ever. No matter what sanctions the army applied to him, they would be overridden by his new benefactor. He was no longer a soldier. He was an undercover operative for an office of congress. He was untouchable.

However, the continuation of his newfound power was dependent on this mission succeeding, and he wasn't about to permit anything to impair his success.

Approaching the prisoner, he stared him in the eye, feeding off his terror. Perspiration fell from the man's brow as he hyperventilated. "Where are they, Nabi?"

No answer.

Drake came closer. "I said . . . where are they?"

Still no answer.

Drake punched the man in the stomach, and the pain on the captive's face was clear. He fought to catch his breath.

"Now, you sure you don't wanna change your mind?"

Nabi shook his head defiantly.

Drake turned around and scanned the hangar. He saw the troops keeping their distance before noticing a tool box at the far corner of the room. He moved across to it and tore it open. It took mere seconds for him to discover a welding torch, the perfect tool for his task. He took it out, turned back to the prisoner, and flicked the switch. A flame appeared. With a twist of the gas outlet, it turned a terrifying shade of blue. He could sense the heat radiating from it as he came closer to the captive.

"Drake, this isn't the way," he heard Spicer say. "Don't do this. We're not like them."

"We've got to stop him!" Stockton said.

"How? You know what he can do."

"We can't afford to be under an Abu Ghraib inquest, Spicer. We've got to do something."

"I'm gonna get Colonel Woodroffe."

His eyes fixed on the blow torch, Nabi screamed before Drake even touched him. When his torturer was upon him, he closed his eyes, bracing himself for the searing pain.

Drake touched the tip of the blue flame to Nabi's bare chest. The bellow that filled the hangar was barely human. "Where the fuck are they, asshole?"

The chilling scent of burning flesh filled the air. Drake held the torch on Nabi for another two seconds before stopping. "We can keep this up all night, you son of a bitch. Now where are they?"

Senseless, with tears streaming down his cheeks, Nabi's body convulsed feverishly with the overwhelming trauma of the excruciating, burning sting in his chest. His torso was painted crimson, punctuated by a black, gaping hole in his breast, his ribcage exposed to the elements. "P-please. N-no more."

"That's up to you."

Finally, the answer came. "Dashti Margo."

Drake grinned gloatingly. "Specifics, Nabi."

The prisoner's voice was faint and his consciousness seemed to be fading. Drake pressed his ear close to his mouth as he muttered the location.

Nabi slumped in his bonds. Drake turned to the troops with his arms outstretched victoriously. "Mission: accomplished. See how fast you can get answers when you don't fuck around, boys?"

Spicer and Stockton hurried past him to attend to Nabi.

At that moment, Woodroffe re-entered the hangar. "What's going on?"

"I just got the location of al Fajr," Drake said.

"Where?"

Before he could respond, Spicer called across from Nabi's position. "Sir?"

"What is it?"

"I think he's dead, sir."

Woodroffe shifted his gaze from the ghastly sight of Haamid Nabi back to Drake, an ambivalence of satisfaction and disgust apparent in his expression.

Drake shrugged his shoulders. "His ticker must have given out." Without another word, he stepped out of the hangar.

***

Drake sat, fully armored with a parachute strapped to his back, in a Black Hawk. Nine other division members accompanied him, including Colonel Woodroffe. The colonel gazed upon him persistently as they flew across the Dashti Margo desert, the translation of its name lending an ominous note to the mission: *The Desert of Death*.

Drake could never make out Woodroffe's viewpoint of him. He was far more permissive than his position should have demanded. He knew the colonel despised him, but his profound disapproval seemed to be tempered by recognition of Drake's necessity on a battlefield. It was as though he saw him as a necessary evil.

Drake turned to Spicer beside him. "When we bail out, I'll go on ahead. You don't die until you settle up with me. Clear?"

Spicer looked back at him with a contempt that overshadowed his fear. "Go to hell, Drake."

"We're approaching drop zone, gentlemen," pilot Steven Wassell said.

Drake eyeballed Spicer. "We'll settle this later. Nobody talks to me like that."

David swallowed hard. Drake was a martial arts champion, and he knew Spicer's thoughts. He didn't stand a chance against him. Spicer had seen him in action. Drake was certain that, right now, al Fajr must have seemed like the easy option. The sense of power gripped him again.

The bay doors opened and the troops bailed out. Drake was the first.

The canopies flared and nine warriors descended. They looked up in unison at the Black Hawk disappearing from their field of vision.

Gliding onto the blistering, desert terrain, they covered almost twenty miles during their descent. When they landed, they hurriedly discarded their parachutes.

Woodroffe approached Drake. "You sure this is the place?"

Drake pointed to a hill approximately half a mile in the distance. "From what Nabi said, they're holed up in a cave just on the opposite side of that hill."

Woodroffe turned back to the men. "All right, gentlemen. We're heading over to that hill. When we reach the top, survey the location, split up, and surround it. Watch out for hostiles."

The men gripped their machine guns and made their way across the sand. The heat was oppressive. The sun beat down on them, literally baking them inside their combat uniforms. As many times as they'd experienced it, none of them ever got used to it.

But Drake's mind was elsewhere. Great wealth was in his grasp, but he had a concern in the immediacy. He was short on cash, having spent much of his earnings on alcohol, prostitutes, and an array of other indulgences. The $500 Spicer owed him wasn't much, but it would help, and more importantly, it was *his*. At all costs, he knew he had to ensure David was kept out of the line of fire.

The team reached the top of the hill. They saw the encampment outside the cave ahead of them. One bearded man wearing a traditional turban patrolled the exterior with a rifle. However, he quickly disappeared inside the cave.

Woodroffe instructed seven of the men to take up positions around the encampment. Drake and Spicer remained with him at the top of the hill. Once their positions were set, they noted the encampment was still unmanned from the outside.

Drake watched as four soldiers approached the base from each side—and they were closing in rapidly.

Woodroffe turned to Spicer. "Take the entrance, but be subtle. We don't want them getting wise to us prematurely."

"Yes, sir."

Drake darted ahead with unusual urgency, but Woodroffe held him back. "Not yet, Drake. On my mark."

"But—" Drake noticed something flying out of the cave in Spicer's direction. Immediately, he knew it was an incendiary.

Disregarding Woodroffe's order, he sprinted across the sand toward David. "Spicer, look out. Incoming!"

David stopped and turned around. "What?"

"Get out of the way." Within seconds, he was upon Spicer, grappling him to the ground. "Get down, asshole."

"Scorp, what the hell are you—"

Drake turned and saw the grenade had landed no more than ten feet from them. With David shielded behind him, panic gripped him. His instinct was to turn around and shield his face, and then . . .

A kaleidoscope of imagery flashed before his eyes, each vision so fleeting his mind didn't have time to register them. Strange, alien pictures shot past him—hundreds of them, including people he couldn't identify. It all happened within the space of a millisecond. What he was seeing made no sense. Finally, there was only the darkness.

***

Frederick DeSouza stood up from the bedside chair and noticed his patient's dawning consciousness. Fascinated, he watched as the awakening warrior groaned. His eyelids flickered, and then, after six weeks of induced coma, Brandon Drake's eyes finally opened.

Two

Scorpion Rising

With labored breathing, Director Andrew Wilmot and Agent Cynthia Garrett hurried along a neon-lit corridor. The heat on the outside was stifling. Wilmot's blue suit and Garrett's matching administrative blue skirt and jacket contributed to their appreciation of the air conditioning.

Wilmot gripped a black, leather briefcase in one hand and brushed his dampened, light brown fringe with the other. He noticed a distinguished older man approaching them from the far end of the corridor. "Doctor DeSouza," he said. "How is he?"

"Charming, as expected."

"What did he say?"

"His first words after he awoke and saw me were, 'Who the fuck are you?'"

"What does he remember?"

DeSouza smiled with a hint of pride. "The grenade in the Dashti Margo desert is the last thing he recalls. He refused to say anything more until he knew where he was. I thought I'd leave that to you."

"You did the right thing. Does he have any idea what year this is?"

"As far as he's concerned," DeSouza said, "it's October, twenty-twelve, six weeks following the incident in Afghanistan. What are you going to tell him?"

"Exactly that. All clocks and date references in the complex have been removed."

Garrett's cell phone beeped.

"What is it?" Wilmot said.

She looked up from the phone, smiling. "Our friend has just landed."

"OK, you go meet him and brief him on the details. I'll reintroduce myself to Drake and assess his condition."

Garrett nodded and turned back along the corridor.

Wilmot followed DeSouza several more steps ahead until they reached the laboratory door.

As they entered the room, Wilmot was seized with tension and doubt. Would he be able to pull this off? Would Drake suspect anything about the year? Everything depended on the truth being kept from him. What would happen if Drake discovered he'd been duped?

They passed the consoles and the glass shelves filled with drugs and medical apparatus. Turning another corner, they came to a door and stepped inside.

Drake turned his head toward them from his bed. Lethargy was apparent in his eyes, which enhanced Wilmot's sense of safety. He was in no condition to pose a threat.

"W-who are you?" Drake said in a barely-audible, hoarse whisper.

Wilmot glanced at DeSouza momentarily, and then turned back to Drake with a manipulative smile. "I'm Director Andrew Wilmot with SDT."

"What's SDT?"

"It's a special department of Homeland Security, which operates from Langley."

"What happened to me?"

Wilmot came closer to Drake with a reassuring smile. "A few weeks ago, you were in Afghanistan. A grenade detonated in front of you. You've been in a coma ever since. Do you remember very much?"

"Yeah . . . I remember seeing the grenade, but I don't remember it going off."

"No, I guess you wouldn't. You caught a shard of shrapnel in your forehead. There were some concussive injuries to your body, but you've healed up nicely."

Drake opened his mouth to speak again but no sound came out.

"Your throat will be dry, Brandon," DeSouza said. "I'll get you some water."

Drake managed to force a few words. "What happened to . . . the mission?"

Wilmot set his briefcase down and perched himself on the edge of the bed. "Your unit went in and took down al Fajr. A few of its members escaped as we planned, but there was an urgency to get you airlifted out of there. You're lucky to be alive."

DeSouza handed Drake a glass of water, which he drank in one, unbroken gulp. He then turned back to Wilmot. "What's going to happen to me?"

"I don't want you to worry about anything. You're safe. You're out of the army, and your cover is ironclad."

Drake looked at him with suspicion. "What do you know?"

"Everything."

"Like what?"

The director grinned. "All right, I'm going to say one thing to you, and then you'll know that we're on the same team."

"What?"

"Operation: Nemesis."

Drake's eyes widened as he attempted to perch himself up. "How the hell do you know about Operation: Nemesis?"

"Because I'm in charge of it now. In case you're wondering, the al Fajr project was a failure. The escapees from the desert camp haven't initiated any retaliation, so we've changed our approach."

"Where's Treadwell."

Wilmot shook his head gravely. "The senator is dead. He was killed in a helicopter crash while you were under."

Drake sank back down with a look that suggested his golden opportunity had died along with Treadwell.

"You're going to be fine," Wilmot said. "The nature of the operation has changed, but you're still a part of it. You'll need some time to get yourself back to full strength, and then I have a few projects I'd like you to work on."

"What projects?"

"All in good time." Wilmot picked up the briefcase, placed it on an adjacent desk, and clicked it open. "This is just for starters." He opened it up to reveal neatly-arranged piles of crisp, new, $100 bills. "How does fifty thousand sound?"

Drake's hungry gaze didn't move from the money, as though the sight of it had miraculously revived him from his weariness.

Wilmot closed the case again and locked it up. "You need your rest. Soon we'll get to work on your therapy. You'll have acquired some muscular atrophy due to your period of inactivity."

"Where am I, Wilmot?" Drake said, his abrasive manner rapidly returning. "What the hell is this place?"

"You're in a clandestine facility in the Mojave Desert. Trust me, you're going to be fine. I've spared no expense to make sure you get the best possible care and everything you need to get back on your feet."

The door opened again and Garrett stepped inside. Wilmot noticed Drake's predatory eyes upon her. She smiled at him, seductively.

Everything is going according to plan. "This is my assistant, Agent Cynthia Garrett," Wilmot said. "You'll be working with her closely, and she will be in charge of your debriefing."

"Can't wait." Drake's throaty voice seemed to enhance his shameless, philandering nature.

"Director, our guest is here," Garrett said.

Drake eased himself up again. "What guest?"

Wilmot walked across and opened the door. "An old colleague of yours. The one who's going to help you get back into shape."

A man who literally filled the doorway entered. His hardened features were made all the more chilling by his shaven head and a deep scar trailing along his right cheek. His cold eyes and twenty-two inch biceps completed the terrifying sight of a destructive force of nature. He looked Drake in the eye but didn't smile. "How're you doin', Scorp?"

Wilmot and Garrett glanced at one another with calculating knowingness. The care and support, the promise of wealth, and the beautiful woman all combined to procure the patient's confidence, enthusiasm, and cooperation.

Now, a familiar face that would, in no way, be sympathetic to official authority, would seal the deal.

Drake fed his elbows into the bed and forced himself to rise as he beheld his visitor. "Slamer?"

Three

New Beginnings

Belinda Reese gazed out a window in her room at the Faraday Ranch's guest house, across sprawling acres of land. The smaller property, one hundred yards behind the main mansion, offered a spectacular view of fields basking in the blistering summer sun for as far as the eye could see. She'd returned from her now-routine, two-hour afternoon stroll around the grounds. Her life was so different now.

Following the death of her lover, Brandon Drake, her sadness and sense of isolation had led to depression and the need to find solace with her new family. At approximately eight weeks pregnant, she needed a support structure more than anything.

Relocating from Denver to Fort Worth, Texas, had required no persuading. She needed Tyler and his father. More than that, she needed her new best friend, Brandon and Tyler's sister, Emily.

Although she was a wealthy woman in her own right, Belinda's money didn't even come close to the billions to which the Faradays were privy. However, the $1.14 million she'd inherited by default from Brandon had grown to $1.63 million in a Swiss investment account since his death. She would not be finding herself wanting financially any time soon. This was truly her new beginning.

But it was Emily who had helped her through her grief the most. Having an escaped nun and human trafficking survivor as a live-in sister, had given her a sense of purpose. Belinda's own past history of abuse at the hands of the Catholic Church, and Emily's disillusionment with her past vocation, had given them a degree of common ground. It also thrilled Belinda that she had the opportunity to introduce such a formerly-oppressed, warm and gentle soul to a world of freedom. Emily could come and go as she pleased, and it had become Belinda's mission to help her *feel* that freedom in her heart. Emily still had far to go. It wasn't only the convent she had to put behind her, but the horrors she'd experienced under the captivity of the Sapphire organization. Even the most elementary of life's freedoms seemed alien to Emily. She still felt the need to ask permission to make the slightest of moves.

Belinda heard the turn of the key in the door. "I'm in here, Em."

The usual, virtually-silent footsteps came closer, marked only by the slightest shoe clicks across the kitchen's marble flooring.

Belinda smiled as Emily entered the room. Emily's head was bowed in typical, submissive fashion. Her wavy hair tied back into a bun, and no makeup whatsoever, demonstrated a clear resistance to worldliness. However, Belinda had persuaded her to start wearing jeans as opposed to long, plain skirts.

Emily looked up finally. Every time Belinda laid eyes on her, she was taken aback by how much she looked like

Brandon. It seemed so contrary to see that particular face—the face of a formidable warrior—on one so timid.

"So, how'd it go today?" Belinda said.

"It was good."

"Meet any good-looking guys." Belinda raised her eyebrows in a faux-display of slyness.

Emily looked up, blushing. "Of course not. It's a homeless shelter."

"Hey, you never know. A guy doesn't need a roof over his head to be hot."

Emily giggled.

"Now, that's more like it. Want a glass of wine?"

"Oh, I don't think I should, really."

Without a word, Belinda walked past her and into the kitchen. After taking a bottle of Chardonnay out of the refrigerator, she took two glasses from one of the cupboards and poured wine into the first glass. Then she remembered she was pregnant. She put the bottle down, opened up the refrigerator, and took out a bottle of soda.

She re-entered her room and handed Emily the glass of wine. "Live, for once." she said with mock sternness.

Emily looked uncertain, but took the glass.

There was a knock at the front door.

"I'll get it." Belinda walked out of the bedroom and approached the front door. Upon opening it, she smiled at the powerful presence that stood before her. "Hi, Charlton. Come on in."

"Thank you, Belinda. Dinner will be served at six-thirty, as usual," Charlton Faraday said in a deep, Texas accent. He followed her into the bedroom, removed his Stetson, and held himself still for a moment. He looked at the two women with a warm smile that was visible through his thick, white beard. "Hi, Emily. How are you?"

"I'm fine thank you, Mr. Faraday," Emily said.

"Emily, would you stop with that 'Mr. Faraday' stuff. Just Charlton is fine."

"I-I'm sorry. You have been so kind to me. I can't tell you how much I appreciate it."

He approached her and held her gently by the shoulders. "It's *me* who should be thanking *you*."

"Why's that?"

"Just having you ladies here is like having a family. A real family. It warms my heart every time I come home. I just can't figure out why the two of you wanna live in this old place. Why don't you move over to the main house with me and Tyler?"

"I . . . I don't know. We really like it here, Mr . . . *Charlton.*"

"Well, whatever makes you comfortable. I'm very proud of you for the work you're doing with the homeless. You humble me."

Belinda kept herself behind them and turned back to the window. She'd been a loner all her life and felt more comfortable with the touch of isolation that came with living in the guest house. Emily had gravitated toward her early on, and the two of them living together worked. It just happened. She needed to be around them, but she wasn't ready for them all to be living under one roof. She just needed a little more time. Nevertheless, Charlton was an extremely kind man, and the last thing she wanted was to hurt his feelings.

"Belinda," he said, "did you say you had a degree in marketing?"

"Yes, I have. Why?"

"Well, no pressure, but if you ever feel like the walls are closing in on you, I'd be happy to set you up with a job, even part time, at the corporation."

She looked at him with a degree of uncertainty.

"Hell, I know you're OK for money, but the offer is on the table whenever you want it."

There was something about his proposition that made her feel uncomfortable. She considered perhaps it was because the last time she was in a corporate environment she'd been scared for her life. "Well, I don't have much practical experience. It was just college. My work experience only took me as far as being a secretary."

"Alex would be more than happy to show you the ropes," Charlton said. "Did I ever tell you I had some dealings with your old boss, Barton Carringby?"

"Really?"

"Yeah, it was back in the eighties. Coldest son of a bitch I ever dealt with."

They were distracted by the sound of Emily's giggling.

Charlton's face turned white, as though he'd realized his language in front of an ex-nun. He turned to her apologetically.

However, it was clear to Belinda that Emily was far from offended, not to mention a little tipsy. She smiled at the funny side of the situation. Emily was actually loosening up.

"No really, it's fine," Emily said.

28

"Well, in that case, I'll see you all at six-thirty." He turned to leave, but suddenly stopped in his stride. "By the way, I don't suppose either of you know where Tyler is, do you? I haven't seen him in two days."

They both shook their heads.

"I never have been able to keep track of that boy." With that, he made his way out of the house.

Charlton entered his office in the main house with deep concern. He hurried over to his desk, picked up his unregistered cell phone, and selected one of his contacts. After three rings it was answered. "It's me. What have you found out?"

A male voice came through the receiver. "I traced him to Chinatown in San Francisco, but he just disappeared, like he melted into the crowd. I'm working on it. I'm sure he's found shelter with one of the families."

"Look, I don't want my son to know anything about this. Right now I don't even know where the hell he is."

"Sir, I'm doing everything I can."

"Well, do it faster. If Han Fong's goons get hold of him, there's a good chance he'll be coming home in a goddamn body bag. Find Fong. When you do, let me know . . . and I'll take care of the rest."

Four

A & Z

"Leavin' home, leavin' home . . . Gonna find my pot o' gold, got to give it all or nothin' at all, on my, on my, on my . . . road of dreams."

Tyler Faraday sat in a mixing booth, tapping his feet to the song and grinning proudly. His girlfriend, Nicole Hawke, stood on the opposite side of the screen singing for her life. Two sound engineers sat to his left, deeply focused on their tasks balancing the digital graphic equalizers.

Tyler had stolen himself away to Los Angeles, temporarily delaying his duties as chief investment specialist with the Faraday Corporation. He wanted to help and support Nicole so badly. In the six weeks since his brother's funeral, they'd fallen in love. Helping her to start a new life gave him a deeper sense of purpose, and acted as a coping mechanism for his own grief.

Nicole was stunning. She captivated him as the overhead light in the studio caught her golden, shoulder-length hair, almost causing it to glow. She'd been through so very much. She'd left her home in Minnesota in pursuit of success as a singer in L.A. only to have fallen into the clutches of a human trafficking organization.

Five years had passed since she'd escaped. During that time she'd been in hiding, finding different jobs in different states, always under an assumed name. She'd finally been persuaded to come out of hiding to help them in the rescue of Tyler's sister from the same slave traders. If anybody deserved a break, it was Nicole.

The door opened behind him and Tamara Quinn, the acquisitions manager of A & Z Records, entered.

He turned to greet her, beaming. "Well? What do you think?"

"I . . . I'm not sure, Ty," she said awkwardly. "I mean, she's got a striking look and an incredible voice, but . . ."

"But what?"

"It's the song."

"She wrote it. I think it's terrific. What's wrong with it?"

Tamara sat beside him and looked through the screen as Nicole built up to the second chorus. "There's nothing wrong with it. It's catchy, inspiring, it has an amazing hook. But . . . what *is* it?"

Tyler frowned, confused. "What do you mean?"

"It's kind of a cross between Martina McBride and Heart. It's neither country nor rock."

"So? It's country rock."

"Not the biggest seller, at least not in L.A."

"Not the worst either."

"No, but . . ." She paused for a moment, seeming embarrassed. "Look Ty, if there's anyone on earth I'd want to help, it's Nikki. Without her, we never would have taken Sapphire down, and she's been my friend for the last five years. I know the hell she's been through."

"So what is it?"

"It isn't up to me. Two weeks ago, we discovered a glitch in our accounts. Our cash flow is seriously down, so much so that we can't afford to take any chances. We need artists guaranteed to sell."

He held her gaze with a deadpan expression, and then slumped back in his chair laughing.

"What's so funny?"

He composed himself, albeit with a look of amusement. "Money? That's the problem?"

"Well . . . yeah, I guess."

He stood excitedly. "I've never had any dealings in the music industry, but I think this is gonna be one of my most fun investments ever."

He noticed the two sound engineers looking up at him hopefully.

Tamara stood, open-jawed. "You're not serious."

"How much do you need?"

"I don't know. We'll have to discuss it with Rob Jacques. He's the CEO, and the final word has to be his."

"OK, let's go talk to him."

Nicole's song reached the end and they all turned back to the screen to see her deliver her closing lyrics:

"*. . . on my road of dreams.*"

One of the sound engineers pressed the mike button on his console. "That's a wrap, Nikki. You can take a rest."

Tyler watched as she nervously removed her headphones and made her way toward the booth. He threw his arms around her before she could fully step through the door. "Baby, you were terrific."

"Oh, boy. I'm still shaking," she said.

"Don't worry about a thing, babe. Everything's gonna be fine."

Nicole glanced over at Tamara hopefully. "Y-you're signing me?"

Tamara shot her an encouraging smile. "You were terrific, Nikki. I didn't know you were as good as that. And your song writing is amazing."

"Seriously?"

"Well, nothing's decided yet. I have to put it to Rob. But with the manager you have, I don't foresee any problems."

"Manager?"

Tamara pointed to Tyler, grinning.

Nikki looked up at him with confusion. "Tyler? What's she talking about?"

"Babe," he said with unbridled excitement, "I just got into the record business."

One hour later, Tyler sat opposite Rob Jacques in Jacques' office enjoying the record producer's astonishment at his proposal. Nikki and Tamara sat on either side of him.

A surge of adrenaline coursed through Tyler. *Being rich is so damn cool.*

Jacques, a middle-aged, slightly-portly professional, showed a ruddy complexion, indicating high blood pressure. His current financial setback was not likely to be helping. "Are you serious?"

Tyler smiled at the realization that what he'd just offered the man would be a boon to his health with which no medication could compete. "I'm very serious, and I also want to look over your books to see where we are. I'm willing to put up the money for Nikki's album and promotion. But, if you're interested, I'd like to offer my help with your other problems."

"You talking about a partnership?"

"Of course."

"How much of a partnership?"

"That all depends on how much money I'm gonna have to throw into this label to make it fly again."

Jacques glanced over at Nikki. "All right. Nikki, you're signed."

Her eyes widened and her breathing deepened. "Oh, my God."

"But you should take my advice on a few things," Jacques said.

"Of course."

"You have a great look, a strong voice, and you are one hell of a songwriter. But there's more to it than that. You need to know your market, and I can tell you, this ain't Nashville."

"Yes, sir, I know."

Jacques was quiet for a moment and appeared pensive. "Your voice does have a touch of the rock gravel. The rock scene is huge in L.A. Do you think you could rearrange your songs in that direction?"

"Piece o' cake."

Tyler felt a sudden grip of sadness. Brandon had been a major-league melodic rock fan, and he knew how much of a kick his brother would've got out of all this.

"OK," Jacques said. "I think we should start working on this right away. How many songs do you have written?"

"Ten, so far."

"We'll need fourteen. You'll need to come up with two more for the US release, and another two for the Japanese bonus tracks."

Nikki's mouth fell open. "Japanese?"

"Yeah, it's a tradition. We distribute internationally."

Tyler reached into his pocket, took out a check, and handed it to Jacques.

Jacques took it and gasped. "A million dollars?"

"I'll sign it when everything is agreed. Once I've figured in recording costs and initial marketing, I might need to throw some more at it if we decide to run TV commercials."

Jacques stood and held out his hand for Tyler. "You've got yourself a deal, Mr. Faraday."

Tyler took the producer's hand with a persistent kid-in-a-candy-store expression.

Nikki got out of her chair and threw her arms around Tyler. "I can't believe you're doing this for me, baby."

"I'm doing it for *us*. Besides, it's business." Tyler turned back to Jacques. "So, while I'm in town, let's have a look at those accounts, shall we?"

Five

Home Security

Charlton Faraday sat in his study, deep in thought. Nobody had heard from Tyler for four days. That wasn't unusual where Tyler was concerned, but the circumstances were different now.

For almost seven weeks, Charlton had suffered in silence. Since the day of Brandon Drake's death at Wilshire Memorial Hospital, he'd been consumed with worry. Wilmot had gloatingly told him Han Fong had escaped the explosion on the docks, and had most likely taken refuge with the Tong. The director had planted the seed in his head that if Fong had the Tong's favor, Tyler might be a marked man.

But how could he tell his son that? What if Wilmot had just been blowing smoke? He'd gone out his way to show what an asshole he was. A cruel prank like that was certainly within his character. But what if there *was* something to it?

In anticipation of the worst, Charlton had taken the initiative and invested in considerable security measures for the ranch. However, that wasn't any protection for Tyler if he was nowhere to be found. Was he safe? Or had something happened to him?

The speaker phone on the desk buzzed. "Yes, what is it?"

"There's a young man at the gate, sir. He says he's your son."

"Can you describe him?"

"Yes, sir. Dark hair, approximately twenty-five or twenty-six, red Ferrari, and he's with a young woman, a blonde knockout."

Charlton exhaled, almost tearful with relief. "Yes, that's my son. Let him through." He ended the call and briskly made his way out of the study.

"Sir, you can go on ahead."

Tyler looked up at a tall, dark-suited security guy, more than a little unnerved by the holstered pistol visible under his jacket. "Thanks a lot," he said with a hint of the sarcasm.

"What do you think's going on?" Nikki said.

"Beats the hell outta me." He gunned the car forward along the quarter-mile-long entrance road. The grass fields on either side of him never failed to fill him with warmth. Whenever they came into sight, he knew his home was where his heart was. This time, a dark shadow had fallen upon it.

As they came closer to the main house, Tyler noticed four similarly-attired guards patrolling the front of the property. "This is crazy. What the hell is the old man thinking?"

He parked the car in his usual space on the gravel as Charlton stepped outside.

Nikki and Tyler climbed out of the car, and Tyler slammed his door as he faced his father. "What the hell is all this, Dad?"

Charlton's face flushed with anger. "Where have you been?"

"What do you mean, 'Where have I been'? What difference does it make?"

"I've been worried sick about you!"

"Why?"

"How could you have been so selfish?"

"Selfish? Since when has me being away for a few days been a problem for you?"

Charlton's eyebrows rose as though he was trying to quickly come up with an answer. "You have responsibilities. We . . . *you* were supposed to be finalizing the McKenzie account."

Tyler turned back to the car, took out an envelope from the glove compartment, and handed it to his father. "You mean this?"

Charlton opened the envelope and took out a fully signed, witnessed, and dated contract.

"I stopped by their offices and got it all finalized on my way home," Tyler said.

"Home from where?"

"Los Angeles."

"What the hell were you doing in L.A.?"

Tyler felt uncomfortable having a private family conversation with the security goons all around him. Seeing a calmness come over his dad, he seized the moment. "Let's discuss this inside, shall we?"

Charlton nodded. Tyler and Nikki followed him into the house.

The door closed behind them, and Charlton wasted no time getting back to business. "What were you doing in L.A.?"

"We were getting signed to a recording label," Tyler said. "What's wrong with that?"

"I want you to stay away from California, Tyler."

"I can't. I bought shares in the record company. I have a vested interest now."

"You what?"

"It was another investment, Dad. Nothing more."

"How much?"

"Two million dollars for Nikki's project, and a fifty-percent share in the company. If they can reach new heights, they'll take her with them, and I'll do all right out of it for myself."

Charlton gestured to the living room and headed straight for the bar. "What do you know about the music business, Ty?"

Tyler raised his hands in surrender and sank down onto the sofa. Nikki sat beside him. "Practically nothing . . . *yet*. That's the whole point. I need to keep my hand in there so I can learn. It isn't the first time I've invested in a business I knew nothing about, and I haven't had a failure yet, have I?"

Charlton sat in the armchair opposite with a glass of bourbon. "No, you haven't."

"So, are you gonna tell me what all this home security crap is about?"

"Think about it, Tyler. You were involved in taking down a human trafficking ring. You're a wealthy young man, and now I have Belinda and Emily's safety to consider. I should have done this weeks ago."

Tyler was about to respond when Belinda and Emily entered.

"Is everything OK?" Belinda said. "We heard what sounded like shouting."

Tyler stood, kissed her on the cheek, and then moved over to give Emily a hug. "How're you doin', Sis?"

"I'm OK," she said quietly.

"Yeah, well, how do you like Fort Knox?"

Emily giggled, typically nervous.

"Ladies, if you'll excuse us," Charlton said. "Tyler and I have business to discuss." He gestured for Tyler to follow him out.

Tyler swallowed hard. The last time he'd seen his father so uptight was after he'd helped Brandon escape from Fort Leavenworth. He'd won his dad over on that occasion. Now, he wasn't as confident.

In an effort to lighten the mood, Belinda took Emily by the hand and over to the window. The guards were still holding their posts, looking particularly intense. "So, Em. Which one do you like?"

"What?"

"The guards. They are kinda hot, don't you think?"

Emily looked away bashfully.

Belinda grinned. "So, there is one, isn't there? Tell me."

Nikki joined them and peered out the window. "That tall, dark one is gorgeous."

Within moments, they were laughing. The atmosphere of a few moments ago was quickly evaporating.

"What were you thinking investing two million into a record company, Tyler?" Charlton said, his tone demonstrating the height of disapproval.

"It was my money, Dad. I didn't use company funds."

"I know, but I don't want to see you losing money on a reckless venture."

"There's more to it than that. I was helping Nikki."

Charlton gently gripped Tyler's shoulders. "It's not your responsibility to save the world, Son. You've only known her for a few weeks."

"I . . . I'm in love with her. Besides, you'd only known me for a few minutes when you decided to save me. Maybe you shouldn't have been such a great teacher, Dad."

As usual, Tyler had his father at a loss for words.

Tyler returned to the living room and joined the women at the window. He watched the guards with them but didn't share their sense of novelty. *What the hell is happening to us?*

Six

Target

Four weeks had passed since Brandon Drake had awoken. Andrew Wilmot strolled along a corridor on the second floor of the Mojave Desert complex, unable to stop a smug grin from cracking the corners of his mouth. So much in life was going his way. He had the opportunity to resurrect *Operation: Nemesis* from the ashes and take it to heights of which Treadwell had never dreamed. Now, with legitimate threats to fight, he had the chance to propose it to Congress, with an elite task force of his own creation as his bargaining chip. It was certain to accomplish his own personal objective in taking his career farther toward the corridors of power.

Kane Slamer would be invaluable to his plans. Slamer, a thirty-eight-year-old, freelance soldier of fortune, was the best of the best with guns, knives, hand-to-hand combat, and an essential lack of conscience. Two years earlier, he'd escaped from captivity by ISIS in Syria. For almost a year, he'd been tortured beyond the endurance of most. Biding his time, he'd waited for the moment he could escape and cause the most damage in the process. That day came when he was being led to his execution—a slow beheading with a knife. He hadn't left one of his captors alive.

Slamer's knowledge of the Syrian terrain made him the perfect operative to assist in covert operations against the terrorists. That, in turn, would provide Wilmot with his sorely-desired acclaim. With Slamer and Drake leading the strike force, he was sure he couldn't lose.

Only two problems gnawed at him. Drake could not learn the truth about what had happened to him during the previous four years. How was he going to keep the truth from him? Drake believed it was now November, 2012. Sooner or later he was going to discover it was July, 2016. Wilmot hoped the legendary temperatures of the Mojave Desert would suffice for creating ambiguity with the weather, at least for now.

But Drake couldn't be confined to the complex indefinitely. It was only a matter of time before he saw a date on something.

Wilmot's other concern was escaped operative, Jed Crane, who knew too much about the operation. Crane knew of Wilmot's connection to Treadwell, his involvement in the murder of Director Elias Wolfe, and the other agents concerned. But where was he? Where had he run to?

Wilmot arrived at a window and looked down onto a basketball-sized arena. Drake and Slamer were sparring, wearing camouflage pants, protective headwear, and boxing gloves. The display was spectacular. Drake, now sporting a military-style crew cut, had recovered and returned to form remarkably quickly. His aerial spin-kicks and acrobatic prowess showed he was clearly the more agile of the two, although Slamer was the more powerful combatant. He was able to deflect many of Drake's sharp and rapid blows, but it was also apparent that the younger fighter was wearing him down.

Wilmot's attention was distracted as Cynthia Garrett turned a corner. She walked toward him in a hurry, briefcase in hand.

"What have you got?" he said.

"Everything."

"What do you mean?"

"At the time of the Hamlin fish factory explosion, there was only one ship that disembarked from the harbor within ninety minutes of the incident." She opened the briefcase, rested it on her forearm, and took out a report. Wilmot took it before she could offer to hand it to him. "Vega Ocean Cargo Express. They were shipping a consignment of fruit to Rio."

"So I see." Wilmot didn't look up from the report as he eagerly absorbed the information.

"He's shacked up in a favela just outside of Copacabana."

His head snapped up.

Cynthia pointed to the report. "It's all there."

He turned the page and came to a loose eight-by-twelve grainy photograph. There was no doubt it was Jed Crane walking along a slum-like street outside one of the hundreds of hillside homes-upon-homes.

"We have an exact address," she said.

He closed the report and briskly walked past her.

"Where are you going?"

"Downstairs to give those two their first field mission."

She came up behind him with a hint of urgency. "Are you serious?"

"Slamer's fine, but I need to put Drake to the test so that I can ascertain his reliability. And it's a test in more ways than one."

"What do you mean?"

"Crane was his friend."

Slamer lunged at Drake, but Drake side-stepped him, flipping his leg out to the left. It caught Slamer just below the knees, sending him plummeting to the floor.

Slamer rolled onto his back and wrapped his legs around Drake's, pulling him onto the ground with him.

The door opened. Wilmot and Garrett stepped inside, halting their contest.

"Nice to see you two are getting along so well," Wilmot quipped. "Since you've floored one another, I'd say it was a draw."

The two combatants got to their feet breathlessly.

"What's goin' on?" Drake said.

"Get yourselves showered, changed, and in the briefing room in thirty minutes," Wilmot said. "You're going to Rio."

Attired in casual clothing, Drake and Slamer made their way along a corridor toward the briefing room.

"What do you think this is all about?" Drake said.

"How should I know?"

"I'm not complaining. I'm just itchin' to get the hell out of this goddamn place and see some real action, like the old days."

Slamer stopped in his tracks. "The old days weren't pretty, Drake. At least not for me." He pointed to the scar on his face.

"If you ask me, it's an improvement."

"We're just in this for the money, Drake. At least we've got that in common. But I don't mind tellin' you, you ain't my favorite person."

"You think I could give a shit? I almost got my ass blown off on account of your screw up."

"What are you talkin' about?"

"Al Fajr. They were onto you. You planted the false attack plans, but they knew. If it hadn't been for that, we'd have gone in and taken them down easily, leaving survivors to initiate the retaliation."

"There *were* survivors. They didn't retaliate. The whole operation was a failure."

"Yeah, but—"

Slamer placed a hand on Drake's shoulder, almost sympathetically. "It's ancient history, man."

Drake brushed his hand away. "Ancient history? It was ten weeks ago."

Slamer was silent and swallowed hard. Drake noticed. It was almost as though he'd just realized he'd said something he shouldn't have. The swallowing and silence were certainly out of character for him.

"Look, let's get in there and find out what they're sellin'." Slamer said.

"Yeah, *let's.*" Drake followed him into the briefing room.

Drake and Slamer entered from the far side of the bare, sterile, windowless room.

Wilmot looked up from an open briefcase on a stretched conference table. Garrett sat beside him. "Take your seats, gentlemen. This operation is important to all of us. We have an enemy. He's the only man alive outside of Operation: Nemesis who knows about it, and I can assure you, he's not sympathetic."

The two fighters leaned forward slightly.

Wilmot took out the grainy photograph of Jed Crane and pushed it toward them. Slamer studied it first and then passed it to Drake.

"Who's that supposed to be?" Drake said.

Garrett took another photograph from the case and took it over to Drake.

Wilmot eased himself around the desk to face them, eagerly gauging Drake's expression as he studied a clear, official head shot of his former ally, Jedediah Crane. But there wasn't even a glimmer of recognition in Drake's eyes.

"His name is Jed Crane," Wilmot said, and then stressed the point again just to see if it triggered anything. "Jed. Crane."

"All right, already. We got it. His name is *Jed. Crane.*" Drake mimicked. "So who is he?"

Wilmot breathed a sigh of relief. *'So who is he?'* *Incredible.* "He's a former SDT agent who discovered what we were doing and fled to Rio. He is your target. Make no mistake, boys, this man is dangerous. I'm making the arrangements to get you flown out there tomorrow."

Garrett placed two copies of the details on the table.

"We'll provide you with the necessary artillery. It'll be a quick hit-and-run operation."

"What about my money?" Drake said.

"I'm a man of my word. Fifty thousand. Twenty-five up front. Twenty-five on completion. Same goes for you, Slamer."

There was a moment of silence as Drake and Slamer's gazes fixed on Wilmot.

"All right, gentlemen," Wilmot said. "I think we're done here. Study your files. I want you both fully apprised by oh-six-hundred, so do your homework." He closed the briefcase and made his way toward the door with Garrett.

Drake stepped out the rear exit of the complex and lit a cigarette. The desert heat struck him immediately. Before him was an endless plain of sand, rock, and cacti. To his left, the edge of a helicopter landing pad was visible from the far corner of the complex, and an aircraft runway in the distance.

Something wasn't right. He didn't know what it was, but something didn't seem as it should. He just couldn't pinpoint it.

Beads of perspiration formed on his brow within moments. Even Afghanistan wasn't as hot as this.

He sensed a presence behind him and turned around. Garrett approached him as he blew out a lungful of smoke. "What are you doing out here?"

"I was going to ask you the same question," she said.

"I'm havin' a smoke. Want one?"

"No thanks."

He dropped the cigarette and stubbed it out with his boot. "You keeping tabs on me, or what?"

"Maybe, but it's not what you think." A seductive smile appeared on her face.

Drake reciprocated with an opportunistic grin of his own. "Oh, I get it."

She moved closer to him and gently caressed his cheek. They held one another's stare for a moment, and then their lips met.

Garrett broke it off, teasingly. "You do this job for us tomorrow, and there just might be more than fifty gees in it for you, handsome." She stroked her forefinger under his chin and walked back inside.

It had been a brief encounter, but Drake was more eager than ever to get this mission out of the way and return. Garrett was an extremely appealing woman, and one he'd been wanting since he first met her. His reservations about making a move on her had been motivated by him not wanting to compromise his financial opportunities. Now, she had taken that concern away.

Once again, he became aware of the heat and his moment of sexual excitement abated. *That* was what wasn't right. The penny finally dropped. *It's November. There's no way it would be as hot as this, even in the Mojave Desert.*

Seven

Flashback

20:04 hrs

Attired in unmarked, black combat fatigues and a utility belt, Drake walked ahead of Slamer toward a sleek, executive-class Learjet 55. He held a protective visor helmet under his arm.

Wilmot came up behind Slamer, gripped his shoulder, and whispered, "When you reach the target site, make sure Drake is wearing his helmet. I don't want Crane recognizing him and letting on he knows him."

"You got it."

"Good. Keep me posted every step of the way."

"Will do," Slamer said, and followed Drake into the Learjet. They faced a twelve hour flight to Rio. With the time zone difference, they would arrive at approximately 13:00 hrs, Brazil time, the following day.

As he ascended the steps to the aircraft, Slamer glanced back to see Wilmot was already heading back inside the complex.

*** *** ***

Drake and Slamer landed at Rio de Janeiro/Galeão– Antonio Carlos Jobim International Airport at 13:37 hrs, owing to a little turbulence en route. They'd slept for most of the journey, and conversation between them had been virtually non-existent.

Wilmot had arranged for them to be received in a military capacity as 'a matter of national security'. It had been such a convenient use of the term.

Upon exiting the Learjet, they were transported, by an airport security official, into the heart of Rio in an inconspicuous sedan.

Once they arrived at the outskirts of the slum, they exited the car and smuggled themselves into a series of alleyways. From there, they made their way into the favela with their helmets under their arms and automatic weapons concealed in leather carriers.

Drake took in the extraordinary scenery surrounding him—hundreds of meager homes piled upon one another. Rising up into the hills in such vast quantities, the properties formed a giant, sprawling cluster. It was the most elaborate example of poverty he had ever imagined, so far removed from the thriving, bustling city. Unique to Rio, the favelas were a sight one would find nowhere else.

Slamer took out a palm-sized satellite navigation device, and Drake looked over his shoulder noticing a flashing red dot in the middle of the map screen.

"We're here," Slamer said. "Crane's apartment is on the other side of this shithole." He tapped the brickwork that made up part of the rear of a dilapidated structure.

Drake looked up and saw a flat roof approximately thirty feet above them.

Slamer took a twelve inch cylindrical tube from his belt. A targeting sight was fixed to the exterior. "You ever used one of these?"

Drake took an identical device from his own belt and looked at it curiously. "Nope."

"It's an upgraded spider cable launcher. Apparently the originals had the cable inside a ball-like container. Pretty clumsy, if you ask me."

"I've never seen one."

"Well, let's get up there." Slamer aligned the targeting sight with a railing close to the edge of the roof and depressed a button on the casing. A high-tensile steel cable shot out of the end and a metallic claw clasped the rail.

Drake aimed and fired his cable. The claw gripped the railing almost a yard apart from Slamer's.

They put their helmets on and secured them. The visors covered their eyes. After hooking their gun-carrier straps over their shoulders, they pulled out hand grips from either sides of the cable launcher tubes and held them tightly. Depressing the quick-release switches at the ends of the grips, motors within the devices reeled the cable in, drawing Drake and Slamer up to the railing.

As Drake held on to the handgrips, a feeling came over him. There was something familiar about the sensation of being pulled up from the ground, but it wasn't exactly a memory. It was a feeling akin to déjà vu, although it seemed as though he shouldn't be pulled *upward*. It should have been a *horizontal* glide.

They arrived at the top, climbed over the railing, and detached the cable claws. Drake shook his head trying to assimilate the strange sensation that had come over him.

Slamer ran across the roof to the other side, took out a set of small, advanced, electron binoculars, and brought them up to his eyes. "Got it . . . Oh, fuck."

Drake hurried over to him. "What's wrong?"

"Take a look for yourself."

Drake took the binoculars. "Which apartment is this guy supposed to be in?"

"Third level. Fifth from the left with the entrance steps at the front."

Drake immediately saw the problem. Crane's was the only apartment in the line where the drapes were closed. If they couldn't see their target, they weren't going to be able to take him out. "Shit."

Slamer removed his helmet, took out his sat-scrambler cell phone, and selected his contact. "Wilmot? Slamer. We're going to have to go directly into the apartment. The son of a bitch has the drapes closed . . . Right, I'll tell him." The call ended.

"Tell me what?" Drake said.

"Switch on your helmet camera and radio. He's gonna be monitoring the operation. We're taking it from the rear."

Wilmot stood with Garrett in the Mojave base's situation room facing a wall filled with monitor screens. Several technicians attended the control panel.

A young male technician approached the director and handed him a head set and mike.

Two of the screens suddenly showed images of the favela. The movements were shaky and difficult to decipher. Drake and Slamer were apparently leaping down onto the balconies of the homes beneath. Occasionally, the screens became blank flashes of white as the two operatives tore through numerous clotheslines of sheets and threadbare towels. Sweeping shots of screaming women appeared for fleeting seconds. The residents were clearly startled by the two aggressively-contemptuous, armored soldiers wading through their homes.

Drake and Slamer arrived at the bottom, and the jerky movements indicated they were running across the street. Perturbed looks on the faces of the pedestrians were cause for concern.

Wilmot gripped the mike. "Boys, you don't have much time. You're creating a scene, and there's a risk of alerting Crane."

Slamer's breathless response came through Wilmot's head set. "You think we don't know that?"

Wilmot rubbed his eyes with anxious tension. "Don't screw this up, Slamer."

The screens became clearer. Drake was ahead of Slamer as they ran along an alley. They turned right and came up behind Crane's complex. A few steps later, they stopped at a rear metallic door.

"This is the one," Drake said. "It's locked."

"Blow it!" Wilmot ordered.

Drake took a small, C4 charge device from his belt, placed it against the door, and it adhered magnetically.

After setting it to five seconds, he and Slamer rapidly moved away a few feet, shielding their faces.

The door blew open. Smoke shrouded the immediate area, accompanied by the unmistakable scent of pitch and burning metal. They drew their automatic rifles, discarded the leather carrying cases on the ground, and ran inside.

Taking three steps at a time, they scaled the stairwell, oblivious to the screams and protestations of the first floor occupants.

They arrived on the second floor. A middle-aged, slightly overweight male wearing a filthy off-white singlet and what appeared to be pajama pants, stood before them angrily. Without hesitation, Drake drove the butt of his rifle into the man's face, breaking his nose, and knocking him to the ground.

Within moments, they were on the third floor. Crane's floor.

Drake heard sounds of commotion coming from below. He looked down three flights of stairs to see a team of police officers entering through the open rear door.

"No, no, no!" Wilmot bellowed through their headsets. "I covered this and ordered them not to interfere. This is a top secret operation. What the hell are those assholes thinking?

"What do you want us to do?" Drake said.

"It's on their heads. Blow out the stairwell."

Drake took a grenade from his belt, pulled the pin out, and dropped it down the stairwell. The first floor steps shattered. The detonation sent two officers flying out through the open door. Two others careened into the walls with bone-shattering force before falling lifelessly to the ground.

Flames rose through the remains of the stairwell, filling the complex with smoke.

Slamer turned around, his rifle poised, ready to dispatch any who might try to interfere.

Drake came to Crane's apartment door and kicked it in, surprised by how easily it came open. It wasn't even locked.

With his rifle raised, he cautiously stepped inside, rapidly aiming his weapon in every direction. It was a basic room with no wallpaper, paintings, or plants. There were only bare stone walls, but nobody was in sight. The smoke impaired his visibility, but it was clear enough to see nobody was there.

He moved around and kicked open the kitchen door. Huddled in the corner was a twenty-something Latina female, weeping and clearly terrified.

"Where's Jed Crane?" Drake demanded.

"I-I no know," she said, quivering in broken English.

"I said where the fuck is he?"

"No know. P-please don't kill me."

Suddenly, an excruciating, stabbing pain shot through his head. It felt as though his skull was being crushed. The rifle fell from his hands and he dropped to his knees, screaming.

The smoke and the woman's words merged into voices from elsewhere:

P-please don't kill me.

I'm not going to kill you.

"Oh, God!" he cried, and tore his helmet off. He grasped his head, unable to bear the pain, and collapsed into a fetal position.

Wilmot and Garrett looked at one another, mystified. They'd seen enough to know Crane wasn't in the apartment. Who the woman might have been was irrelevant. A neighbor? A prostitute? Crane's roommate? It didn't matter. Whatever was happening to Drake had negated the operation.

"Slamer, abort the mission," Wilmot ordered. "Something's happened to Drake. I'm having you picked up out front. Get him the hell out of there!"

Slamer headed into the room and saw the writhing figure of Brandon Drake on the floor. The pain in his eyes was so extreme he almost felt a surge of pity for him. "What the hell . . . ?"

He picked up Drake's rifle and gripped his hand to pull him up. Drake slapped his hand back to his temple immediately, and Slamer realized he could barely stand.

He glanced at the hysterical woman, but she wasn't important. Looking out onto the balcony, he recalled the front entrance steps. The purpose of taking the rear entrance was to reduce attention to a minimum, obviously to no avail.

He placed his head under Drake's armpit and lifted him across his right shoulder. With two heavy rifles braced under his free arm, he headed for the outside stairwell. He was heavily weighed down with little opportunity for grasping the railing. *Hell, this is gonna be a joy.*

57

Jed Crane emerged from an alleyway and fed himself through a crowd of stationary onlookers. He hadn't shaved for over a week. His hair had grown and was visibly protruding from beneath a baseball cap. Using an assumed name, he'd survived, since his arrival in Rio, working in a meat-packaging plant on the far side of town for the minimum wage. He'd managed to subsidize his income by sharing his apartment with Juanita, his roommate. She was a poor woman who worked in a souvenir store, but every little bit helped. It was only intended as a temporary measure until he could figure out a way to expose Wilmot and return to his position at SDT. So far, he hadn't formulated a plan.

His heart ached for the touch of Patricia, his fiancée. Forced to live on the run, he'd lost everything, with no idea how he would restore himself to his former life.

He saw smoke coming from his apartment and froze. *Oh, God! They've found me.* He was seized with horror at the thought of harm coming to Juanita. She had nothing to do with any of this. Frantically, he made his way to the front of the crowd, keeping his head bowed.

A man wearing a helmet, with another man over his shoulder and two automatic rifles under his free arm seemed to be struggling to reach the end the outside stairwell.

Jed took out his iPhone, set it to camera, and aimed it in the direction of the man in the helmet. He then selected the zoom option.

A white sedan pulled up outside the apartment. The man in the helmet awkwardly prized open the rear door with his fingertips and threw the rifles inside. He eased the other man from his shoulders. As he helped him into the car, the face of the other guy appeared up close on the zoom screen. Jed's eyes widened. "Brandon?"

But how could that be? Brandon Drake was dead. What was wrong with him? His face registered pain, even though he seemed barely conscious. And what was he doing working for Wilmot, in what was obviously an assassination attempt?

A memory came back to Jed. On the day he'd helped Drake to escape in Nevada, they'd been racing away from Wilmot. Brandon told him Treadwell had subjected him to a memory revision operation. Could they have done it to him again?

In the moments before Brandon's face became obscured by the car door, Jed snapped three photographs of him. Combined with the date and time recording of the shots, he finally had something he could use. Wilmot had fabricated the death of a fugitive, and had most likely brainwashed him.

However, his sense of hope was diluted by his concern for Juanita. The sedan sped away, ensuring his safe return to the apartment. He ran to the steps, filled with apprehension of the horror he might find when he arrived.

Eight

The Voice in the Darkness

Drake lay unconscious in a hospital bed in the Mojave Desert facility. Fifteen hours had elapsed since the incident in Rio.

Wilmot looked at Drake, puzzled. Dr. DeSouza stood over him in a white coat with a hypodermic syringe in his hand. Slamer, having showered and changed, stood watching in the doorway.

"The sedative I've administered should keep him unconscious for approximately twelve hours," DeSouza said. "At least it will spare him any further pain."

Wilmot turned to Slamer. "Did he give you any indication that anything was wrong on the way down there?"

"He was asleep most of the time. We both were. But he seemed fine to me."

Wilmot tapped his fingers on his lips, shaking his head. "What the hell happened?"

"I think I may know," DeSouza said.

"What?"

DeSouza glanced up at Slamer, and then back at Wilmot. "Do you think we could discuss this in private?"

Wilmot took the hint and approached Slamer. "Go home. Take some time off. I'll call you as soon as we've got this sorted out."

"OK." Slamer exited the room and disappeared along the corridor.

After closing the door, Wilmot ensured his displeasure was apparent. "I want to know what the hell happened out there."

DeSouza chuckled, demonstrating his lack of concern for the director's anger. "You may recall, during our first meeting, that I told you there was no known way of completely eradicating a previously-experienced persona. A memory revision simply relocates it to the subconscious."

"Go on."

"I believe something happened to Brandon in Rio that triggered a flashback."

"A flashback?"

"Yes. Something that reminded him of an incident that occurred during the four years he was living under the other personality."

Wilmot lowered his head in thought. DeSouza's words made no sense. "How the hell would a recollection cause him to fall down in agony?"

"It's what's known as phantom pain. There was nothing wrong with him in the physical sense. The pain was a manifestation of his mind, caused by a moral conflict."

"Dammit! That means he's utterly useless."

"Everything he did, and everything he experienced during those years, is recorded in his muscles. In his bones. He will not remember them, but he will *feel* them."

"Why didn't you tell me this before?"

"I did tell you, and as I recall, you said that you 'always paid attention in class.' Perhaps you should revise your position on that."

Wilmot grimaced in defeat. He knew he wasn't justified in taking it out on DeSouza. He'd been provided with comprehensive information about what he was doing, but in his arrogance, he'd chosen to ignore it.

DeSouza rested a sympathetic hand on his shoulder. "To the best of my knowledge, the reversal of a memory revision had never been attempted before. It was experimental."

"So, what can be done about it?"

"I honestly don't know. What we are dealing with are two conflicting personas occupying the same mind. One is violent and malevolent, and the other is a compassionate rescuer. Anything could trigger a conflicting episode."

"All right. Take care of him for now. I've got to figure this out." Wilmot walked out the door and made his way to the elevator.

His descent to the lower floor was a thought-filled period of angst. He couldn't fulfill his plan for Operation: Nemesis with Kane Slamer alone leading the team. They needed Drake, who was now an unreliable, ineffective option. That presented a serious problem. What were they going to do with him?

He walked out of the elevator and along another corridor until he reached the situation room. Stepping inside, he saw Garrett preparing a slew of report files.

She looked up. "What did the doctor say?"

"Basically, that it's over. It seems the personality Treadwell created is still inside him, and they're at war. If he does something that the other doesn't approve of, it will knock him down, just like we saw."

"So, what are we going to do with him?"

"What else can we do?"

Garrett shrugged.

Despondency filled Wilmot's heart as he summoned the courage to answer her. "We're going to have to put him away. The world will be none the wiser."

Garrett came closer and kissed his cheek. "Leave it to me."

***

Drake looked around him. There was nothing but blackness. No light. He couldn't make anything out. He looked down and saw he was standing in exactly the same darkness, as though he was suspended in a void of nothingness.

A chill gripped him. He didn't know where he was, and he could see no way out. He moved forward but it was more of the same. Everywhere he looked, there was nothing but darkness. *Is this Hell?*

He felt his heart racing and ran forward, panic-stricken. However, his legs didn't move as they should. It was like trying to run through water.

Finally, panic got the better of him. "Help!" he cried. "Somebody. Anybody!"

He continued to fight through the strange, fluid-like emptiness, but the blackness persisted. There were no discernible shapes or anything that represented existence. How could he even see the blackness if there was no light? He raised his right arm and could see it as clear as day.

He wandered aimlessly through the void, unable to assess how long he'd been in this place. A minute? A day?

A year? Many years? Time had no meaning here. It seemed eternal.

He sank to his knees in despair. Only then did he feel the presence. He looked up sharply. "Who's there?"

There was no answer.

"I know someone's there. Show yourself."

Hey, Scorp. How're you doing?

The voice echoed throughout the void. It sounded familiar, and yet unfamiliar. "Show yourself, you son of a bitch!" Drake roared.

How do you like Shitsville?

"Where are you?"

Did you really think I was gonna let you hurt that girl? She reminded me so much of . . . her.

"Who?"

I stopped you once. I will stop you again.

Drake felt a cold gust of wind blow past him with dazzling speed and knew it was the one who was talking to him. He still couldn't see him. It was just him alone with the voice in the darkness. "Who are you?"

The voice didn't answer.

Rage and frustration filled Drake's heart. "I said who the fuck are you?"

You know who I am.

Drake's eyes opened, and he shot bolt upright in his hospital-style bed, coated with perspiration. What was it about the voice's last words that had affected him this way?

Ultimately, he was forced to admit that he was afraid.

Nine

Comic Book Hero

Emily attended to a pot of stew in the kitchen of her workplace, The Sanctuary Street Mission in downtown Dallas. A humble and mundane occupation, it provided her with a sense of purpose and joy. It was a secular continuation of her previous vocation, but without the baggage and personal restrictions of the convent. She was free to come and go as she pleased, and under the domination of no one.

Day by day, she felt the changes in herself. Belinda had been a tremendous friend, and the source of some envy. Belinda was strong, humorous, and a pleasure to live with. Emily constantly wished she could have been more like her from the beginning. Nevertheless, she was finally sensing the spark of confidence within.

She looked out through an open porthole into the very basic dining hall with minimal décor. She noticed Jake, a young man who'd arrived a week ago. He was nineteen, and had fled from a violent home without a penny to his name. Emily couldn't deny she was attracted to him. Despite Belinda's constant encouragement that she should embrace that part of herself, it was extremely difficult. It had been her most troublesome challenge, having spent her life suppressing such feelings.

A line of disheveled, hungry men and women formed outside the porthole. With a compassionate smile, she filled the bowl of each person. Jake was the last.

"Hi," he said. He was the only one who spoke to her.

Blushing, she looked into his striking grey eyes. His brown hair hung limp across his forehead, and he had a chiseled bone structure. He was so good looking, yet the sadness in his eyes was apparent. She ached to put her arms around him. "Hi," she said.

"I . . . I really appreciate this."

"Oh, it's my pleasure, Jake. Are you OK?"

He held her stare for a moment, as though he knew she liked him. "I'm fine." He smiled nervously, and then made his way back to his place at the table.

Emily watched him, tormented by her own inability to know how to help him.

It had just turned four o'clock in the afternoon. Emily took her denim jacket from a cloakroom hook and headed toward the exit. At that moment, a familiar, smartly-suited male in his mid-fifties stepped inside.

"Oh, hi, Mr. Eisley," she said.

"Emily. I'm glad I caught you."

"Really? Is something the matter?"

"Not at all."

She felt confused. Why would Glen Eisley, the founder of the shelter, and the administrator of a nearby Samaritans organization, be keen to come over just to see her?

"I have a proposition for you, if you're interested," he said.

"What's that, sir?"

He smiled heartily. "How would you like to try out working the phones at The Samaritans?"

She looked at him, surprised. Why on earth would he think of her for something like that? "I . . . I really don't think I'm qualified, sir."

"The only qualifications you need are compassion and a sympathetic ear. I can't think of anyone finer. Consider what you've been through and the horrors you've survived. If anyone can understand suffering and despair, it's you."

She looked away in deep thought. Could he be right? The gnawing pangs of doubt still plagued her.

"I'm just asking you to try it, that's all. You'd sit in with a few of our counselors first to get the feel of it, and I promise, you'll be under no obligation."

His words made her feel a little easier. It sounded like something she would find truly fulfilling, but her heart ached with uncertainty.

"Give it some thought, OK?" he said. "You have an extraordinary counselor in you. I can feel it."

"Thank you, Mr. Eisley. I'll certainly give it some thought."

"You do that." He smiled and turned back through the exit.

Emily stood motionless in the foyer for a moment, trying to assimilate Eisley's suggestion. Finally, she walked toward the exit. Her hand pressed against the door as Belinda showed up.

"Hi," Emily said. "What are you doing here?"

"I finally decided to pay Charlton a visit," Belinda replied. "I've been with Alex all afternoon discussing this marketing job, so I thought I'd come down and see you."

They stepped out onto the walkway.

"How did your discussion go?" Emily said.

"Great, actually. I think I'm gonna take the job. It's what I set out to do originally, but just never had the opportunity. It was rejection after rejection, until all I could find were secretarial jobs. Wanna grab a coffee?"

Emily smiled. "Yeah, that would be great. I've got some things to tell you."

Belinda sat opposite Emily in Starbucks, pregnancy-consciously holding a large cup of decaf. After discussing their respective new job offers, it was Emily's second revelation that prompted Belinda's intrigue. "You're kidding! You've actually got your eye on someone?"

Emily giggled bashfully. "Well . . . yes, I suppose. But, what do I do? I have no experience with things like this."

"Nobody does in the beginning. Just go with your heart. Talk to him. Chances are he's just as nervous as you."

"Well, how was it when you met my brother?" Emily asked the question with more than a little eagerness. It was clear she'd wanted to ask Belinda about Brandon for weeks, but had been afraid of saying anything that might upset her. Perhaps she felt the conversation had just presented the perfect opportunity.

"Oh, boy," Belinda said. "Don't take my relationship with Brandon as a guide to normalcy." A thought came to her and she laughed.

"What?"

"The first thing I ever said to him. I can't believe I just remembered."

"What did you say to him?"

"'Please don't kill me'. How romantic is that?"

"'Please don't kill me'?"

"I know. I thought he was one of the terrorists. You wouldn't believe how scared I was."

"Actually, I would."

Belinda cringed. *Damn. Why didn't I think?* "Of course. I'm sorry, Em. What you went through with those Tong jerks must've been unimaginable."

"It was horrible in the beginning, but I don't remember much of it after that. I think they . . . *did things* to me. I was drugged up all the time so it's just a haze."

Belinda placed a comforting hand on Emily's and closed her eyes at the thought of her friend's terrible experience.

"But I *do* remember seeing Brandon in the parking area," Emily said with a more spirited tone. "He was on the floor. I think I remember his hair was quite long. He looked up at me. I just knew he was my brother and that he'd come to save me. What was he like?"

"What *wasn't* he like, is more like it. There were so many sides to him. When I first met him, he was kind and considerate. He seemed strong, yet so vulnerable, and then—"

Emily leaned forward with eager eyes. "What?"

"Whenever we were in serious danger, this thing came over him. He became this incredible fighting machine who was consumed with rage. It was terrifying to see, but he protected me. After each episode, he didn't remember a thing."

"What was it?"

"At first we didn't know. Then, one night, we returned to the cabin and found Treadwell sitting there. He told us

Brandon's memories and personality had been manufactured in a mind control experiment. In reality, he'd been a psychopath they called The Scorpion, and his blackouts were remnants of his true personality coming through. It completely crushed him when he found out."

"I remember some of this from the funeral, but I didn't really understand it. What happened then?"

"After he escaped from Leavenworth, he developed a serious drinking problem. I guess he just couldn't come to terms with his life being a lie, and the truth being the worst of all truths. His intoxication damn near jeopardized our chances of finding you and getting you out."

Emily shuddered and placed her hand against her mouth.

Belinda tilted her head slightly and shot her a pensive smile. "I often wonder who your brother might have been if he hadn't been abused as a child, and hadn't been brainwashed. I think about it every day. Who was the *real* Brandon Drake? His two personas were products of what others had done to him, not who he was naturally."

Tears welled up in Emily's eyes. "It's really incredible. I wish I could have been there for him."

"Oh, Em. I don't think anyone could have helped Brandon. His circumstances were so extraordinary. It was something he had to work out for himself. The thing that pisses me off the most is that he was beginning to find himself, just before . . ."

Emily looked at Belinda with profound sadness. "I'm so sorry."

"Hey, you have a chance to help people in distress now. You're gonna make a terrific counselor, Em. I know it.

People can come through the most terrible tragedies. You did. I did. *And* Brandon did. Just look at the effect he had on the rest of the world."

"What do you mean?"

"He divided the country. He had fans and followers across America. They even turned him into a comic book hero."

Emily laughed, spontaneously coming out of her sad slump. "I remember your celebrant saying something about him being in a comic book?"

"I hadn't seen Brandon laugh for weeks before he saw that first issue. They call him *The Interceptor*."

"The Interceptor?" Emily chuckled, almost choking on her coffee.

"Yes. I've still got the first issue back at the ranch. Tyler picked it up in Nevada when we were trying to find you. You can read it if you'd like."

"OK, but . . ."

"But what?"

"I've never read a comic book before."

Belinda laughed again. "There's not much to it." She took another sip of her decaf and gazed into the ether, her mind becoming flooded with wishes and the possibilities of what might have been. *Oh, Brandon. If only you were still here.*

Ten

Deadly Seduction

Drake moved back into his own room after waking from his drug-induced sleep. Uneasiness had a constant hold over him. So much was wrong, but he couldn't figure it out. It was too hot for the time of year. He'd remembered something he couldn't identify. And there was the voice inside him trying to tell him *something* in his dreams. It felt as though a part of his life was missing. But how could that be? What had happened to him in Rio? There was something he felt he *knew* in the pain that had taken him down. It was as familiar as the voice in the darkness. But what was it?

He paced the room aimlessly, stopping finally to cast his gaze through the gap in the drapes across the desert. The room was on the third floor, thirty-five feet above ground, and he didn't even have means of getting out without a security clearance. He would occasionally sneak out the back for a cigarette if the rear exit was open. Personnel were often coming in and out, but as soon as the back entrance was closed, he was locked in. That didn't sit well with him in the least.

Wilmot stepped out of his Mojave office with Cynthia Garrett. In contrast to Garrett's professional attire of a white shirt, a blue skirt, and a jacket, she wore extremely alluring make-up. Bright red lipstick complemented her bronze-hued skin tone and flawless black eyeliner. Seduction was her intention, not that it would have taken much with a predator like Drake. However, this particular task required that she present herself as the ultimate distraction.

"Are you sure about this?" she said.

"I'm not happy, obviously, but I'm sure," Wilmot replied. "Just be careful. What you need is under his mattress."

"I know." She kissed him tenderly and then headed toward the elevator.

The doors opened on Drake's floor. She arrived at his room and knocked. There was no answer, so she tried the handle to find it was locked. She knocked again.

The door opened, and Drake's towering frame stood before her. "What's going on?" he said icily.

She shot him a sultry smile. "Hi. How are you feeling?"

He held her gaze for a moment with a suspicious demeanor. Without warning, he gripped her shoulders and thrust his lips onto hers. He hungrily pulled her into the room, probing her mouth with his tongue. With one stab of his foot, he closed the door.

Their lips parted for a moment. "You move fast," she said.

"Why wait?"

"Why, indeed?" She dropped to her knees and set about undoing his belt buckle. "I've been waiting weeks for this."

She noticed his impressive bulge tenting forth underneath the denim. *Damn, he's eager.* Pulling down his jeans, she was startled as his sterling appendage sprung out. Leaning back slightly to take it all in, she lightly grasped him, at all times conscious of her macabre task. *What a waste.*

She slowly took him between her lips, and his primal impatience became apparent almost immediately. His hips rocked back and forth aggressively, causing her to gag. "Hey, take it easy," she said. "Do you have a license for this thing?"

"I want you."

She stood again and smiled at him sensuously, bringing the moment back round to where she wanted it. Knowing he wasn't the type to waste time on foreplay, she cast off her jacket and quickly unbuttoned her shirt. His hands were upon her within seconds, tearing her bra away. He gazed upon her firm breasts for only a moment, giving her the time necessary to remove her skirt. She wasn't wearing any underwear.

"You came prepared," he said.

Garrett didn't respond. For the first time, she was beginning to doubt she could pull off her mission. There was nothing in Drake that even remotely resembled vulnerability. He was cold, compassionless, and animalistic.

He circled around her and she shivered. There was a momentary pause, as though he was taunting her.

Suddenly, he grasped her hair and thrust her over the bed. For the first time in her life, she felt helpless.

He prized her legs apart and entered her, thrusting with violent savagery. She gasped with shock and a stabbing pain, but forced herself to endure it. However, this wasn't the position she needed to be in.

Her gaze fell upon the widescreen HD television set on the cabinet. It was nothing. It was irrelevant. But it was enough of an anchor for her attention while she formulated a plan.

Relentlessly, he ravished her, grunting with every thrust as they consummated their loveless union. It was the most distorted experience of sex she had ever known. It wasn't a type of mission to which she was a stranger, but it had never been like this before. Now, it was personal. Drake was brutally violating her, and she wanted nothing more in that moment than to kill him.

He relaxed his hold on her head, giving her the opportunity to ease herself up a little. "Wait," she whispered.

"I don't want to wait."

She forced herself to stand, and he slipped out of her. She was unable to prevent a gasp of relief from escaping her lungs. "I need to rest for a moment," she said, and tapped the bed. "Lie down. I need to get off too, you know." *Please, go for it.*

He nodded, despite his constant, hard, savage expression.

Garrett watched with a subtle sigh of relief as he lay back on the sheets. At all costs, she knew she had to keep him there.

Quickly, she climbed on top of him and guided him inside her. She sank down onto him, angling her knees into the mattress in order to move her hips up and down on him with ease. "Just relax and let me do all the work."

For long minutes she rode him, watching his expression for even a hint of vulnerability. Of *surrender*.

Finally, she saw his eyes rolling slightly. The pleasure was actually breaking him down. It stunned her that she was deriving some pleasure from it herself now that she had a degree of control.

She sensed a sudden, steel-like rigidity inside her and knew he was about to come. *Now or never.*

He cried out with the raptures of climax. Garrett threw herself down onto him, capturing his cries with her mouth. His eyes closed, and she knew that wave after wave of pleasure was coursing through him. But it would be fleeting, and she had virtually no time to do what she had to do.

She grasped the back of his head with her left hand, pressed her lips to his, and dropped her right hand down to the side of the bed. Her fingers slid under the mattress, gliding along frantically as she distracted him with a deep, faux-passionate kiss.

Within seconds, her fingertips came into contact with a hypodermic syringe. She drew it out and let her hand hang over the bed for a moment. Her mind raced. The paralysis would kick in first and within a couple of seconds. However, he wouldn't need any longer than that to break her neck. She had to get the needle in him and then move across the room rapidly.

His eyes were still closed with the faint hint of a satisfied smile creeping from the corners of his lips. She raised the needle and angled it toward his neck . . .

The world exploded. Stars appeared before her eyes for a fleeting moment before the veil of oblivion claimed her.

Drake threw Garrett off him, sending her flying into the television set. It fell upon her as she collapsed onto the carpet.

He leaped off the bed and picked up the syringe. Studying it for a moment, he wondered what was in it. There was no doubt it would've been the instrument of his death, had he not kept his wits about him.

He stared at Garrett's limp form. She was merely unconscious, albeit with a broken jaw. Perhaps he should use the needle on her. Then he considered he might have a use for it. It was, at the very least, a weapon.

But why would she have been trying to kill him? It seemed to fit with the mysteries that filled his mind. Perhaps now, he had the opportunity to find some answers.

He moved around the bed and picked up Garrett's jacket. Sifting through it, he came to her iPhone. He questioned why should that be of interest to him? Could it be that he'd not been provided with one? Whatever it was, there was something about it he was sure contained an answer. A clue.

He switched it on and waited a few moments for it to boot up. In an instant, his clue was displayed on the screen: July, 30th. *Ten weeks ago was September. This should be November.*

His heart quickened, prompting him to search through her other pockets. The inside pocket contained a credit card wallet. He found two cards—her security key card and an American Express card. His eyes widened. Her American Express card bore an expiration date of August 16th, 2017. The start date read: August 17th, 2015.

Immediately he realized, in all the time he'd been living in the complex, he'd never seen a date on anything. *What year is this?*

He could hold Garrett's head under the cold faucet to wake her up, interrogate her, and find out what the hell was going on. But if they were trying to kill him, they'd be waiting for her to leave his room. There was no time. He had to get out of there.

He spun around, grabbed the bed sheet, and wiped Garrett off him.

Hurriedly, he threw his clothes back on, placed Garrett's key card into his pants pocket, and ran across to the closet. After taking a key out of his pocket, he opened it up and grasped a backpack. *The bastards had better not have ripped me off.* He unzipped it and saw it was filled the $25,000 in cash that Wilmot had paid him up front. Satisfied it was all there, he fed his arms through the backpack straps.

He looked around and realized he was unarmed. There were no firearms in the room. He would have to acquire them on route.

He returned to the bed and picked up the syringe. As he made his way to the door, he knew that between the room and the main exit, there would be bloodshed.

Eleven

Unleashed

Drake quickened his pace with the hypodermic syringe concealed under his fingers. The needle rested against the sleeve of his jacket. The corridor was deserted, and the elevator was right ahead.

He stepped inside the elevator and selected the ground floor option. As it descended, his eyes were fixed on the doors. Security guards would be everywhere, as would security cameras.

It stopped on the ground floor, and he braced himself as the doors opened. All he saw before him was a bare wall. But what might be on either side of the doors?

He stepped out and glanced around. Behind the myriad of doors were offices, conference rooms, and the gym. Off-shoot corridors led to the laboratories and underground research facilities.

He gritted his teeth with annoyance. He'd woken up in the medical lab ten weeks ago with the promise of wealth as his first 'welcome back' message. He'd been blinded by the gold.

But what was this place? He'd never asked that question before. By all appearances, it seemed like a miniature Langley, but why had questioning it evaded his attention? Confusion as he came around, perhaps? His heightened focus on new opportunities? They'd duped him, and the reality finally dawned on him. He'd been a prisoner whose captivity had been enabled by his own unawareness of the fact.

He turned left and noticed a CCTV camera above him. *Just keep going.*

A security guard turned a corner at the end of the corridor toward him. He was young, perhaps mid-twenties. Drake vaguely recalled his name was Jack. His eyes immediately fell upon the guard's pistol in the belt holster.

"Is something the matter, Mr. Drake?" Jack said.

"Just trying to find the men's room."

They drew closer.

"The men's room?"

"Yeah. I'm gonna piss all over this shithole." Drake revealed the syringe.

Jack immediately reached for his gun, but Drake moved with the speed of a cobra, plunging the needle into his neck. The young security guard's hand relaxed on his holster, and his eyes rolled back within seconds.

Drake cradled his back and eased him onto the floor. After waiting for ten seconds, he saw the lifelessness in the man's eyes. In that moment, he knew. *Lethal injection.*

He took Jack's gun and placed it in his inside jacket pocket.

Security officer Adam McCann glanced at his monitor in the observation room at the moment Drake appeared on the screen. He'd been told Drake was a V.I.P. But what was he doing down on the ground floor with a backpack?

McCann used the console controls to adjust the position of the camera. Jack's motionless form came into shot.

Urgently, he picked up the phone beside him and punched in an extension.

Wilmot sat in his office, anxious to hear from Garrett. His concern became heightened now that the moment of her perilous task should've passed, and he still hadn't heard from her.

His desk phone rang and he picked it up. "Wilmot."

"Sir, this is Adam McCann in the observation room. Drake is on the ground floor, and one of the guards has been taken out."

Wilmot's heart pounded. *Oh, my God. Cynthia.* He knew he had to get to Drake's room immediately to ensure she was all right, although that was extremely unlikely. It was also imperative that Drake didn't leave the complex. "McCann, send through a command to security. Under no circumstances is Drake to leave the facility. Tell them to shoot to kill, if necessary." He slammed the phone back on the receiver and ran out of the office.

Drake's room was only one floor down, but Wilmot couldn't bring himself to wait for the elevator. He hurled himself down the stairwell, taking three steps at a time.

He arrived at the third floor entrance door, thrust it open, and sprinted along the corridor. Drake's door was ajar just ahead of him. *Oh, please, please, please.*

After entering the room, his gaze immediately fell upon Garrett's motionless, naked body. *Oh, dear God, no.* Devastation coursed through him as he approached her.

He knelt down and noticed her severely swollen face with blood tricking from the corner of her mouth. "Oh, baby," he muttered tearfully, and gently cradled her head.

Garrett groaned and Wilmot's spirits soared in an instant. "Oh, thank God you're alive." He wiped the tears from his eyes and held her to his chest, overcome with relief.

Ten security guards covered the ground floor in three groups. They examined the main corridor, then the corridors and offices shooting off it. There was no sign of Drake.

A group of four took the corridor to the lab. Still nothing.

They were about to turn around when they heard a rustling noise. There were no other sounds as they looked around them.

They barely had enough time to register a crashing noise above them. Drake landed behind them from an air vent grill. He grasped the head of the first guard and broke his neck. The corpse fell from his grip, and Drake took his gun.

The remaining three recoiled instinctively, but it was too late. Drake opened fire.

Drake picked up the pistols from the hands of the dead security guards and took the cartridges from them. He heard the clatter of running feet coming from the main corridor and braced his back against the wall.

Three guards were about to pass the lab corridor when one of them noticed him. "Look out!"

But it was too late. With rapid fire, Drake took them out with inerrant shots to their heads.

He ran across the corridor as three more guards came toward him from the far side. This time, he knew he didn't have the advantage of surprise.

Their footsteps grew nearer. He estimated they were approximately twenty feet behind him. Bracing his chest against the opposite wall, he fired, missing his first target. He sprung back as a bullet blew out a section of the concrete wall. Reaching around again, he fired, taking down the gunman. The remaining two seemed distracted by the shock of their colleague falling dead. *Amateurs.*

He took the other gun from his inside pocket and stepped out into the open. The guards looked at him fearfully, and he held their stares for a tense moment.

The guard on the left raised his firearm a fraction of an inch, but Drake ensured there would be no chance of him firing. He squeezed the triggers of both guns simultaneously and fired into their hearts without hesitation.

Turning around, he continued his journey toward the exit.

A door opened at the end and DeSouza stepped out. Drake slowed his pace. This was the man with the answers. He needed him alive, at least for the moment.

"Brandon, you don't have to do this," DeSouza said. "Let's talk about it. What happened?"

"What happened? Are you for real? You bastards tried to set me up with that bitch and kill me."

DeSouza raised his hands peacefully. "I know nothing about that, Brandon. Please. Let me help you."

"Help me? *Help me?* After what you've done? After what you've been keeping from me?"

DeSouza swallowed hard. "Brandon, all is not as it seems. We gave you *yourself* back."

"What are you talking about? How long was I under, DeSouza? What year is this?"

"It's twenty-sixteen, Brandon. We were going to tell you gradually. It's extremely complicated. You weren't *under*."

Drake lunged for DeSouza, gripped him by the throat, and pinned him up against the wall. The doctor's face flushed a deep shade of purple. A certain resignation came across his eyes, as though he was accepting his own end. "Y-you . . . were a hero . . . Brandon. You just . . . don't remember."

"If it's twenty-sixteen, I've lost four years, you son of a bitch! Now, what happened?"

DeSouza seemed to smile, even through his fear. "He's . . . still inside you. W-Wilmot . . . wanted me to bring you back . . . and to destroy him. But . . . The . . . Interceptor . . . stayed with you."

Drake loosened his grip. "What the fuck is The Interceptor?"

The doctor caught his breath. "He's the voice inside you, just as you were the voice inside him. The world thinks you're dead, Brandon. Now, you're unleashed, out of control, and it's my fault."

Drake gripped his throat again, consumed with rage. "Tell me, DeSouza. Where have I been for four years?"

"He'll . . . save . . . them . . . from . . . you." DeSouza's eyes rolled back and assumed a lifeless glaze.

Drake realized his fingertips were buried deep into the man's throat and knew he'd crushed his windpipe. He released him, and the body of Dr. Frederick DeSouza fell to the floor.

His mind was awash with questions. He'd lost four years, but he'd apparently had a life outside of . . . *himself?* What was that supposed to mean?

He heard an elevator beep in the distance. The exit was only a few yards away. He ran to the key card reader and slipped Garrett's card into it. A green light came on accompanied by a faint beep. The main doors opened.

A Mercedes pulled up at the front of the complex. A familiar, middle-aged man stepped out and smiled at him. Drake recognized him as one of DeSouza's colleagues. "Hi, Matt," Drake said.

"Hi, Mr. Drake. What are you doing out at this hour?

"Just thought I'd go for a drive."

The man frowned. "I didn't know you had a car on site."

"I don't. You do." With blinding speed, Drake drew out a pistol and shot the man point blank in the forehead. The car key slipped from his grip onto the asphalt.

Drake picked the key up, threw his backpack onto the back seat, and climbed into the car. Tires screeched as he reversed.

He looked to his right and saw Wilmot heading for the entrance door, pistol in hand. Rage surged within him again. He picked up the gun from the passenger's seat, aimed it out the open window, and fired. The bullet blew out the windows of the complex's entrance. Wilmot leaped behind the corridor wall for cover.

Drake hesitated for a moment. He wanted Wilmot to die for what he'd done, but he knew he was losing time.

He'd made it off the grounds, and the freedom of the uncharted desert was right ahead of him. "Another time, asshole."

Gunning the Mercedes forward, he headed for the runway. He hit ninety miles an hour, his mind consumed with questions and hate-fueled determination. Maybe now he'd find answers to what they had done to him. To any who'd get in his way, he would show no mercy.

Twelve

Cover Up

Slamer's blood-drenched fingers reached through a wound into the skull of the last dead security guard. He retrieved the fatal bullet and cast it into a Perspex container beside him. He'd soaked every ground floor room with gasoline and the stench filled the air.

He heard footsteps behind him and turned to see Wilmot and Garrett. Garrett's severely swollen, disfigured face took him by surprise. She'd always been a stunning woman, now reduced to the vision of a monster to rival even his own aesthetic misfortune.

"You almost done?" Wilmot said, his tone tempered by heightened distress.

"That's the last one. I buried DeSouza in the desert. We can't afford for him to be identified if this bullshit story is to be believed." Slamer picked up a towel next to the container and wiped the gore from his hands.

"This has been devastating, I don't mind telling you, Slamer. But we're all in it, and this has to be covered up."

Slamer stood to face him. "With the bullets removed, the explosion will blow the corpses to four points of the compass. Forensics won't even know where to begin to find a cause of death, other than what it looks like."

Wilmot looked around the place pensively. "Did you know this base never even had a name?"

"Yep."

"M.O. five-zero-six is all it was ever referred to on paperwork. It's been an intelligence-gathering and covert training center for twenty-five years. Now it's all about to go up in smoke."

"We have no choice, Wilmot," Slamer said. "These men have families. You need to give them an explanation for how they died without telling them the truth."

"I know. Drake's been gone for six hours already. He could be anywhere by now."

"I'll find him."

"Make sure you do, Slamer. All of our asses are on the line here."

"OK. You two get out of here. I'll set up the event." Slamer looked across at Garrett. "What about you? How are you gonna explain that broken jaw?"

"She can't speak," Wilmot said. "We're saying she got hit by a chunk of debris outside when the place blew."

"Gotcha. Good thinkin'." Slamer made his way past them, his gaze falling upon the corpses all around him. *Thirteen dead. Eleven guards, DeSouza, and his assistant.*

He headed along the walkway, opened the door to the lower floors, and descended the steps.

He came to the door of a particularly hazardous power supply room, which was the main source of gas for the facility. An explosion would cause a cataclysm, and the ground floor would collapse. Fire would rise rapidly, creating a chain reaction of secondary explosions from the electricity supply and the gas contained within the pipes through the upper floors. Very quickly, the complex would collapse in on itself like a house of cards.

He picked up a large wrench from a toolbox beside the door and took it across to the main gas feed pipe. His herculean biceps bulged as he loosened the bolts around the central collar. He soon realized they were so tightly fixed, they might as well have been welded on, and he had five more to remove.

It was an arduous task, but he finally drew out the final bolt as perspiration dripped from his brow. After removing the collar, he forcefully prized open the pipes a fraction of an inch. Exposed to the air, fumes hissed as they escaped.

Slamer took a small device, no larger than the end of his thumb, and a length of thread from his pocket. He slipped the thread through the back of the casing, gripped the severed pipe, and tied the device to the point of separation. With the touch of a button, it was armed—a small, fragile, incendiary that would do no more than create a spark. The device would be burned into vapors. There would be no trace of evidence. He had five minutes to get away from the complex.

Slamer ran back along the corridor with a sense of urgency. Wilmot's undercover plan had always been haphazard at best, but he paid well, as Treadwell once had. The director's assumption that an elite team of operatives who had proven their worth would bypass intelligence protocol might have had some merit. A slap on the wrist followed by a golden handshake was what Wilmot had counted on. They would've had no knowledge that Operation: Nemesis had always been Treadwell's pseudo-terrorist cell.

But success was no longer an option. The entire project had failed spectacularly. A formidable killer was now on the loose, having left a bloodbath behind him. Drake's very existence jeopardized them all. If the truth was discovered, there would be no defense to their mutual involvement in an undercover mind-control operation, an illegal fabricated death, and countless unauthorized assassinations over the years. Slamer and Wilmot had been principle members of Treadwell's team, which would finally be discovered, leading to charges of treason. At all costs, Drake had to be neutralized.

Slamer stopped momentarily to pick up the container of bloodied bullets and the towel, and then continued briskly toward the exit. He glanced at his watch: three minutes fifty-seven seconds to detonation.

Wilmot and Garrett stood beside a top-of-the-line BMW. Anticipation was apparent in their eyes as Slamer ran toward them.

Slamer looked at his watch again. "Three minutes. Get the hell out of here."

Garrett climbed into the passenger seat, and Wilmot approached Slamer with a briefcase. "Here. The other half on completion. I need to get Cynthia to the hospital."

Slamer took the money, although given his other concerns, the cash was a moot point. It would, however, be useful. He threw the case, the towel, and the container of bullets into his passenger's footwell and fired up his Camaro.

Seconds later, the two cars raced away from the complex and into the night.

With one hand on the wheel, Slamer took out a piece of paper containing the details of the Mercedes Drake had escaped in. Casting it onto the passenger's seat, he glanced at his watch again. *One minute remaining.* With his foot firmly pressed on the accelerator, he sped along the dusty, desert road. *I'll find you, Drake, no matter what it takes. You're a dead man, bud.*

The night came alive with a violent shock wave. He glanced in his rear-view mirror and saw a cloud of flame in the background, accompanied by repeated, distant explosions. The Mojave complex had breathed its last.

Thirteen

Road Kill

Drake had driven over three-hundred-fifty miles since his escape from the facility. He checked the digital clock on the dashboard: 05:37.

He needed sleep, but he'd already decided where he was heading. To find answers to questions he didn't even know, the most logical place was for him to go back to the beginning. That meant two-thousand miles. In the meantime, he had to dispose of the car. They knew what he was driving, including the license plate.

He kept his focus on the desert road ahead of him and estimated he couldn't be far from Flagstaff, Arizona.

Through the dim, half-light of the dawn, he noticed a blue Chevy Impala up ahead, parked on the side of the highway. *Breakdown.*

As he drew closer, he could see the car owner crouched beside the rear right wheel. The man stood and waved his hands. The hopeful glint in his eyes was visible, even through the dim light.

Drake grinned darkly and slowed down. Looking to his left, he noticed a mountainous edge where a flat remnant of land ended. The road had been built through a patch of desert, and the clear drop gave him a macabre idea.

Rapidly planning his strategy, he stepped out of the car and approached the man. He appeared to be approximately Drake's own height, and around twenty-five. *Perfect.* "Hey, bud. What happened?"

93

The man beamed. "Oh, thank God. I've been stuck out here for two hours. Yours is the first car I've seen. My rear tire blew, and I discovered they sold me this thing without a jack in the trunk."

Drake lowered his gaze. The tire was completely shredded. "Do you have a spare?"

"Yeah, just no jack."

"I'll see what I've got in the back." He walked back to the Mercedes and cracked open the trunk. After peeling back the upholstery, he spotted the jack. With a sinister, opportunistic grin, he took it out and held it up for the young man to see. "Happy birthday."

"Oh, man, you've just saved my life."

Don't count on it, asshole.

"By the way, I'm Luke." The man held out his hand, but Drake didn't take it.

"Fred."

"Nice to meet you, Fred."

"OK, let's get this thing propped up, and then you can be on your way."

Drake jacked up the car, removed the lug bolts, and changed the wheel with Luke's spare. After twenty minutes, the last bolt was tightly secured. "There you go. You're all set."

The relief in Luke's eyes oozed with gratitude. "Oh, man. Thank you so much."

Drake stood and gave him a chilling smile. "Don't mention it." His hands shot up with dazzling speed and gripped Luke's head. Rotating them counter-clockwise, he broke his neck in a flash. Luke's body fell from his grip and slumped onto the road.

With cold calculation, Drake hurriedly formulated his plan. He had to move fast. Another car could appear at any moment. Ideally, Luke could pass for Drake's remains if disfigured sufficiently by fire, although it was unlikely the authorities would fall for a trick like that. It was also possible they would identify Luke through his dental records since the teeth wouldn't burn. That would, in turn, give them the information on what car Drake was driving. He had to stall them as long as possible.

Crouching down beside the corpse, he picked up the wrench and repeatedly bludgeoned Luke's face, shattering his teeth. The rear molars were the most difficult to knock out. With every blow, Drake glanced around him, listening intently for engine noise. Nothing was coming.

He reached into Luke's mouth, pulled the last of the loose teeth from his gums, and tipped the head into his hand. After collecting all of the teeth, he thrust them into Luke's jacket pocket, which he noticed had a hood hanging from the rear. *That'll be useful.* They were both wearing jeans, so there was no need to switch pants, although Luke was wearing a checkered shirt. Hurriedly, he removed his own jacket and t-shirt and set about switching clothes with his victim.

Finally, he dragged the body along the road and placed it in the Mercedes passenger's seat. He then took the backpack with the $25,000 from the back seat, carried it to the Chevy, and secured it in the trunk.

He returned to the Mercedes and fired up the engine. *The tracks will be examined. It needs to look like an accident.* He reversed the car several hundred yards and gunned it forward, twisting the wheel, intentionally skidding across the rocky patch of land beside the road. He accelerated toward the edge and hit the brakes at the moment he was about to go over the edge. The tip of the hood protruded over the precipice. He put the car in park and pulled on the hand break, but left the engine running.

After stepping out of the car, he pulled Luke across into the driver's seat, and secured him with the seat belt for authenticity.

Reaching into the inside pocket of Luke's jacket, he took out a wallet. He counted two hundred and ten dollars and looked through the credit cards. *Luke Smith.* There was also a business card. Luke had been a computer repair technician. Just an ordinary guy.

And then he found a photograph in one of the side slots—a picture of Luke with an attractive young brunette. They looked so happy together.

The pain shot through Drake's head again. He dropped the wallet and fell to the floor, grasping his skull. It wasn't as bad as the last time, but sadness soared through him, paralyzing him where he knelt. Tears poured from him as he looked up at the dawn sky with a cry of anguish. It was something about the picture. All he could feel was that this man had done nothing to harm him—and he was *real*. He had a life, people who loved him. Drake knew he'd just taken his life from them.

But why should that affect him? He'd killed many men. It was a vocation to him. However, the sadness was debilitating. DeSouza's words rang out in his head:

The Interceptor is the voice inside you, just as you were the voice inside him.

Consumed with grief, he vomited onto the rocky ground. After a moment, his rage returned. "You son of a bitch! You aren't gonna win. I'll beat you, whatever you are."

He picked up the wallet and photograph. Wiping his face, he reached inside the Mercedes, put it in neutral, and released the hand break. The car rolled forward slightly. When he moved around to the back, he realized he had nothing to brace against the accelerator. Luke's lifeless foot would simply slip off.

Pushing it with all his might, he forced the front wheels over the edge. It continued for more than half the length of the car when the chassis became braced on the rock. Nevertheless, it was tilting precariously. Drake coughed as the exhaust fumes hit his lungs, but the engine had to be running in order to increase the likelihood of an explosion.

Using the leverage, he gripped the back of the car, gnashing his teeth with exertion. *Just a little more.* The weight of the car finally took over and tilted it farther. The rear wheels left the ground and the Mercedes drew itself up into a vertical position. It seemed to hesitate for a moment. And then, it was gone.

Drake moved over to the edge and watched the car descend down the canyon. It struck the bottom and exploded on impact.

As he turned and made his way toward the Chevy, the sadness struck him again. *Leave me alone. Get out of my head.*

He wiped his eyes again, climbed in, and turned the key in the ignition. The car fired up, but he couldn't bring himself to drive. He placed his forehead onto the steering wheel and succumbed to tears.

Suddenly, reality hit him. He couldn't afford to be there. He was already pushing his luck, having been out there for almost forty-five minutes. No cars had driven by, but it was only a matter of time.

He pressed his foot onto the accelerator, assuming complete focus again. The answer to the mystery of The Interceptor was just a few days ahead.

He pulled the hood of Luke's jacket over his head almost fearfully, as though he was hiding from . . . *himself.*

He gunned the Chevy along the desert highway with one thought fixed in his mind: *I'm coming home.*

Fourteen

Brenham

Andrew Wilmot paced his office in Langley. Never before had he experienced such excruciating anxiety. Garrett was on leave nursing her wounds, and Slamer was in pursuit of Drake. There was no guarantee he would track him down, much less defeat him in mortal combat.

And in ten minutes, he had an appointment with the 'old man', Jack Brenham, director of the CIA. Pre-empting the questions—why had he been spending so much time in a rarely-used facility? What had caused the gas explosion? Thirteen people dead? Garrett's injury? None of it appeared favorable. Wilmot's confidence in his own fabricated history and imaginative, overly-rehearsed revisionism was not great.

He halted in mid-stride, startled by the entrance of an older man in his late fifties. The man's authoritative demeanor, immaculate black suit, white shirt, and blue tie, offered the definitive image of a leader. "Sir?"

"I thought I'd spare you the ordeal of the trek up to my office, Wilmot," Director Brenham said. "Would you like to tell me what the hell has been happening? Because right now, we've got an incident on our hands."

"I know, sir."

Brenham came closer to him with a stern expression. "I was never in approval of you taking over SDT, Wilmot. You inherited your position from Wolfe by default. I was hoping his treachery would have ended. Now, it seems it's been replaced by your incompetence."

"Sir, I could have been killed, myself. Cynthia was injured. We had no way of knowing the gas pipes were corroded."

"You've been disappearing for days at a time for weeks, leaving Kerwin and Rhodes in charge of your office. What have you been up to?"

"ISIS."

Brenham frowned. "What about ISIS?"

"I intercepted a tip from a mercenary outfit in Syria eleven weeks ago. It seemed they were planning a strike against the US. I initiated an investigation into possible cells that might have been threats."

Brenham threw him a harsh glare. "And you didn't think to tell me about any of this? What were you thinking?"

"I couldn't entirely trust the source, sir, and until I was absolutely certain, I wasn't about to call upon further resources. I was acting in the best interests of the CIA."

"It's not your place to decide that."

"Sir, I . . ."

Brenham made a dismissive move with his hand. "What did you find out, now that you've decided to share your intel?"

"Nothing. It was all a lot of hot air, in my opinion."

"Well, you've wasted a hell of a lot of time on hot air, Wilmot, and thirteen people are dead."

"I know."

"It's your mess. You clean it up, or I swear, I'll propose that the president closes you down."

Wilmot looked up at Brenham sharply, his heart pounding.

"SDT," Brenham said sarcastically. "The Strategic Detection of Terrorism. It was set up under Treadwell's encouragement. Wolfe turned out to be a traitor too, and I still agreed to let it run from here under my supervision. You want to know why?"

"Yes, sir."

"Because I believed in it. It gave us a loophole for performing conventional investigations on select cases without having to call on the FBI. Despite its origins, I still believed it was useful. You have access to CIA equipment and facilities, but you're under my jurisdiction. One more screw up, and I'll have this department closed down for good. Are we clear?"

Wilmot gulped. "Yes, sir."

"Good. Now do your goddamn job and contact the families of those dead security guys. It's your responsibility." Brenham looked at his watch. "I've got a breakfast meeting."

Wilmot held his breath as Brenham exited the room. Only after the door was closed did he exhale with the most powerful sense of relief he'd ever known. *Call me, Slamer. Please call me with something.*

***

Kane Slamer entered the Coconino County Morgue in Flagstaff, Arizona at just past noon. His pursuit of Drake hadn't taken him long to stumble upon the commotion on the roadside. The Highway Patrol and a clearance crew dominated the scene of the crash. A crane had brought the burned-out Mercedes back to the top of the cliff by the time he'd arrived. Three digits on the license plate were visible, matching what he had written down. The cop he'd spoken to wasn't forthcoming with any answers and had been more concerned with telling Slamer to stand back. However, it was clear, even from a distance, that there was a body in the driver's seat. The morgue was now his only remaining option for finding answers.

A petite blonde receptionist looked up from her desk, her expression conveying a modicum of distress at the sight of him.

Slamer knew his appearance was not an advantage in this situation. He was aware he couldn't even smile at someone without looking like he intended to tear their throat out. "Hi," he said, attempting to sound as cordial as possible. "You just brought in someone I think I might know, and I was wondering if I could speak with the coroner."

"Yes, sir. What's the name of the deceased?"

"If it's the guy I think it is, his name was Matthew Bush. He was a research scientist. Apparently, his Mercedes went over a cliff a few miles back along the highway."

"I think I know the one you mean. Would you mind waiting for a moment? I'll get the coroner for you."

"Thanks."

Slamer paced the reception area as he waited, already convinced it wasn't Drake's body in the car. He knew him too well, but he needed something concrete to tell Wilmot.

If the real victim could be identified, they would have a lead on the car he was driving.

A tall, dark-haired, distinguished-looking man in his late forties appeared at the end of the corridor wearing a long white coat. "Yes, sir? How can I help?"

Slamer turned to him eagerly. "I'm looking for information on the guy they just brought in here from the Mercedes crash."

"Are you a relative?"

"Colleague, but only if it's the right guy. Is there anything you can tell me?"

"Not much. He was completely burned. There wasn't a patch of him untouched by flame. Total immolation. No fingerprints. Not even any teeth. That's the weirdest part."

Slamer frowned. "No teeth?"

"That's right. Most of the skeleton is still intact, but the teeth are gone. The jawbones are completely shattered. I've never seen a fire that could completely incinerate all of the teeth. There's no way of positively identifying him."

"That's just terrible," Slamer said, feigning a convincing 'horrified' act.

"If you think you know who he is, I could sure use your help with the paperwork. Otherwise, all I've got is a John Doe."

"Sure. I'll be with you in a moment. I need to make a call." Slamer made his way out of the reception room into the parking area, and hastily took out his cell phone.

Wilmot was startled out of deep thought by the vibration of his unauthorized cell-phone in his inside pocket. He knew the call couldn't be from anyone other than Slamer. With a combination of eagerness and trepidation, he opened the line. "What have you got?"

"Can you talk?"

"For the moment, yeah."

"It's not good."

Wilmot closed his eyes in dismay. "What happened?"

"He switched cars with some poor schlub just outside of Flagstaff, and then rolled the Mercedes off a cliff with the other guy in it."

"Do you have an ID on this other guy?"

"My thoughts exactly, but there isn't enough left of him to fit in a cigar box."

"Dental records?"

"Not a single tooth left. He must have smashed his face to pieces to get 'em all out. Apparently his jaw was completely shattered and every inch of the rest of him was burned to a crisp. Not even a fingerprint survived."

"Damn!"

"All we've got here is a John Doe, who's gonna join a long line of missing persons."

"What do you have planned for your next move?"

"We don't know who this other guy was, so we have no idea what the hell he's driving. There's only one thing I can do."

"What's that?"

"Follow the blood trail."

"Keep me posted." Wilmot's hand came up to his forehead despairingly. His brow was damp and he felt the blood draining from his face. He sat back in his chair infused with dread.

Fifteen

Invisible Protector

On the second night following his acquisition of the Chevy, Drake checked into a run-down motel in Oklahoma. A rural backwater on the approach to Arkoma, it provided him with another remote location to sleep. The night before, he'd slept in a similar motel on the New Mexico/Oklahoma border.

After showering, he took one hundred dollars from the money in his backpack and locked the remainder in the closet. He'd noticed a biker's tavern a mile along the dirt road from the motel, and decided a few drinks would be in order.

With the hood over his head, he sat in the corner of the biker's bar, appropriately called *Choppers*. It had turned 9:00 p.m. and was growing darker outside by the minute. He stared at the empty glass before him. It was his second beer, but they'd had little effect on him.

A rockabilly band played at the far side of the room. The wooden, dusty floor and the upkeep of the place left much to be desired. Biker regalia adorned the walls, covering much of the eroded paintwork, but the patrons seemed unconcerned, even comfortable. They were a fraternity of leather-clad, bearded, long-haired and balding bikers, whose only agenda was to get hammered, as shown by their intoxicated mirth.

Drake caught sight of an attractive brunette dancing with one of the male patrons. Garrett had been his last screw—an experience he'd found far from satisfying. He gazed with predatory lust at the woman on the dance floor, estimating she was perhaps twenty-five and in particularly good shape. Scantily-dressed in hot pants that rode up her buttocks, and a low-cut blouse, her ample cleavage was totally exposed. Red lipstick and heavy makeup made it clear she was out to seduce. Her companion appeared to be somewhat conservative and out of place in the bar.

But what was it about her that had captured his attention so profoundly? The style and color of her hair seemed familiar somehow. He just couldn't place it.

He stood, approached the bartender again, and pointed to the beer dispenser.

"You want another?"

Drake nodded but didn't speak. He simply kept his head bowed, his eyes shadowed over by the hood. The bartender handed him the beer, and Drake placed the cash on the bar.

After another couple of beers, he felt the effects of the alcohol finally, although he was conscious of not taking it too far. He still had a considerable journey ahead of him and wanted to reach his destination by the following night.

He glanced at the digital clock on the wall, which now read 11:23. *Time to get some sleep.* He finished his fourth beer and made his way out of the bar.

He stopped to inhale the night air in an attempt to clear his head. The music from the bar drowned out all other sounds.

As he moved away toward the road, the sound grew quieter, revealing another noise coming from the darkness along the opposite side of the road. Curious, he turned and made his way toward it. Somehow, it sounded like a scream.

Jane Marabel crawled backward, pushing with her hands and heels, away from two youthful attackers.

She was an impoverished woman with a young daughter to support. She'd been moving from bar to bar all afternoon, in the hope of attracting a man who might have had the means to support her. She thought she'd found him. He wasn't attractive to her in the least. He was too clean-cut and timid-looking, but he appeared to be someone who was educated, and most likely had a good job. All she knew about him was that his name was Brian. Her plan had been to lure him back to her trailer and captivate him with her sexual charms.

That was, until *they* attacked them.

Two hoodlums punched Brian repeatedly in the head while he held his jacket tightly closed. What he lacked in brawn, he clearly made up for in courage. He wasn't about to let them take his wallet. He looked at Jane and cried, "Run!"

Despite being under attack, he was undeniably concerned for her safety. She wept with shock and a tinge of guilt at her predatory agenda. This was a man who was willing to take a beating in order to save her.

A dark silhouette, formed eerily by the moonlight, fell across the street. Jane looked up and saw a huge man wearing a dark hood, which concealed his face in shadow.

One of the two young punks turned to him. "Hey, beat it, asshole."

The shadow man's foot shot up, taking the thug's nose clean off. The other man turned to the interloper and attempted to lunge at him, only to be met with the blade of his hand to his throat. The punk fell to the ground, choking.

The stranger knelt down, grasped them by their hair, and held their terrified gazes for a second. He then drove their skulls into one another with ferocious force before discarding their unconscious forms on the road.

Jane stood, shaking and sobbing hysterically. "T-thank you."

Brian pushed himself up off the ground, his face cut, and bloodied. A hint of swelling around his eyes was already becoming apparent. "Oh, man, am I glad to see you. I can't tell you how much I appreciate what you just—"

The man in the hood struck Brian in the jaw, rendering him unconscious.

Jane staggered back. "Oh, my God!"

He came toward her slowly. Terrified, she ran into the trees. She was blind with fear and sprinted aimlessly, too afraid to look back.

Hysteria and terror were impairing her reason as she scurried through the woods. There were so many trees. So many obstacles. Every time she thought she'd found her stride, another tree or protrusion of twigs would slow her down.

What was happening? She'd met a nice guy in a bar and was taking him home. They'd been attacked by two muggers. And then a man without a face arrived to save them. He was remarkable. The speed with which he'd taken down the two punks was astonishing. But then he turned on them too. It was as though she was in a nightmare. It couldn't be happening.

She glanced back and caught sight of him through the trees. He was so close, and no matter how hard she tried, she couldn't get away from him. There was so much forestry in the way. Waves of terror came over her as she struggled to escape through the woods. Breathlessness and panic continued to impair her ability to think rationally, and her actions became frantic.

Her foot hit a rock, sending her plummeting onto the ground. Panicked, she hustled onto her feet again, and glanced back for the briefest of moments. He was standing above her. She tripped again and fell onto her back.

He grasped her flimsy blouse and tore it in two.

"P-please. Don't do this," she said. "I'm begging you. Don't do it."

The man suddenly fell, gripping his head. She looked at him bewildered. What was wrong with him? It didn't make any sense.

But neither did it matter. She got to her feet again and ran, leaving her strange assailant in agony.

"Oh, God," Drake whimpered as the debilitating pain crippled him. Again, the voices in his head echoed:

I can't do this. Please, I'm begging you. I can't do it.

You don't have to. I do. Now, take it steady and join me here.

Oh, God, please don't let me fall.

You're not going to fall.

He screamed with the pain. It was unbearable.

Hold on!

"No!" he cried.

Hold on!

"No!"

Gradually, the sharp, piercing agony in his head began to ease enough for him to get back on his feet. His vision was blurred and the pounding in his head was nauseating. He knew he had to get back to the motel.

He staggered back through the trees, falling sporadically. The pain was draining him of every iota of energy.

He soon came to the edge of the forest and saw the road ahead of him. He tried to hurry toward it, but fell onto his face. Struggling to get onto his feet again, he crawled onto the roadside.

The bar was right ahead of him, and the motel was a mile past it. The way he felt, it might as well have been a thousand. With slow, weakened steps, he moved forward. Every step was an ordeal. All he could think of was collapsing onto the motel bed.

He glanced at the two unconscious thugs and the woman's friend. He couldn't even remember why he'd done it. He barely noticed the blood-spattered face of the one who didn't have a nose.

As he made his way along the road, he scarcely recalled the lustful urge he'd felt toward the woman when he'd first seen her in the bar. He'd wanted to take her. To *own* her. It was as though it was his right. Now, all he could feel was crushed.

It took him an hour to reach the motel. His fingers trembled when he took the door key out of his pocket and inserted it into the lock. He pushed the door open and almost fell into the room. Bracing himself against the walls, he reached out for the bed.

His eyeballs felt like they were about to explode. He needed to close them. He threw the hood from his head, fell onto the bed, and sank into the pillow.

Drake walked through the void of darkness, and the fear tore through him again. It was a horrifying, endless vacuum of nothingness. Every direction led to nowhere. No matter which way he turned, no matter how hard he tried to see a ray of hope, there was nothing except the darkness.

Hey, Scorp!

He turned to the sound of the voice, but once again, there was nobody there. "Show yourself!"

I can't. You won't let me.

"What do you mean, 'I won't let you'?"

More of it is coming back to you, but not enough, yet. There was just enough for me to stop you again.

"Are you the pain I felt?"

Kind of.

"Are you The Interceptor?"

That's what they call me.

"What are you?" There was no response, but at least the voice was giving him some semblance of sensory experience in this place. "Tell me who you are."

I'm the one who exists to stop cruel, raping, predatory scumbags like you.

For the first time, the voice demonstrated a hint of aggression. Before, he'd seemed fairly light-hearted.

She reminded you of her, didn't she? You tried to take her. It was only because of her that I could protect that woman.

"Reminded me of whom?"

I had no connection to that other poor kid you killed, and I wasn't strong enough to stop you. But this time, you came so close to remembering.

"I came so close to remembering what?"

Hold on!

He shivered at the sound of those words. "What does that mean?"

It means everything I am, and everything you're not. It means hope.

The fear gripped Drake again. "P-please. Show yourself."

You sure you can take it?

"I don't know what you mean."

Can you remember?

"Remember what?"

Think. Think deep and hard. Remember hope.

The words that had taken him down in the woods came back to him:

Oh, God, please don't let me fall.

You're not going to fall.

A shape appeared through the darkness and came closer. It seemed to be a man walking upon the dark air. Or at least, he *thought* it was a man. Within moments, he became clearer. He was wearing a black suit of some kind, with a belt around his waist that seemed to contain an array of technological gadgets.

And then the helmet came into view. It was like a motor-cycle helmet, but more slender, as though it was molded to his head.

"Interceptor," Drake said. "So, you're my enemy."

"Depends how you look at it."

Why does his voice sound so familiar? "Take the helmet off."

"I can try, but I don't think I'll be able to."

"Why not?"

"Because you won't let me."

"Why do you say that?"

"I'm breaking through slowly, but it's taking time. You're in the stronger position."

"Take it off!"

The Interceptor reached up to the helmet and gripped the sides. "OK. Here goes." He moved his hands upward. The helmet began to come loose . . .

Drake awoke abruptly, coated with perspiration. He shivered uncontrollably, terrified by knowing, and yet *not* knowing. "Oh, Jesus. What are you?"

For the first time since his childhood, he wept. And yet it was to the last one who'd made him weep he had to return.

In the place where it all began.

Sixteen

Premonition

Jed Crane sealed a suitcase and took it from the bed in his favela apartment. His heart fluttered with apprehension.

"Do you have to leave?"

He turned to Juanita, his roommate of the last three months. She'd been a good friend to him, and he knew she was secretly in love with him. It hadn't been easy for him to resist. She was appealing and sensual, but he had a life and a fiancée back home. His sojourn in Brazil had only ever been a temporary hideout while he tried to come up with a solution to his plight. Now, one had been handed to him.

Juanita was a poor woman as he was now a poor man. Together, they'd managed to pull enough money together to finance living in a run-down apartment in a favela.

"I have to go, Juanita," he said. "We both knew this day would come."

"How are you getting back?"

"I've got a job on a cargo ship. It docks in Florida, and they didn't ask any questions. I'll just do my job and get off when we arrive." He walked over and held her. "Once I've got all of this sorted out, I'll do whatever I can to help you."

"Is it about the men who came here?"

"One of them."

"The one who collapsed in front of me?"

"Yes."

"But . . . who is he?"

Jed looked away sadly. "He was my friend. A courageous hero who put himself on the line to save innocents."

"But he came here to kill you."

"That wasn't *him*. That was what they did to him. It's what I have to stop. There is an evil running amok in America, and it operates from the highest levels of intelligence." He picked up his suitcase and kissed her on the cheek. "Goodbye, my friend." He turned and walked toward the door.

***

"Samaritans, Emily speaking. How can I help?"

A tearful male voice came through the receiver, barely coherent. Emily's eyes moistened at the mere sound of it. She'd had so many of them and it was beginning to wear her down. She could feel his pain without even knowing the cause of it. Every call was another voice of heartbreak and devastation. She questioned if she had what it took to continue with her new position. She felt too close to the callers for comfort. Conversely, she considered, perhaps, that was how she was able to empathize with them. She knew she couldn't abandon them.

"Can you describe what you're feeling right now?" she said. "Can you tell me what happened to you?"

"They took everything from me. My whole life."

"Who did? What did they take from you? Can you tell me your name?"

"M-my name's Mark. I live in a rough part of town. A gang came into my home and robbed me blind. I live alone. I haven't seen my family for five years. They took my hope chest. Every last photograph I had of them was in it, even my mom and dad, and they're no longer alive. I don't have a penny to my name, and I can't pay my rent. I have nothing left."

She could tell he was desperate and knew she had to keep him on the line. "OK, stay with me, Mark. We can work this out. I know you're terribly sad. I understand that." *Focus on his strengths and find hope for him.* "I will alert my director and try to get you set up in the shelter here. You don't have to be out on the streets. Then we can work on getting you back on your feet. There is always hope, Mark. Believe me, I know."

"How?"

"Mark, this isn't about me. This is about you. All I can tell you is . . . you feel like you don't know what you can do when you're on the edge of it all. You feel like your life is over, and nobody is coming to save you. Somebody saved me, and I want to be there for you. Now, do you think you can trust me?"

"I . . . I guess so."

"OK, what skills do you have? Tell me about yourself. We *will* find a way out of this."

As the conversation continued, Emily began to feel stronger. She'd been flitting between the heartbreak caused by her own innate compassion, her doubt that she could continue, and then to knowing she could. In an ironic way, it was helping her through her own traumas and personal issues.

During the call, she learned everything she could about Mark, just as she learned as much about each of the callers. It was a huge responsibility—far more so than when she was a nun. Back then, her every move arose from orders. This time, she was subservient only to her own heart, making it such a trying task. If anything went wrong, it would be on her own head. But she was getting better at it with each passing day.

By the time the call had ended, she'd persuaded Mark to make contact with his estranged siblings and advised him on how to approach them. She put in his mind the likelihood that they would have copies of his lost photographs, from which hc could take duplicates. It didn't take her long to get him to realize, not only could he get his life back, but a life that was far better than the one he'd been living.

Eisely had spent much time training her in procedure, teaching her the pattern of questions, and the temperament a distraught person responded. Finding common ground she could empathize with, and offering no judgment, was essential. She was beginning to realize he had chosen her wisely. Who could possibly empathize with hopelessness more than her, after being a victim of a human slavery ring? And who would have had more of an aversion to judgment than one who had escaped from a convent? Finally, she was finding her true self.

She stood up from her desk, walked across to the hook on the wall, and took her coat. Belinda said she'd meet her outside.

Belinda was on her mind often. She was everything she'd ever dreamed of in a friend: spirited, funny, supportive, loving, and most of all, free. She was her late brother's lover, but in Belinda, she'd found a sister of her own.

She walked out of the room. At that moment, Glen Eisley stepped out of his office and came toward her. "Emily. How was it today?" he said.

"It was . . . good, sir."

"You sound uncertain."

"I don't know. There are so many people with problems, and sometimes it overwhelms me. But then . . ."

"Yes? Tell me, Emily."

"It makes me feel so good when I can help them. They really seem to hear me. Ideas come to me when I talk to them that help me show them there are alternatives to . . . suicide."

Eisely smiled warmly. "This is why I asked you to do this, Emily. I've been involved in this for many years, and I know an empathetic person when I see one. Those who have suffered are those who have the most kindness in them. I knew this would help you too."

"Thank you, sir."

"*Glen*," he said. "And I'll be here whenever you need me."

"Thank you, si—*Glen*." She chuckled.

He patted her shoulder affectionately, and moved on.

She walked down the steps and saw Belinda waiting for her at the bottom. "Hi."

"Hi, Em. How did it go today?"

"Same as usual. Emotionally trying, but rewarding."

They turned and walked out the door. Emily could sense Belinda was not her usual self. "Is everything OK? What have you been doing today?"

Belinda replied, "Alex and I have been going through reams of engineering reports for quotes in a new ad campaign for the *Air Shark Four*. Charlton's launching it next year. He wants to really push the improvements to the corporate community."

"Wow. That sounds pretty complicated."

"It is, but Alex has been an invaluable help. He really knows about this stuff. I have to admit, it feels great to have a job where I have some responsible input. When I was a secretary, I felt like a spare part."

"So, why do you seem so glum?"

They continued along the street and Belinda's brow furrowed. "I've . . . not been able to concentrate much. Something's bugging me, but I don't know what it is."

"That's odd."

"I just can't shake a feeling I've been having the last the few days."

"What feeling?"

Belinda stopped in mid-stride and turned to her. "I keep feeling like . . . something terrible is about to happen."

Seventeen

Origin

1:14 a.m.

Under the cloak of darkness, Drake walked around the back of a once-well-kept, three-story house, just outside Rock Hill, North Carolina. Rage began to consume him again as he looked upon the property for the first time in over a decade. There were so many memories, none of them heart-warming.

Fixed to the wall beside the back door was a key safe. *Is the code still the same?* He punched in the digits that were permanently fixed into his mind—numbers he'd spent his childhood in fear of punching in. He'd been dependent on the house for his survival, but inside had been nothing but terror and pain.

The key safe came open and he smiled. *You're such an asshole, Joe. You couldn't even be bothered to change the code after all these years.*

He opened the back door and stepped inside. Through the moonlight, he could see the place was neglected. The furniture and fittings were the same, but the place looked as though it hadn't been cleaned in months. Formerly, it had been impeccable. His foster father, Joe Cassidy, had been a successful property developer. Drake immediately deduced the revelations that had come out about the man at the trial of nineteen-year-old Brandon Drake had destroyed him. He knew Cassidy had been legally barred from fostering children for life. Clearly, the bad publicity had seriously affected his property business in the process.

With slow, vengeful steps, he entered the house through the kitchen. He entered the dining room and noticed the antique, oak dining table remained. It was scattered with litter, and a coating of dust was illuminated by an almost-exhausted candle flame. A smell of musk and dirt permeated the air, with a slight garnish of whisky. *Oh, you really fucked up, didn't you, Joe?*

He looked up at a replica Samurai sword hanging from a hook on the wall, and chuckled. Joe had always seen himself as some kind of warrior 'hard man', but only with little kids.

He continued into the hallway and heard footsteps coming from the landing at the top of the stairs.

"Is somebody there?" a female voice said.

He braced himself behind the stairwell in the shadows. *Stay out of it, Gretchen. I don't want you involved in this.*

More memories came back to him, giving him a moment of pause. Gretchen Cassidy had tried to protect him from Joe, but she was always rewarded with a punch in the mouth. Resentment toward her festered in his heart. She was weak, and she'd still stayed with the son of a bitch. She was a born victim.

He caught a glimpse of her as she reached the bottom of the stairwell. She seemed so much older than the ten years since he last saw her should've allowed. However, he couldn't let her see him.

With dazzling speed, he emerged from the shadows and punched her—a precision strike to the base of her skull. She fell to the floor, unconscious. *I'm sorry, Mom.*

Joe would be appearing any minute if he was even remotely sober. Drake returned to the living room and took a seat at the head of the table.

Within moments, he heard a groaning voice coming from the landing. "What's goin' on down there?"

Drake waited as the sound of footsteps came down the stairwell. His first view of Joe Cassidy through the candlelight was that of an unkempt man in his late fifties. Cassidy's dirty white vest, blue and white-striped pajama bottoms, and apparent obesity, gave him the appearance of a man who'd given up. *You really are a pathetic asshole, Joe.*

Drake watched in silence as the man crouched down over his unconscious wife.

"Gretchen!" Cassidy said. "Gretchen, wake up."

"Hi, *Dad.*"

Cassidy froze as though he couldn't believe his own hearing. He slowly turned and looked up. "N-no. It can't be."

"What's wrong, Dad? You look like you just saw a ghost."

"B-but . . . you're dead."

"Clearly exaggerated."

Cassidy stood, while Drake walked over to the liquor cabinet and helped himself to a bottle of brandy and a glass.

"What are you doing here?" Cassidy said. "And what did you do to Gretchen?"

Drake poured himself a generous glassful and sat down again. "A carefully-controlled blow to the base of the skull. It jars the brain. She'll be out for awhile, but she's all right. I wanted to talk to you privately."

"What do you want?"

"Answers."

"What answers?"

Drake took a mouthful of brandy. "You said you thought I was dead. I want you to explain that to me."

"Why do you need me to explain it? It was all over the news."

"Yeah, well, it ain't quite that simple. I've been out of it for awhile, and I wanna know what the fuck is going on."

Cassidy sat in the chair at the opposite side of the table. They faced one another through the eeriness of the candlelight, the aura of hostility ever present.

"According to the news, you died in a crash in Los Angeles," Cassidy said.

Drake frowned, bemused. "Los Angeles?"

"Yeah. Some kind of test aircraft. It happened apparently after you and your brother broke your sister out from some slavery ring. The army and some intel agency were involved, too."

Drake's mind became numb with what Cassidy had just told him. It was too much. "Brother and sister?"

"What's wrong with you? Some kind of amnesia? Yeah, your natural brother hooked up with you after you broke out of Leavenworth."

"Leavenworth?"

Cassidy looked at him pensively for a moment. "You really don't know, do you?"

"No, I don't, and that's why I'm here."

"You were all over the news for a couple of years. Before that, the last I heard, you were injured in Afghanistan. Can't say I was sorry to hear it."

Drake laughed angrily. "Keep talking, asshole. What happened to me after Afghanistan?"

"Why should I tell you?"

Drake stood and walked over to the Samurai sword on the wall, removed it from the hook, and drew it from its sheath.

"Put that down, *boy*!" Cassidy said with a growl.

"Are you being serious? You really think you can tell me what to do?"

"I can still give you a whooping, kid."

"How deluded can a man be?" Drake spun around and held the point of the blade to Cassidy's neck. "You remember how you used to stick me and cut the soles of my feet with this thing? It was agony for me to walk for days afterward."

Even through his sudden fear, it seemed Cassidy wasn't going to repent. "Apparently, I didn't do it often enough. It's obviously what you could have done with a lot more of."

Drake shook his head in disbelief. "You are so obscenely stupid. I am what I am because of you. Hatred and rage drive me. After you, it was the army. Always authority. Always someone trying to control my life. I hate the fucking world, Joe. I know what I am, and *you* are responsible. You created me."

Cassidy was quiet, his gaze on the sword at all times.

"Now talk, ass-wipe. What happened to me after Afghanistan?"

"I . . . I only know what happened from the papers and the TV. They sent you to work at some weapons development facility in Washington. Mach Industries. After that, you went crazy and tried your hand at becoming some kind of superhero. They even turned you into a comic book." Cassidy laughed. "You, a comic hero. That's got to be the joke of the century."

"What comic hero?"

Cassidy looked up at him with tears of laughter running down his cheeks. "The Interceptor."

Interceptor. Interceptor. Interceptor. The word rang out in Drake's head causing him to stagger backward. *No, it can't be. It can't be . . . me.* But deep down, he knew it was. He suddenly realized he'd always known.

He stepped forward again. "You'd better tell me what you know, or I swear, Cassidy, I'm gonna kill you. What did I do? What were these *superhero* things I'm supposed to have done?"

"Carringby Industries in Denver. You saved the Reese woman. It was all about her. You went across the country with her. You were on TV together. I saw it."

"Who?"

"Belinda Reese."

A faint hint of the pain in his head struck him when he heard her name. *Belinda Reese. Belinda Reese. Belinda Reese.* He was now certain this was the woman who'd been tormenting him. *She* was his Achilles Heel. He could finally see the connection between The Interceptor and 'the woman'. He just couldn't process it all.

"What's wrong with you?"

Drake shook his head. "It's nothing."

"You're pathetic, you know that? You always were a sniveling, snot-nosed little shit. You cost me everything. My business. My position in the community. I hate you, Brandon."

Satisfied he'd just received more information than he'd expected, Drake raised the sword. "Then consider this your retirement, Joe."

Cassidy's eyes widened in terror.

"Go to hell, motherfucker. I'll see you later." He slashed the sword across in a horizontal movement, decapitating Joe Cassidy in one clean stroke. The head fell onto the floor and rolled.

Drake watched for a few seconds as Joe's heart pumped the last of his blood through the remnants of his lower neck. Finally, the headless body slumped off the chair.

Drake looked on, almost mesmerized as blood dripped from the sword. He tilted it one way and the other in the realization that it was the tool of his own creation. The brutal cruelty of it was what made him who he was. In a decision to embrace his former fear, he chose to make it his own.

Kneeling down, he grasped Cassidy's vest and wiped the sword clean. After sheathing it, he hooked it across his back with the strap.

Looking around the room, his mind reeled with the information Cassidy had revealed. He needed to know more—something that would provide him with further answers.

He switched on the lights and hurried around the living room, but there was nothing he could use.

He ran up the stairs and scanned each room in turn. When he came to Gretchen and Joe's bedroom, he moved around the bed and found a laptop computer, complete with a power pack.

Drake took the laptop and power leads and ran back down the stairs, quickly becoming fingerprint conscious. *What have I touched?* The sword was on his back. He'd used the door key, which was in his pocket. *The glass and brandy bottle.*

He reached the dining room, picked up the bottle and glass, and put them in the side pockets of his hooded jacket.

After hurrying out through the kitchen, he slipped his hand under the sleeve of his hoodie and wiped the outside door handle, then the key code buttons.

The Chevy was parked behind the trees on the other side of the garden. With the sword on his back, he pulled the hood over his head and made his way across the clearing.

Now, he could assimilate his thoughts. He'd somehow found his brother. *I can't believe I found Tyler. And . . . I have a sister?*

But something had been done to him to give him a different persona. Under the spell of this other identity, he'd become this *Interceptor*, and saved some woman named Belinda Reese. From his experiences in his visions and dreams, The Interceptor had always drawn reference to a woman. She was the one who kept bringing him down. She had to be the cause of the pain that debilitated him. But who was she? To him, she was merely a pain in his head. He couldn't associate her with a living person.

Where was she? What was she to him that could induce such excruciating pain?

The government had taken four years of his life from him, brainwashed him, kept him prisoner in the Mojave Desert complex, used him for their own ends, and then tried to kill him. He had to have his revenge. But how would he accomplish such a mission if the pain in his head kept bringing him down?

With the laptop, he could now search and find out everything about what he'd been doing during his lost four years. He had to locate the one who was weakening him. It was the only way he was going to survive.

He knew he had to kill Belinda Reese.

Eighteen

The Stranger in the Mirror

Drake drove aimlessly through the night, his mind awash with what he'd learned. He had no choice but to get out of North Carolina. Gretchen would've revived before long to discover her decapitated husband, and would've contacted the authorities. Drake had no desire to kill her. She'd tried to be kind to him when he was a boy, but she never had the guts to stand up to Joe. Maybe now she'd have the opportunity to live her own life, all by virtue of a blow to the back of her head. It surprised him that he still retained a degree of regard for Gretchen Cassidy.

At noon the following day, he pulled up at a motel in Danville, Virginia, close to the border with North Carolina. It was a random stop, but it was far away from where he'd killed his foster father, and he needed sleep.

He awoke at 9:00 p.m., went out to an adjacent truck stop for a burger, and then returned to his motel room. A burning question plagued him: *Who was I?*

He connected Cassidy's laptop to one of the room's plugs and opened up an internet search for 'Brandon Drake'.

Images of him appeared in the sidebar on the screen. The first was a close-up shot of him being led across the courtyard at Fort Bragg. Enlarging it, he saw it was him. But it wasn't *him*. He had no memory of what he was looking at. The face on the screen was so much gentler than his. It seemed to be imbued with compassion and

130

much vulnerability. *He* was so unlike *him.* It was like looking in a mirror, but seeing a total stranger. *Is this you, Interceptor?* He studied the image of his doppelganger for long moments before noticing the article beneath entitled: 'Death of a Hero.'

He read the story of how he'd rescuing Belinda Reese from Treadwell's operatives at Carringby Tower, and their escape from the police in a flying car . . . "What the hell?"

The article continued with an account of his escape from a Wyoming police cell and a chase with the army.

Something about that was familiar. Wyoming. The woods. An image of him kicking the crap out of some guy in a suit flashed before his eyes. It was as though he was remembering something he'd actually experienced, unlike the sounds of the voices in his head.

Then it dawned on him. The guy he'd kicked the crap out of in Wyoming—was Wilmot. He could see his face as clearly as he was seeing the computer screen. *The son of a bitch was there. It was him. He was a part of all this from the beginning.*

He kept reading and came to a story about an attack at Channel 7 studios. That felt familiar too. It was something about a gang, running through the streets with a woman, and a derelict building.

Then he came to the story of his arrest and trial at Fort Bragg, and his escape from Fort Leavenworth. It concluded with the account of his involvement in a rescue attempt in Los Angeles—a human trafficking organization set up by fragmented members of one of the Tongs.

He looked away from the screen trying desperately to allow the memories to come back to him. The feeling that he was close to recalling the events was overwhelming.

And then he read the details. The rescue had occurred in an abandoned fish factory situated on Los Angeles Harbor. There had been a conflict between him, the army, and SDT. That was when he'd supposedly died. He'd been in an experimental aircraft. The flying car. It had crashed into a jeep at the site of the conflict.

Fish factory. Tong. Those two points seemed familiar to him. He tried to focus on them to see if anything came back to him.

He sensed a pain in his shoulder as though it was being squeezed, but it was more than that. It was an intense, penetrating, burning pain. It wasn't like the flashbacks he'd had through the Interceptor's memories. As with his memory of Wilmot in the Wyoming woods, he was actually remembering it as a personal experience.

He saw a flash of something. There was darkness, and then he was firing a machine gun, blowing a Chinese man's head to pieces. Then he was driving the nozzle of a machine pistol into the shattered knee of another Chinese guy.

One flash led to another. There was a huge Chinese man gripping him, pinning him against a wall. He could feel the hatred he'd felt toward this man, but he couldn't put it together in any context. Had he broken the giant's neck? He couldn't be sure. There was someone else there too. Through a blurry haze, he was sure he could remember a young man. *Could that have been my brother?*

He returned to the search page and came to an older post dated April 26th, 2014 from the website of *The Wall Street Journal*: 'The Trial of Brandon Drake.' It began with another account of that which had been covered in the other article, but delved more deeply into the details of his trial. There was a mention of him taking on a team of MPs in the courtroom. That also triggered something. Once again, he could remember with his own mind. The courtroom flashed before his eyes. There was the woman through a haze, although he couldn't make out her face. All he could see were the MPs. He was leaping across the tables, kicking and punching them into oblivion—and he loved every minute of it.

Something like an electric shock seized him, and the memory ended.

He continued reading about who had given evidence at his trial. There had been Woodroffe, police officers, an agent from the FBI, and Professor Abraham Jacobson, from Mach Industries. He remembered Cassidy mentioning that place. It was some kind of complex in Washington D.C. where they'd sent him to after Dashti Margo. *Why can't I remember any of this? How could they have done this to me? How could I have lived another life and not remember it?*

He came out of the page and entered 'Belinda Reese'. With shaking hands, he clicked the search button. Instantly, a thumbnail of a woman's face appeared in the sidebar beside a long list of article entries. He swallowed hard, clicked on the thumbnail, and her face filled the screen. As his gaze fell upon her fully, the pain throbbed in his temples. But this time, it was accompanied by his ultimate Achilles Heel; that which was the very antithesis of who he was. He felt *sadness*. Tears poured along his cheeks at the sight of her. *What are you? What are you doing to me?* He clenched his fists as a means of suppressing the feelings her image was causing.

Unable to bear it, he came out of the web page, and returned to the articles about her. *Where was she?* There was nothing to indicate her whereabouts. It was clear there was a desire to keep her location anonymous. She'd become a media sensation, all on account of him.

As he read further, he came upon details of his brother and sister. Tyler's name was now Faraday, and he'd been adopted by a helicopter mogul.

But it was his sister that offered the greatest intrigue. She'd been raised in a convent and she'd escaped, but was then kidnapped by a human trafficking outfit. It seemed he'd been responsible for rescuing her just before his supposed death. There were references to a brief interview with her when she said she'd become close to Belinda Reese.

Another search, this time for 'Emily Drake', offered a recent interview in *The Dallas Morning News.* Emily had stated she lived with Belinda, although it didn't say where. The focus of the small article was Emily's new posting with The Samaritans.

Drake smiled. An end to his vulnerability was now in sight, but there was another he needed to meet during his search for Belinda Reese. And that man would provide him with the weaponry he needed.

***

Kane Slamer approached the reception desk on the first floor of the Piedmont Medical Center in Rock Hill, North Carolina. Reports of Joe Cassidy's ghastly death had been all over the news. The knowledge that Cassidy had been Brandon Drake's foster father presented the likelihood that Drake was the killer.

"Yes, sir. Can I help you?" a young blonde receptionist said.

"Hi. I understand a lady was brought in here yesterday. A Gretchen Cassidy."

"Are you a relative?"

"No, I'm a . . . private investigator. It would really help me if I could have a few moments with Mrs. Cassidy."

She looked at him with more than a degree of reservation. He knew, once again, his appearance was the cause.

"I'll call the doctor," she said. "Wait here."

"Sure."

Several minutes later, the receptionist returned with a tall man wearing a white medical coat. "I'm Doctor Grant-Reason," the man said. "How can I help?"

"Nice to meet you, sir," Slamer said. "If possible, I'd like to ask Gretchen Cassidy a few questions about the man who attacked her. I'm a private investigator."

"I'm afraid that won't be possible. She's under sedation right now. When she was brought in she was suffering from shock."

"I can imagine."

"However, it wouldn't do much good to talk to her. All she remembers is walking down the stairs and then waking

135

up with a pain in the back of her head. She was struck at the base of the skull. She never saw her attacker."

"Well, thank you for your time, Doctor." Slamer turned and made his way out.

In the parking lot, he climbed into his car and took out his cell phone. He selected his contact and the response came in seconds. "It's me."

Wilmot's impatient voice came through the receiver. "I know it's you. Who else would it be? What have you got?"

"I drew a blank again. The Cassidy woman is under sedation. According to her doctor, she never saw her attacker. This guy Cassidy wasn't popular, so there's no guarantee it was Drake that killed him."

"It's likely, though."

"Yeah, and that's all I've got to go on."

"What are your plans?"

"Guesswork is all I have. If Drake killed Cassidy, I can only try to pre-empt what, if anything, he may have told him. If they spoke, it's probable Cassidy told him about the life he can't remember. If he did, there's a good chance he'll be out there trying to trace those who knew him."

"That's a lot of 'what ifs', Slamer."

"Look, you got any better ideas? He could be hiding out in Central England for all we know. I'm not even doing this in an official capacity, Wilmot. I can't talk to the police, so why don't you use your divine influence and find out what the story is with the Cassidy house. Did he leave fingerprints? Was anything taken?"

There was a momentary pause on the line, and then Wilmot said, "All right, I'll do what I can. Let me know where you're headed."

"It's like I said in the beginning, Wilmot. I'm following the blood trail."

"All right, Slamer, just find him."

"Oh, I'll find him. And when I do, he'll become a distant memory pretty damn quick." Slamer ended the call and fired up the engine.

Eighteen

The Visitor

Emily sat at her desk at the Samaritans gazing at the phone. She'd only taken three calls all morning. The lines seemed to have gone quiet.

There was a knock at the door. "Come in."

A twenty-something blonde female entered with a coffee in her hand. "Hi Emily. I brought you a coffee. How's it been today?"

"Oh, thank you, Jessie. You're very kind. It's been really quiet. How about you?"

"Weird, actually."

"Weird how?"

"We've been having calls from someone who keeps dropping the phone as soon as we answer. Laura had one, and Amber had it twice. I just had one too."

"Well . . . some people are seriously distressed with their lives. Too distressed to even talk about it, I suppose."

"I guess so."

Emily's phone rang.

"I'll leave you to it. Maybe you'll have better luck," Jessie said, and left.

Emily picked up the phone. "Samaritans. Emily speaking. How can I help?"

There was silence on the line, but it remained open.

"Please don't hang up," Emily said. "Maybe I can help. What's your name?"

A deep, resonating male voice came through the receiver. "It's . . . John."

To Emily, he sounded quite strong, unlike the majority of callers. They were usually quiet, weakened, and defeated. "Hi, John. I'm here to help. Can you tell me how you are? How you're feeling?"

"I'm . . . lost."

"Lost in what way?"

"I've never really had a family. I have no one. No one at all. I'm totally alone."

Emily felt compelled to do whatever she could to keep this caller on the line. "John, I understand what you're saying, believe me. I grew up without my family, too. But I found my brother, and we're very close now."

"You're lucky you found your brother. It's more than I have."

"Maybe you have family and you just don't know it."

"Maybe. How did you find your brother?"

"That isn't important. What's important is helping *you*."

"You are helping me just by talking to me. It's nice to know someone else who has suffered too. Maybe if you tell me your story, it will make mine seem not so bad."

"That isn't why you called. Why don't you tell me *your* story?"

"There's nothing to tell."

"Then why *did* you call?"

There was a short silence. Emily thought he'd hung up. Then, he spoke so softly she almost didn't catch what he was saying. "I-I'm not sure. Maybe simply to get some reassurance that my problems aren't as bad as they seem. Isn't that why most people call The Samaritans?"

"Hopefully yes, but they don't ask us about our problems. I shouldn't have mentioned my family."

"I think you were trying to show me you understood. Well, I also understand, Emily. You found your brother. What happened to the rest of your family?"

She inhaled and decided to break the rules. Mutual empathy was a tactic she'd been considering, although she knew it was a gamble. "It's a long story. Apparently, my father got drunk and killed my mother. I had two brothers. We were all split up when we were infants. I grew up in a convent, but I was very unhappy there. A few months ago, I escaped."

"You escaped?"

"Yes."

"And now you're working for The Samaritans?"

"That's right. Now I can help people *and* have my freedom. I wouldn't change my life now. I love it. If we work on it, maybe we can find a new life for you. Let me help you, John."

"I . . . I think I'd like that, Emily. Would it be all right if I called you after awhile? I need some time to think."

"Take all the time you need, John. Just ask for me when you call back, all right?"

"All right. Thank you, Emily."

The call ended.

Emily placed the phone on the receiver and sat back thoughtfully. She questioned if it had been right to disclose personal details of her own life to that particular caller. Was it unprofessional of her to have done so? Or was it exactly the right thing in order to procure his trust? She was certain John was the caller Jessie had told her about. Perhaps she'd just been desperate to keep him on the line. *Oh, boy. I sure hope he calls back.*

***

Night had fallen by the time Professor Abraham Jacobson returned to his home in Lyon Village, Arlington County, Virginia. At sixty-eight, he was beyond retirement age. However, the loneliness of being a widower had driven him to keep working until late every night. Coming home to an empty house was the most harrowing part of his day.

Having parked his Lexus in the garage, he made his way up the steps between the porch pillars of his impressive, secluded home beyond the suburbs. His presence activated the light sensors.

He took out his front door key and hesitated before inserting it into the lock. He could sense someone was there. He turned around and could barely make out a dark figure crouched in front of the garden bush. "Who's there?"

The figure stood and came closer, his face overshadowed by a dark hood.

"Who are you?"

The visitor raised his hands in a peaceful gesture. "Professor, it's me."

Jacobson's heart missed a beat at the sound of the voice. *No. It can't be.*

The man peeled the hood back and stepped into the porch light.

"Brandon?" Jacobson said, astounded. "But how—"

"I need to talk to you. I know this is going to sound strange but . . . I don't remember you. I need you to help me."

Tears welled up in Jacobson's eyes as he walked back down the steps. He threw his arms around Brandon in a display of deep affection for his most unexpected visitor. "I'm so happy you're alive, Brandon."

Drake did not return the embrace.

"Come inside with me. Let's talk, OK?" Jacobson said.

"Thank you."

They ascended the steps together and entered the house. Jacobson placed his keys on a small counter beside the door and turned back to Drake. He immediately noticed a darkness in his eyes that he'd never seen before. But what was to be expected? Brandon was supposed to be dead, and there was no saying what he'd been through in the meantime. "Come into the living room, Brandon. Can I get you a drink?"

"Yeah, I guess."

"I have a vintage Cognac, and I've been waiting for a special occasion to open it."

"Sounds great."

Jacobson led him into an ornate, opulent living room. An array of classic paintings adorned the walls, which complemented a collection of antique furnishings. "Take a seat, Brandon," he said, and poured two brandies.

Jacobson's history with Brandon came back to him. He recalled the first time he'd met the handsome young soldier. Brandon's genius had been so unexpected. With his IQ recorded at one-hundred forty-four, and the extent to which his technical ideas had accelerated their research, it had been a phenomenal vocational experience for the professor. Brandon's knowledge of aviation mechanics, combined with the technology he had access to at Mach Industries, had helped them to design a supersonic VTOL vehicle. The Turbo Swan's powerful miniaturized engines had been Brandon's handiwork. That technology had gone through two further advancements since he'd fled from the facility.

"You say you don't remember me. How did you find where I lived?" Jacobson said.

"A lot of internet research. I've lost four years of my life, and I've been spending a lot of time trying to find out what happened to me. Apparently I worked with you."

"Oh, indeed you did. We were very close, in fact." Jacobson handed him a brandy and removed his suit jacket. After loosening his tie, he sat opposite Brandon. "I can't believe you're here. Tell me what happened and we'll take it from there."

"Well, most of what I know is from what I read. I just can't remember any of it. The last thing I remember was being in the desert in Afghanistan. That was four years ago. The next thing I knew, I was waking up in a facility in the Mojave Desert."

"Mojave?"

"Yes. They seemed to be caring for me, but after about ten weeks, they tried to kill me. I had no choice but to escape."

"Kill you? Who were they?"

"As far as I could tell they were some kind of government operation."

"You don't remember the crash in Los Angeles?"

"Only what I read on the internet."

"All right, Brandon," Jacobson said. "I can certainly tell you what I know. You were sent to my department at Mach Industries by Senator Garrison Treadwell after you were released from the hospital. Do you remember Senator Treadwell?"

"Yes."

"Not my favorite person, I must say, but working with you was extraordinary. You created the engines for the Turbo Swan. Does any of this sound familiar?"

"No. What's the Turbo Swan?"

"An experimental test aircraft. It was as small as a car."

A glimmer of recognition appeared in Drake's eyes. "Is that the flying car I've been reading about?"

"Yes. After you discovered Treadwell's plans to attack government facilities, you fled from Mach Industries in it. It's what you crashed in during the fiasco in Los Angeles."

Drake shook his head as though attempting to assimilate his thoughts. "That's amazing. And I don't remember a thing."

"Well, it's clear to me that you're suffering amnesia from the crash. But that still raises the question of why they wanted the world to believe you were dead."

"I have no idea."

Jacobson squinted his eyes inquisitively. "Forgive me, Brandon, but there's something I must ask."

"What's that?"

"You say they faked your death, and then tried to kill you. You must have discovered a wealth of information about Treadwell's activities. Mach Industries is a military operation. How can you trust me?"

"When I was researching my missing years, I discovered reports about my trial at Fort Bragg. I couldn't access any transcripts, but there seemed to be a strong indication that you spoke in my defense."

Jacobson smiled. "Yes, I did."

"Thank you."

They continued talking for another hour. The professor conveyed his sentiments toward Brandon, and the feeling of betrayal he'd suffered after Brandon had fled from Mach Industries in the Turbo Swan. It was only after his reasons for doing so became apparent that the professor's sense of disappointment became one of great pride.

Jacobson sipped his brandy and lowered his head in thought for a moment. "How would you like to pay a visit to Mach Industries? Just to see if it triggers anything."

Drake's eyes widened excitedly. "Are you serious? When?"

"Tonight. Most of the personnel will have gone home. There won't be anybody there who knew you. Even the security boys are all new."

"Are you sure it's safe?"

"I'll get you in. Trust me."

Drake stood eagerly. "I do, sir. Maybe you shouldn't have any more of that brandy if you're driving us there."

Jacobson looked down at his glass and smiled. "You're right. Shall we go?"

"You got it."

Drake lay concealed under a dark blanket on the back seat of Jacobson's Lexus, unable to see anything. He could only hear.

After a twenty minute journey, the car finally came to a stop. He heard one of the front electric windows lowering and seconds later, a male voice could be heard.

"Professor? It's past ten. What brings you back at this hour?"

"Oh, I apologize, Leon," Jacobson said cordially. "There's some business I need to attend to in my lab. Could you let me through?"

"Sure thing, sir."

The mild hum of the window rising was followed by the car moving on again.

"Brandon? Are you OK?"

"Yes, I'm fine."

"Good. We're going to take a slight detour around the complex. There's an entrance at the rear that takes us to a corridor leading directly to the lab."

"OK."

Drake smiled under the sheet with narcissistic coldness. His vulnerability act had enabled him to avoid even asking Jacobson to bring him to Mach Industries. *That stupid, balding idiot bought it, hook, line, and sinker.*

The car pulled up and Jacobson turned off the engine. Drake heard the front door close, and then the back door opened.

"You can come out now, Brandon."

Drake threw the sheet off him and climbed out of the car.

"Stay close to the wall." Jacobson pointed to a rooftop camera. "You need to stay out of range of that camera."

As the professor used his key card to open the rear entrance door, Drake glanced around him and gained a sense of the magnitude of Mach Industries. He estimated it covered at least a quarter of a square mile.

Jacobson quietly said, "We're in. Come on."

Drake lowered his head and followed him. His eyes rose in a sinister glare as he prepared himself to acquire an arsenal of the most advanced weaponry in existence.

Twenty

Mach Industries

Drake followed Jacobson along a corridor of lights that seemed to extend far into the complex.

Eventually, they stopped at an electronic chrome door. Jacobson slipped another key card into a reader. The door opened from the center to reveal a lattice of formerly-invisible, curved components, which retracted back into a flush break either side. Blue electronic lights lined the inner margins. Drake was stunned, never having borne witness to technology such as this. At least, not that he could remember.

They stepped inside and the door sealed itself shut with dazzling speed. Ahead was a studio the size of a large, car showroom. Everything about it was pristine and sterile in appearance. The ceiling was thirty feet above them, and the room was bare, save for a strange black craft, approximately the size of a Mercedes. However, that was where the comparison ended. It was set upon a platform a mere twelve inches above the ground within a shining, circular base.

"I wanted to show you this, Brandon," Jacobson said, "just to see if it triggered anything."

"What is it?"

"This is how far we've taken Turbo Swan technology since you left." He gestured to the strange craft before them. "This is the TS-3. The third generation of the original Turbo Swan. Come and take a look."

148

Drake followed him over to the craft, and Jacobson lightly touched the underside of the right door handle. The door rose upward to reveal a technological spectacle within. It appeared extremely shallow inside, which explained the necessity for reclined seats. The dashboard was at the front of the inner-roof and lit up the moment the door was opened.

"It flies as a VTOL aircraft, and the controls are touch-sensitive." Jacobson pointed to the digital control panel. "It's larger than the original Turbo Swan because we're gradually increasing the weight that can be taken by the miniature engines. We've also corrected some of its vulnerabilities."

"What do you mean?" Drake said.

"The alloy shell is still the same. It can withstand the concussive force of bullets and a detonating incendiary, but the original had an Achilles Heel. You went down in Los Angeles because one of the engines was struck by a rocket."

"And this one?"

"The engines are shielded by precision-angled, alloy guarding."

Drake gazed upon the TS-3, fascinated, but he could sense Jacobson looking at him.

"Is anything about this familiar to you, Brandon?"

"I . . . I feel as though it is, but I just can't remember." Drake looked around the vast room and soon realized there was nothing like an opening. "Is this the place I took the Turbo Swan from?"

"Yes it is. Can you remember that?"

"Not really. I just can't figure out how I would have gotten it out. I mean, we're boxed in here."

Jacobson smiled shrewdly. "Let me show you." He walked across to a chromium wall at the far side of the room, which measured approximately fifty feet in width and twenty feet in height. He punched in a code on a touch-sensitive keypad beside it. The wall broke apart in the center the same way the entrance door had, and retracted into itself. A runway appeared beyond it, leading to a forest in the distance. "Remember that?"

Drake shook his head.

Jacobson came closer to him excitedly. "Then I think I should show you where you spent most of your time. The look of it really hasn't changed."

"You lead the way, Professor."

Jacobson headed toward another one of the strange, wall-like doors at the side of the room.

Drake glanced at the gaping exit Jacobson had left open in his eagerness, and a broad grin crept from the corners of his lips.

Another electronic door opened. He followed Jacobson along a corridor, which led to two flights of steps down to the lower floors. Everything about the place was futuristic, with a spotless, luminescent appearance.

They came to the bottom and Jacobson led him through a glass door. A series of laboratories separated by windows and further glass doors came into view. The same sterile 'whiteness' persisted, varied only by shelves and tables containing an array of extraordinary gadgetry.

Jacobson turned to him. "Do you remember it, Brandon? You worked here every day for a year."

Drake looked around him, trying to recall any of it, but there was nothing there. "No."

"Well, let me show you around. You never know. Something might spark a memory."

Drake stepped toward a strange, circular table with a transparent, Perspex screen on the top. He looked down and noticed some kind of projector beneath the screen. "What's this?"

Jacobson touched a sensor on the side and a ghostly vision formed above the table. It was the image of a man wearing some kind of silver armor with black epaulettes, and a matching midsection. The helmet was black and silver with a bizarre arrangement of seven blue lights positioned in the center of the mask. Two were set in the position of the eyes.

"What the hell is that?" Drake said with sincere awe.

"I thought you'd like it," Jacobson said excitedly. "I can't tell you how many times I've daydreamed you were still alive and working with me, just so that I could show you this."

"But . . . what is it?"

"It's a hologram, naturally. A design for the potential soldier of the future. The technology doesn't exist yet. We're twenty, maybe twenty-five years away from it." The professor's eyes lowered in sadness. "I very much doubt I'll live to see it happen."

"Well . . . what's it supposed to do? What are those blue light things on the helmet?"

"As you know, infrared and thermal imaging has been in existence for almost a century. As an aid to night vision, it's served the military extremely well. Unfortunately, it

151

only offers images in two tones, or in a form of red and yellow negative." He gestured to the blue lights on the hologram helmet. "We're developing a new system that will enable the wearer to see in pitch darkness and in full color, as though it were daylight. Those blue lights will be the photo-generators that enable it."

"That's amazing."

"The armor will be fully mechanized and constructed from the same alloy the Turbo Swan and TS-3 are made with. It's lightweight and not only bullet-proof, but incendiary-proof. It'll contain its own built-in weaponry, which will spare soldiers the burden of carrying heavy artillery across a battlefield. It'll also enable *whomever* to cross the chasm between two skyscrapers without the use of a spider cable and power-glider." He winked at Drake mischievously.

"Incredible."

"As a matter of fact, I have a fully functioning breastplate right here." Jacobson moved over to a mannequin in the corner of the lab, which bore a breastplate identical to the one on the hologram, extending from collarbone to waistline. "The sections connect electronically and can be released with this." He took a small, remote control device from a metallic pocket fixed to the side of the mannequin.

Drake kept an opportunistic eye on the breastplate and remote control.

"I think the best thing to do would be to retrace your steps," Jacobson said. "You took considerable materials from the lab when you took off, and concealed them in two attaché cases." He took one of the cases from a shelf. "Look familiar?"

Drake shook his head again, far less interested in remembering than in what was on offer. "What did I take?"

Jacobson began to collect samples of equipment from the shelves. The first items he placed on the counter were what looked like small, golden paper weights, and a radio receiver. "You took a few of these. They're bugging transmitters, resistant to all known detection devices."

Always useful.

More items appeared on the counter—an original spider cable launcher, an EG-9 wire glider, a portable laser torch, a sonic force emitter and power charger, a diamond-laced glass cutter finger pad, sachets of corrosive putty, digital macro-binoculars, magnetic long-range homing devices, and a sat-scrambler phone. The latter was the only item with which Drake was familiar. "I took all of this stuff?"

"Yes. Still nothing?"

"No, I'm sorry."

"Oh, don't apologize, Brandon. It's not your fault."

Drake turned around to the breastplate mannequin again. On a shelf beside, some kind of rifle in a larger case caught his eye. At least a hundred rounds were set in individual sponge cut-outs in the top half of the case. "What's this, Professor?"

"That's an MZ-five-oh-seven. It's a high-powered rifle with a thermal imaging sight that can detect the enemy through mortar. The bullets are an advanced titanium design. They can take out the enemy at long range, and through the same mortar."

Drake's heart quickened. He'd never even imagined the possibility of a rifle so powerful.

Jacobson turned back to the items on the counter. "If only I could figure out some way of helping you to remember."

With Jacobson's back turned to him, Drake seized the moment. He took off his hooded top and shirt, and hurriedly took the breastplate from the mannequin. After dropping it over his head, he sealed the magnetized sections together, marveling at how lightweight it was.

Jacobson froze at the sound of the breastplate clicking together. Something was very wrong, and he was afraid to turn around. Brandon had no reason to steal from the facility this time.

And then he remembered the strange darkness in Brandon's eyes—the darkness he'd forced himself to ignore in his euphoria that his dear friend had returned from the dead. It was the same joy that had caused him to act with such recklessness, throughout. "You're going to kill me, aren't you, Brandon?"

"I have no choice. You've seen me."

Finally, the professor turned around. Drake was pulling his hooded top back over his head. Jacobson watched as he took the rifle from the case and quickly figured out how to load one of the bullets into it.

"Why, Brandon? Why?" Jacobson said, his voice choked with devastation.

Drake trained the rifle on him with maniacal rage in his eyes. "You wanna know what really happened, Jacobson? Do you?"

"Yes. Please, Brandon. Tell me. Let me help you."

"Nobody can help me. When I was sent here, I'd been brainwashed. New memories. New personality. Everything about me had been erased. The person you knew wasn't me. They then faked my death and brought me back to who I always was. After that, the bastards tried to kill me!"

"Then let me help you find justice."

"There is no justice. *I* am justice. All my life people have tried to control me, abuse me, and drive me into the ground. No more. I hate this fucking world, old man, and now I'm gonna start a war!"

"Don't do this, Brandon."

"I have to." Drake's finger tightened on the trigger.

"I love you, Brandon."

The pain shot through Drake's head again. He dropped the rifle and fell to the floor, screaming.

"Brandon, what's wrong?" Jacobson said.

Voices from nowhere echoed in Drake's mind:

How did you find Sergeant Drake as a person?

He was a joy to work with. He was a true pioneer, a unique individual, and the most unlikely candidate for such brilliance. I grew close to him in the year that I worked with him and . . . I loved him like a son.

Tears ran down Drake's face. The sadness was overpowering. The voices sounded like Jacobson and Captain Hugo Arrowsmith. He subconsciously knew he was remembering something from his trial at Fort Bragg.

I loved him like a son.

"In-ter-cep-tor. P-please, don't . . ." He felt Jacobson's hands cradling his face and looked up into the man's compassionate eyes. He was losing the will to fight, but clenched his fists in desperation.

"It's all right, Brandon. I'm here. Let me help you."

Everything was turning black, and he began to feel so different. The rage had abated so quickly. What he was feeling was alien to him. He gently touched Jacobson's face. "A-Abraham?"

Twenty-One

Last Flight

Drake faced The Interceptor in the darkness and leaped into the air, twisting and kicking his heel toward his adversary's helmet. The Interceptor instantly vanished. He looked around, but there was no sign of him.

He sensed a hand on his shoulder and spun around. Roaring, he lunged forward, but The Interceptor disappeared and instantly appeared behind him again.

"I thought you were supposed to be hot shit, Scorp," The Interceptor said tauntingly. "Must've been a lot of hype."

Drake punched toward the helmet but struck only an empty vacuum.

"Come on, Scorp. Catch me if you can."

The battle continued for what seemed like an eternity. Drake relentlessly struck out at the figure in the black combat fatigues, only for him to vanish and appear behind him, like a cat chasing its own tail.

Finally, he spun around, but The Interceptor had disappeared completely. "Where are you, you goddamn pussy?" There was no response. He continued to spin around in the void trying to catch sight of him. But he was alone, stranded, with nothing other than his own, gnawing frustration. "Interceptor!"

Brandon, I'm here. Stay with me, Brandon.

157

He looked ahead in the direction of the echoed voice and could make out Jacobson's face gazing down at him.

And then he was no longer in the void. He could feel the hard, cold floor of the lab beneath him. Looking up at Jacobson, he pressed his fists into the floor, summoning every iota of strength he had to stand. "S-stay away from me."

"Brandon, you remembered me. I could see it in your eyes. You called me Abraham. You were the only assistant I ever had who called me that. We were *that* close, Son."

Without a word, Drake gripped the rifle and got to his feet.

"Brandon, please."

Struggling to gather his thoughts, he staggered over to the mannequin and took the armor-release control mechanism. *What do I need? What do I need?*

He saw the bullets in a sponge cut-out strip that filled the top half of the rifle's case, but the case itself would present an unnecessary burden. He removed the strip of bullets, took it to the attaché case on the counter, and threw it inside. He then crudely cast all of the devices Jacobson had shown him on top of the bullets.

"Brandon, stop!" Jacobson said.

Drake looked behind the counter and noticed a display of familiar, palm-sized silver spheres. Each sphere was circled by an indentation, which housed activation lights. Bracing the rifle under his armpit, he took all eight of the spheres and threw them into the case.

"Please, Brandon, I'm begging you. Those are not grenades," Jacobson said. "They're thermo-neutron detonators. They're devastating."

Drake clasped the case shut. "I know what they are."

"You could be killed, Brandon."

"I've been dead once. It's not as bad as you think." He took Jacobson's access key card from the counter, then the rifle and attaché case, and heading out of the lab.

"Don't take the TS-3, Brandon. *Please.*"

Drake paused in mid-stride and turned to Jacobson one last time. "I have no choice. It's the last flight out of here." Staggering with the pain in his head, he exited the lab and headed up the steps.

He came to the corridor at the top and headed toward the electronic door at the end. Every step was an ordeal. His temples pounded, and his emotions consumed him with confusion and inconsistency.

He arrived at the door, placed the attaché case on the floor, and slid Jacobson's key card into the reader. Once the door opened, he picked up the case and struggled to walk across to the TS-3.

Halfway to the craft, he was startled by the deafening sound of sirens all around him. Clearly, Jacobson had sounded the alarm.

Quickening his pace as much as possible, he reached the TS-3. With its side door still raised, he threw the attaché case and rifle over the seats into the back.

He climbed inside and pulled the door down. Closing his eyes, he tried to focus. The Interceptor had flown something very similar, but he had no conscious memory of doing so. The Interceptor's memories came to him only as fleeting feelings.

He opened his eyes again and stared at the control panel above him. Jacobson said it was a VTOL aircraft, but nothing inside the craft resembled one. Second-guessing the design, he scanned the digital display and his right hand rose, almost by instinct. His forefinger gravitated toward an illuminated red and yellow touch sensor bearing the letter 'S'. *That has to be Start.* With a light touch of the sensor, the engines fired up. Immediately, he could feel the craft rising. *How do I fly it out of here?*

A squad of security guards appeared in the open exit with their rifles trained on the craft. One of the guards was heading for the code pad, and Drake's heart pounded. If they closed the door, he'd be trapped inside.

Desperately, he turned his attention to the TS-3 and used the standard controls to move it forward slightly. *Where's the turbo controls?*

The guards opened fire, but the bullets bounced harmlessly off the alloy shell.

Panic took over, and his finger automatically touched a sensor. The TS-3 shot forward as the electronic door began its rapid closure. He cleared the gap with barely a microsecond to spare. *How did I know which button to push?*

He flew away from Mach Industries, across trees and homes. Drake knew he had to get his bearings. He couldn't deny how appealing the TS-3 was, and he sorely wanted to steal it. But with what he had to do, it would attract attention. His priority was to get back to the Chevy.

He quickly got the feel of the craft and discovered the navigation screen, which enabled him to get a fix on his location. The navigator showed he was already thirty miles away from where he should've been. He tapped in his destination coordinates and switched over to autopilot. The TS-3 turned itself around and flew him toward his destination.

The world became a speeding blur of lights as he flew along the highways between traffic. An overwhelming sense of déjà vu came over him. It was all so familiar-but-unfamiliar.

Minutes later, he came to a deserted wooded lot, approximately three miles from Jacobson's home. *This is it.*

He slowed down and descended from fifty feet. When the navigator showed he was close to the ground, he looked around for the landing gear, but there wasn't anything that resembled it. *Shit, where the hell did they put it?*

The TS-3 spun out of control and the underside hit the grass, just ahead of the trees. "Son of a bitch!"

Only then did he realize he couldn't even feel an impact, due to the concussion-resistant design

Finally, he collected himself, shaking with adrenaline.

After climbing out of the TS-3, he reached into the back, and pulled out the rifle and attaché case. He then made his way toward the Chevy on the other side of the wooded lot.

He walked through the trees trying to process what had happened to him. He was beginning to understand the dynamics of his unique condition with greater insight.

Belinda Reese wasn't his only vulnerability. It was also anyone to whom The Interceptor had been close. He'd been struck down when he was preparing to kill Jacobson, but it hadn't been as severe as something that simply reminded him of Belinda Reese. She was the one The Interceptor loved the most. Taking her out was still the key to overcoming him.

But how could he do it if The Interceptor could knock him down and debilitate him before he could act? There was no doubt The Interceptor persona was growing stronger, but he couldn't give up. He had to destroy what they had done to him. It would require intense focus and control. It would take everything he had. If he was to survive, this woman had to die. By killing The Interceptor's most beloved, nobody would ever impair him again. She was the one who had the greatest hold over his mind.

He arrived at the Chevy and threw the case and rifle into the trunk. Looking around, he satisfied himself that the area was deserted and there were no witnesses.

He climbed into the car, started it up, and drove on. Soon he'd be on the highway en route to his current motel in Columbia Heights.

***

The phone rang and Emily picked up the receiver. "Samaritans. Emily speaking. How can I help?"

"Hi, Emily. It's John."

She took a sharp breath, relieved he'd called back. "Hi, John. How are you feeling today?"

"Not great, but I'm bearing up. I really wanted to talk to you."

"I'm glad, John. I'm sure you'll feel much better if you get a few things out. Tell me more about yourself. Do you have a profession?"

"Not anymore."

"What did you *used* to do?"

"I was . . . a pilot and a technician, but the company I worked for kinda went up in smoke."

"What do you mean? Did they go out of business?"

"Yeah, kind of."

"I'm sorry to hear that. You have no job and no family?"

"I have a brother and a sister somewhere, but I don't know where. That's why I'm so alone. No job. No family. No future. I'm constantly depressed. I just don't know what to do."

"I feel for you, John. I really do, and I want to help you. Sometimes, when we're ready to give up, the most amazing surprises can come our way."

"Like they did for you?"

"Oh, boy. You wouldn't believe it."

"Would you mind telling me about it? It might give me something to hold onto."

Emily was silent for a moment as she contemplated her response. How much should she disclose about herself? She felt a connection with this man that she couldn't explain. *Keep it general. No specifics.* "Well, soon after I escaped from the convent . . . after they locked me in my room, I . . . I was kidnapped by a human trafficking organization."

"Oh, my God."

"I know. But what I didn't know is that my brothers had found one another after twenty-five years, and they came looking for me. They saved me, but my older brother was killed. I live with the guilt of that every day."

"I'm so sorry, Emily. Do you still see your other brother?"

"Actually, I live with him and his father. My other brother who died? Well, his girlfriend lives with us too, and she's the best friend I've ever had."

"That's wonderful."

His tone sounded more spirited, and Emily felt she'd made the right choice by telling him her story. "That's what I want you to take from this, John. No matter how bad things seem, you never know what's around the corner. In a heartbeat I went from finding myself in slavery, to having a family, a terrific roommate, and a rewarding job here at The Samaritans. I'm only able to talk to you right now because of all this. I believe everything happens for a reason."

"It's certainly a remarkable and inspiring story, Emily . . ." He stopped in mid-sentence.

"John? You still there?"

"Darn. Can I call you back? I think someone's at the door."

"Sure," she said.

"Thank you." The call ended.

Emily put the phone back on the cradle and sat back proudly with a feeling of hope and self worth. The evidence that she was helping John was apparent in the rapid change in his tone.

In his motel room, Drake switched off his burner phone and threw it into the bedside trash basket. *So, Emily. You live with Belinda Reese and my brother. That has to mean Belinda Reese is at Faraday Ranch.*

With a cold grin, he began to gather his belongings in preparation for another long drive. This time—to Dallas.

Twenty-Two

Massacre

Drake parked the Chevy behind a cluster of trees and stepped out. The midday Texas summer heat was intense, but nothing was about to deter him.

It had been another exhausting day-and-a-half journey. After driving across three states the day before, a stopover at the Arkansas border, and a two-and-a-half-hour drive to Fort Worth, he'd finally arrived at his fateful destination.

He brought the set of digital binoculars he'd taken from Mach Industries to his eyes and focused them on the ranch, a couple of miles in the distance. There were eight security guards patrolling the grounds, plus one posted at the entrance. Inside that ranch was his quarry.

Everything was at stake, and he knew he'd have to become stronger than ever to accomplish his objective. If he succeeded in overcoming the pain, the fake persona lurking within the darkest recesses of his subconscious would no longer have any power over him.

Lowering the binoculars, he considered his strategy. There was only one way. He would have to kill them all.

He walked around to the trunk, cracked open the attaché case, and cast the binoculars into it. There were the two pistols he'd taken from the Mojave facility, and enough bullets to deal with those clowns at the ranch. He wasn't about to waste sophisticated weaponry like the MZ-507 rifle on a cadre of bottom level rent-a-cops. However, the laser torch might have a use.

His gaze fell upon Cassidy's Samurai sword—that which had been the creator of his rage. With macabre glee, he took it out and hung it across his back with the shoulder strap.

Scrabbling through the jumble in the case, his fingers tripped over the small transmitters. *Just in case*, he thought, and took one.

He closed the trunk and placed the pistols in the rim of his jeans, concealed by the hooded top. Pulling the hood over his head, he made his way along the deserted road toward the ranch.

A brisk, determined pace enabled him to reach the entrance of the ranch within ten minutes. From twenty feet away, he saw suspicion in the security guard's eyes. It was hardly surprising. A hooded man wearing a Samurai sword was never likely to inspire confidence.

"Can I help you?" the guard said.

"Is Belinda Reese here?"

The guard angled his head in an obvious attempt at gaining a clearer view of the face beneath the hood. "And you would be . . . ?"

Drake raised his head and noticed the sudden, shocked expression on the guard's face.

"Oh, my God. Y-you're—"

"Death." Drake reached over his shoulder and gripped the sword's handle. Drawing it out, he decapitated the guard in one sweeping movement. The headless corpse slumped to the ground.

Drake wiped the sword on his sleeve and sheathed it before making his way forward along the entrance road. Halfway along, he drew the pistols.

Four security guards brandished their weapons and ran toward him. With a quickening pace, he raised both pistols as they opened fire—but he continued toward them. As he came closer, he could see fear in their eyes. He permitted them one more shot, but it simply bounced off the breastplate beneath his clothing. With that, he fired, taking down four of them with clean shots to their heads.

Four more guards hurried around to the side of the house and braced themselves behind the walls. They reached out to fire at him, but he drove them back with more shots.

He arrived at the front door through exchanged gunfire. One of his pistols was empty, which gave one of the guards the opportunity to emerge from behind the wall. The guard fired, but the bullet struck the breastplate. The terror in the guard's eyes appeared only for a moment before a shot to the head erased all expression from his face.

One bullet left.

A guard on the left attempted to come out from behind the wall but was driven back by Drake's last shot. A shower of concrete exploded as the bullet struck the corner of the wall.

Drake thrust the two empty pistols into the rim of his jeans and drew the sword again. Standing in the doorway, he knew there were armed guards behind the walls on either side of the house. He headed to the left and stopped at the edge, knowing he was inches away from one of them. His gaze darted from side to side while he waited.

A pistol crept out from behind the wall, and then the hand gripping it appeared. Drake raised the sword and brought it down, severing the hand at the wrist. The security guard's scream pierced the air. Drake turned around into his path.

Crouched down in agony, the guard looked up. "P-please . . ."

In a flash, Drake shot the blade across the man's throat, semi-decapitating him. *Two to go.*

He walked along the side of the house, peering through the fencing that enclosed the rear open porch. It was deserted. *They've regrouped at the other side.*

He crept around the porch, glancing through the windows fleetingly for signs of life, but it was empty.

As he came to the end, he braced himself. There was only one thing for him to do. *Go for it.*

He turned into the path of the two security guards and stood before them.

The one on the right aimed his pistol at him. "Don't come any closer."

Drake shook his head at their ineptitude. The guard's hand was shaking to the extent that he couldn't hold the gun straight. "When are you assholes gonna learn?" He held their gazes for a moment, and then lunged toward them with a bestial roar.

The guard discharged the pistol, but the bullet bounced off the breastplate. Drake reached them, slicing them both across their midsections with one stroke. Bloodlust rose inside him, fueled by the joy of the kill.

He ran around the house again to the front door. After trying the door handle, he discovered it was locked. He took out the laser torch and aimed it at the handle. With the touch of a button, the beam cut through the wood and metal within seconds. He then kicked it with his heel and the door swung open.

Rampaging through the house, he kicked open doors all across the ground floor, but all rooms were vacant.

Next, he scaled the stairwell and frantically entered each room on the first floor. Nobody was there. The same applied to the second and third floors. It was an empty house, consisting of the most appealing luxuries: spotless, beautifully-furnished bedrooms, Jacuzzi bathrooms, an indoor swimming pool on the ground floor, a sauna, steam room, gymnasium, offices, and a huge living room with a bar. But no human being in sight.

He returned to the ground floor, exited the house, and looked to his right. *What's in that guest house?*

Using the laser torch again, he entered the guest house and looked around. He noticed it was more humble than the main house, but he quickly found the first bedroom. It was empty.

He walked through the kitchen, and then entered the other bedroom. The moment he stepped inside, he knew.

A photograph of *her* on the counter caught his attention. He picked it up and gazed into her eyes. The sadness began immediately. *No! I have to fight this. I have to beat him.* He forced himself to look at her photograph, but the feeling only grew stronger. It was all-consuming. Tears ran down his cheeks until he could bear it no longer. *Oh, God!*

He dropped the photograph and found just enough strength to reach into his pocket and take out the transmitter. It was an effort for him to even peel away the plastic adhesive backing. However, he managed to switch it on and crouch low to look around for a dark corner underneath the counter.

Once the transmitter was in place, he staggered out of the guest house and gradually gained speed as he made his way across the field.

Twenty-Three

Shock

Belinda sat with Emily in the back of a cab as they returned home from work together.

Emily turned her attention to Belinda's midsection. "You're really starting to show now, you know."

"Well, I'm nearly four months along."

"How do you feel about it?"

Belinda's smile beamed. "Wonderful. The doctor says I should feel the baby kicking soon."

"I've got to tell you, I can't wait to be an aunt."

"And you'll be great too, Em."

Emily lightly tapped Belinda's lap and chuckled. "Oh, I forgot to tell you. I read the first issue of *Interceptor*."

"And what did you think?"

"Well . . . I'm quite embarrassed, actually."

"Why?"

"Well, at the end it says 'To be continued' and I want to know what happens next. Do you have the next one?"

Belinda looked at her surprised, and then burst into laughter. "No, I haven't. We'll have to look on eBay."

They turned the corner to the ranch to discover their passage was blocked by a police car. Then they saw the place had been cordoned off by yellow tape around the perimeter. A squad of police cars and an ambulance were parked in front of the house in the distance.

"Oh, my God!" Belinda said. "What's going on?"

Emily shook her head with deep concern in her eyes.

Belinda barely had the presence of mind to pay the driver before exiting the car with Emily. "You remember when I told you I sensed something terrible was going to happen?"

"Yes."

"I have a horrible feeling this is it."

Through the crowd, Belinda saw Tyler talking to two police officers. Charlton was at the back talking to a tall, burly man in a police uniform. She assumed it was the sheriff.

Tyler looked across at them and excused himself from the officers.

"Tyler, what's going on?" Belinda said.

Without answering, he hugged them both together. "Damn, we were so lucky," he said, his voice quavering. "You just missed the TV crew."

"But what happened?"

"We don't know. We don't even know how many there were, but all the security guards are dead. Some of them decapitated."

Belinda's hand came over her mouth with the horror of having to process something so ghastly.

"Who would have done such a terrible thing?" Emily said, shaking her head vacantly.

"I don't know, Em. That's what we're trying to find out."

Sheriff Aldo Malloy's intense stare burned into Charlton Faraday's. "So, you have no idea who did this?"

Charlton had been cagey throughout—uncertain of whether he should disclose what he knew. Finally, he realized he had no choice, and ushered the sheriff away from the crowd. Away from Tyler, in particular. "Al, we've been friends for many years."

"We sure have. Charlton, tell me something truthfully. Do you know who did this?"

He looked at the sheriff darkly, and whispered, "I can't be absolutely sure, but I think so."

"Tell me about it."

"You remember the incident in Los Angeles a few months ago."

"With Tyler, his brother, and the slave traders?"

"Yes. At the hospital, I had a tip that one of them, Han Fong, had escaped, and that we should watch our backs. That's why I had the security set up here."

The sheriff became pallid and looked away for a moment. He then turned back to Charlton. "And you think this Fong guy had something to do with this?"

"Like I said, I can't be sure. It wouldn't have been him by himself. He's affiliated with one of the Tongs. I've had an investigator looking into it. One of the best."

"What's his name?"

"Adam Brody. He's been on the case for weeks in San Francisco, but he hasn't been able to locate Fong yet. I called him after I called you. All I got was his answering service."

"Will you let me know as soon as you hear anything?"

"Of course. I didn't want to say anything in front of Tyler."

"Why not?"

Charlton eased his mouth closer to the sheriff's ear. "Because he's the one they're looking for, and he has no idea. That's the way I want to keep it. It was Tyler and his brother who helped take them down."

"Thanks for telling me this, Charlton. I'll do whatever I can, but I think this is way over my head. Forensics said something was used to break in through the back door and the door to the guest house. Whatever it was *burned* through the wood and the lock mechanisms. They'd never seen anything like it."

"It's way over everybody's head, Al," Charlton said. "Even SDT didn't wanna be involved."

"What's SDT?"

"Some investigative division that operates from Langley. That's who I got this Tong information from."

The conversation was interrupted by Charlton's cell phone ringing. "Lemme get this, Al. I'll be with you in a moment."

"You bet." The sheriff turned away to rejoin the officers.

Charlton answered the call. "Faraday here."

"Mr. Faraday, it's me, Adam Brody. I just got your message."

"Brody? Where the hell have you been? I called you hours ago. I thought they'd got you too."

"I'm sorry, sir. I don't quite follow you. Who did you think had got me?"

"The Tong, who else?"

"No danger of that, Mr. Faraday."

"How can you say that? I've come home to a goddamn massacre. All of my security boys were slaughtered."

There was a moment of silence on the line, and then Brody said, "I'm so sorry, sir. That's terrible. But I can assure you, it wasn't the Tong. Fong had nothing to do with it."

"How do you know?"

"Because he's dead, sir. They burned him weeks ago, that's why I couldn't find any trace of him. He's been a John Doe in the morgue all this time."

"Well . . . what happened?"

"It took me awhile to get to the bottom of it. After Los Angeles, he went to San Francisco to find safe haven with the Tongs. Seems they weren't in favor of the business he'd been doing in L.A. They considered his actions a disgrace to their names, and they killed him."

Charlton shook his head in bewilderment. "Then who—?"

"I don't know, sir, but the Tongs are not your enemy, I can assure you."

"OK, come on back to Dallas. I have to go. There's half the damn police department here."

Charlton ended the call and looked ahead into the horizon. All this time he'd feared the Tongs without knowing they were his allies where Fong was concerned. *So who, or what, attacked the ranch?*

Twenty-Four

Interrogation

Jed Crane pressed 'send' for the tenth time and disconnected his iPhone from the computer. It had been an essential task. Creating ten anonymous email addresses to send copies of his photos of Brandon Drake would ensure the data, complete with their time and date of origin, would be preserved. He had every intention of taking the phone to the highest level of government, although he knew he couldn't place his complete trust in anyone. Using a Florida internet café ensured the location of the duplicates would be untraceable.

He picked up his backpack and stepped out onto a Fort Lauderdale street, pondering his strategy. He'd just spent a week working on a ship importing coffee to Port Everglades for a private corporation. The job had given him access back to mainland America. His payment for services rendered would enable him to afford a bus fare to Washington, D.C.

Nevertheless, he knew he would be placing himself in serious jeopardy. He faced immediate arrest the moment he appeared, notwithstanding the possibility of interception by Wilmot's goons.

Walking along the busy street, he thought of Juanita and how alone she must've been feeling since he left. He was determined to do whatever he could to help her, once he'd exposed Wilmot.

He passed an electronics store and saw a caption on the screens of each in a line of high-definition display televisions:

Massacre at Faraday Ranch

Jed froze and watched through the window as a female reporter interviewed Tyler and his father. He couldn't make out what they were saying, but the caption told him enough.

He hurried along in search of a newspaper vendor, and found one within minutes. The story was front page on all newspapers.

After purchasing a copy of *The Washington Post,* he walked away reading the story. A chill went through him. The article focused on the mystery behind the attack and the confusion caused by it. Nobody had a clue who was responsible.

But *he* knew.

In a heartbeat, his agenda changed. Washington D.C. would have to wait. He needed to get to the Faradays in Dallas, and cursed the fact that he couldn't fly due to his fear of being identified.

***

Abraham Jacobson sat, exhausted, in a depressing, Langley interview room. The bare, white walls seemed to be closing in on him. He'd slept very little during the last four days while under the detention of, first the FBI, and now the CIA. He didn't know how many more times he could endure the same questions. Overnight, his entire world had been turned upside down.

Agent Wentworth Cullen, a thirty-something operative, had been particularly trying in his approach. He undoubtedly didn't believe him, which had led to mind-numbing repetitions of the questions. Jacobson knew the agent was trying to trip him up. He'd been locked in the interview room alone for the last two hours, and was beginning to lose track of time.

Suddenly, the door opened and Cullen entered. Jacobson looked up, startled.

"All right, Professor. Let's do it one more time." Cullen activated the recording equipment on the table. "Who broke into Mach Industries?"

"One more time, Agent Cullen, I told you. And why was I brought here? I told the FBI everything that happened."

"Mach Industries is a military operation. If someone pulled a heist, we need to ascertain which foreign power was responsible, and your story is just the wrong side of ridiculous. Now, let's try it again."

Jacobson shook his head in despondency. "Brandon Drake came to my home with apparent amnesia. I took him to where he used to work in an attempt to prompt his memory."

Cullen flicked his thick black hair from his eyes and leaned forward with an intimidating glare. "Brandon Drake is dead and buried."

"Then I suggest you save us all a lot of time, go out to Aspen, and exhume his grave. I can assure you, you won't find Brandon Drake in there."

"Yeah. We might just do that."

"I really wish you would."

"Even if what you say is true, you smuggled an unauthorized man into a top secret facility, and a fugitive, at that."

"I'm aware of that, but what was I supposed to have done? This was a man I'd worked closely with for a year, loved like a son, and trusted implicitly. He needed my help. I had no way of knowing what he was planning. He wasn't the man I once knew."

"So, what did he tell you?"

Jacobson exhaled, his patience at an end. "Only what I've already told you. He said he had no memory of me, or of the last four years of his life. The last thing he recalled was the grenade in Afghanistan, and then he said he woke up in a facility in . . . the Mojave Desert, I think he said."

Cullen's eyebrows rose. "Mojave?"

"Yes. He said the Brandon Drake I used to know was a manufactured persona created by Garrison Treadwell, and that intelligence personnel faked his death and restored his true persona."

"And this happened in Mojave?"

"According to him."

"So you took him to Mach Industries to see if anything prompted his memory, then he went psycho, looted the joint, and took off in the TS-3 with the items we've logged?"

"That's right."

Cullen stopped the recording and removed the memory card. "Thank you, Professor. You've been very helpful."

"That's wonderful. Now, when are you going to release me?"

"Soon, hopefully. But you're not off the hook, yet."

"I figured as much."

Cullen stood and made his way toward the door.

"Are you saying you believe me now?" Jacobson said.

"Let's just say . . . I'm keeping an open mind. If it makes you feel any better, we've found the TS-3."

The professor looked up eagerly. "You have? Where?"

"It'd been abandoned in a wooded lot, north of Route 29."

Jacobson felt a note of relief. It wasn't a surprise that Drake had discarded the TS-3, given its size. It was larger than the original Turbo Swan, and would've required a large truck if he'd wanted to ferry it around. But at least it was safe.

"I want a lawyer," Jacobson said.

"All in good time, Professor."

Cullen exited the room, leaving Jacobson to his thoughts. The mention of Mojave had changed the young agent's attitude almost immediately. It had to have been why he'd disclosed the information about the TS-3. Jacobson cursed himself for not remembering about Mojave sooner. For now, he could only sit in the tedious room, contemplating his potentially-bleak future.

Cullen moved briskly through the corridors. He arrived at the office of Deputy Director April Hayes as she was stepping out. A reasonably attractive woman in her late forties, her shoulder-length, dark blonde hair complemented a conservative, impeccably-professional appearance.

"Agent Cullen," she said, surprised. "What can I do for you?"

"It's important."

After a moment, she opened her door again. "I have a meeting in ten minutes. It'll have to be brief."

"Sure." He followed her inside and took the memory card out of his pocket. "I've been interrogating Professor Jacobson. He's just told me something I think the director should be aware of."

"Oh?"

"He's still adamant about Brandon Drake being alive. But now he's remembered something Drake allegedly told him." He handed Hayes the memory card. "It's all on there. According to him, Drake said he woke up in a facility in the Mojave Desert, and that he'd been subjected to some kind of mind control operation by intelligence personnel."

Hayes' eyes narrowed.

"SDT Director Wilmot was involved with the Mojave facility when it exploded, wasn't he?"

"Yes, he was."

"Well, what if there was more to it than he's letting on?"

"You believe the professor?"

"Being realistic, a man in his position would have no reason to assist in a heist. His record is cleaner than the Blue Lagoon, his story hasn't faltered once, and now this."

"You think Director Wilmot is dirty?"

"I don't know what to think, except this demands further investigation."

Hayes agreed and glanced at the memory card. "I'll get this to Director Brenham. In the meantime, I don't want you mentioning this to anyone. Are we clear?"

"Of course."

"All right," she said. "I have to go."

"Yes, ma'am."

The atmosphere was particularly tense as they exited the room.

At 8:00 p.m. Director Jack Brenham sat alone in his office listening to Jacobson's interview for the seventh time. By now, he was no longer hearing it. His mind reeled, certain that Jacobson was telling the truth. Everything fit with Mojave and the mind control claim. He'd kept a lid on his discovery of Treadwell's brainwashing experiments. Only a select few of his highest-ranking officers had ever been made aware of it. If it ever got out, it would have created a national panic.

If Drake had been subjected to memory revision in Mojave, Wilmot had to be at the helm. That would mean he'd been with Treadwell's outfit all along. If Wilmot was running Treadwell's faction, it stood to reason that Wolfe had not been a traitor. It had been a devastating revelation at the time, but what if it wasn't true?

Brenham needed hard evidence to support what he now suspected, although it would have to be handled shrewdly. Wilmot could not be alerted. Brenham had no idea how far this corrupt faction extended, but it had to be rooted out and destroyed, once and for all.

Despite Jacobson's appalling judgment, his actions might have unwittingly uncovered a serious threat to national security. It was essential that the professor be brought into the fold. He was now a vital witness.

Brenham sat back contemplating his strategy. It wouldn't be easy. If an internal terrorism movement was operating, everyone in the intelligence community was a potential suspect. At all costs, the press had to be kept in the dark, although Brenham knew Wilmot had to be taken down, no matter what.

Twenty-Five

Bombshell

Tyler gazed out the window in his office at the Faraday Corporation, his mind numb with the effects of shock. It had been four days since the massacre at the ranch, but he was unable to focus on work. They had no access to their home while forensics were combing the place. Consequently, he had no choice but to stay at the Ritz-Carlton with his father, Belinda, and Emily. The hotel was beautiful, but the dark cloud that hung over the circumstances quashed any sense of novelty. Tyler loved his home more than anywhere in the world.

The office door opened, and he turned with a start. He smiled just as quickly when he saw whose head was poking through. "Hey, Alex."

"Belinda and I are gonna grab a bite. Wanna join us?" Alex Dalton said.

Tyler shook his head. "Thanks, but I really don't have much of an appetite."

Alex stepped through the doorway with a sympathetic stare. "You've got to eat something, Ty. I know you're not doing great, and that's understandable. Belinda's going through it too. Her mind isn't on anything."

"I know. I haven't seen my dad today. He left the hotel early. Have you seen him?"

"Briefly. He's workin' his ass off, nose to the grindstone, but I could tell he wasn't himself."

"He's a strong man. The strongest I've ever known."

185

"You got that right."

Tyler's desk phone rang. "Let me get that?"

"Sure."

Tyler pushed the speaker button. "Tyler here."

"Hi, Mr. Faraday. This is Sandy at the front desk."

"Yes, Sandy."

"There's a man down here who says he needs to see you."

"Who?"

"He didn't give his name, but he says it's extremely important he sees you."

Tyler looked across at Alex feeling particularly intrigued.

"Maybe it's someone who knows something," Alex said.

"My thoughts exactly." Tyler turned back to the speaker phone. "All right Sandy, send him up."

Belinda stepped into the office behind Alex. "Hey, are we doing lunch?"

"Yeah, but I think we should stick around for a minute," Alex said. "Tyler's just had a call."

"Oh? From whom?"

"That's what I'd like to know," Tyler said. "Whoever it is, they're on their way up."

They waited anxiously for several minutes until an unshaven, un-groomed man with a backpack appeared in the doorway. His casual clothing seemed almost tattered.

However, Tyler's jaw dropped as he recognized him. "Oh, my God . . . Jed?" He walked across the room and hugged his former comrade-in-arms. "Where the hell have you been?"

"It's a long story. We need to talk," Jed Crane said.

"Hi," Belinda said, and held out her hand. "We met briefly before. It's good to see you again, Jed."

"You too, Belinda."

Alex offered his hand to Jed. "Hi. I'm Alex Dalton. I work with Tyler."

"It's good to meet you, Alex. I hope I don't sound out of line, but I have some extremely personal information for Tyler and Belinda."

"You got it. Belinda, I'll be in my office."

"OK."

Alex closed the door behind him. Tyler, Belinda, and Jed sat at the desk.

"So, Jed. What's going on?" Tyler said.

Jed looked at Belinda, and then back to Tyler. "What I have to say is going to come as a shock to both of you. I want you to be prepared."

There was a tense pause. Finally, Tyler said, "OK, let's hear it."

"Brandon . . . is alive."

Belinda's mouth fell open and her hands began to tremble.

Tyler stood rapidly in response to the most heart-wrenching bombshell he'd ever heard. "What?"

"I have proof, Tyler."

"But how can that be? Belinda and I saw the crash. There's no way he could've survived."

"Did you see his body?"

"No, they said he was a mess. They said he didn't even have a face left, so they advised against it."

"He's alive, Tyler, and his face is just fine."

Tyler sank back into his seat, unable to process what he'd just heard.

"Let me take it from the beginning," Jed said. "Back in Utah, Agent Cynthia Garrett tracked me down to a motel. I woke up in the night to find a bomb under my bed."

"Oh, my God."

"Yeah. Anyway, I diffused the bomb and took it with me to L.A." Jed was quiet for a moment, almost cagey, and then said, "I was the one who blew up the fish factory. I just couldn't live with the idea of those child-raping monsters getting away."

"You'll get no argument from us there," Belinda said.

Jed continued. "Anyway, Wilmot was after me and I had to get out of there. I stowed away on a boat that was about to set sail. I had no idea where it was headed, but we arrived in Brazil. That's where I've been all this time."

"Brazil?" Tyler said.

"Yeah. I had no money, but I managed to find a menial job and earn enough to live in one of the slums. It wasn't fun, but I had to bide my time while I figured something out."

"And what happened?"

Jed took out his cell phone with a USB cable and gave them to Tyler. "Hook this up to your computer."

Tyler took the phone and cable while Jed stood and moved around to the other side of the desk. Once the phone was connected, Tyler opened it up.

"All right, go to photos." Jed pointed to the icon. "Now, the second row down, click on any one of the first three images."

Tyler clicked on the first of the three shots and an image of his brother appeared on the monitor screen. He immediately noticed Brandon appeared to be unwell, and he was being helped into a car by a particularly formidable-looking brute.

"I took those in Rio, two weeks ago," Jed said.

"Two weeks ago?"

"That's right."

"Let me see," Belinda said.

Tyler turned the screen around for her, and saw her becoming tearful.

"Oh, God," she muttered through her hand.

"What were the circumstances of these photographs?" Tyler said.

"Brandon and that other clown came to the favela where I was staying. According to Juanita, the lady I was shacked up with, they burst in there with machine guns looking to kill me. They shook her up pretty badly. I happened to catch these shots from a distance when I was coming home from work."

Tyler shook his head. "But . . . why would Brandon want to kill you?"

Jed sat down again. "I've been thinking long and hard on that. When I first met your brother, he told something about his personality being the product of a mind control experiment. He said that in reality, he was some kind of psychopath called The Scorpion. In L.A. I saw a sample of it, myself. It wasn't pretty."

"I know. I was there, remember?" Tyler said.

"Well, if he survived that crash and Wilmot got hold of him, what if he did it to him again, only this time, turned him back into who he was originally?"

Tyler and Belinda looked at one another with deep concern.

"I think that's what they've done. It would certainly explain why he'd come to take me out. Wilmot could've created an assassin with no memory of me, or any one of us."

Belinda gazed at the screen in disbelief. "Why does he look like he can't stand up?"

"I don't know. Juanita said he had her at gunpoint, and then he fell down holding his head, screaming."

She looked at the image intently. "He's fighting it."

"If so, he's not fighting hard enough. When I arrived in Florida, I saw the news about the attack on the ranch."

"Wait a second," Tyler said. "You think that was Brandon?"

"I'm sure of it."

"Why would he do that?"

"I don't have all the answers, Tyler. I just know it was him, and I believe you are both in serious danger. You can't go back to the ranch."

"But that's crazy."

"It might be, but I believe it's true."

"What are you gonna do now?"

Jed's gaze lowered with clear signs of trepidation. "I have to turn myself in with that cell phone." He took out a slip of paper and handed it to Tyler. "In case I get taken down, those images have been uploaded to these email addresses. The passwords are on there."

Tyler glanced at the paper and placed it on his desk. "If we can't go back to the ranch, what are we supposed to do?"

"I have to expose Wilmot and tell the authorities everything I know. Your lives are in jeopardy, so until this situation, and Brandon, are diffused, there's only one thing you can do."

"What?"

"Run!"

Twenty-Six

Aftershocks

Tyler sat on the bed in his Ritz-Carlton hotel room. The TV was on, but he wasn't fully conscious of what was showing. He gazed through the screen, his mind racing. The brother he'd believed dead was alive. Surely it wasn't possible to imagine news so fantastically joyous.

And yet, in a unique twist, the dream appeared as the worst of all nightmares. His resurrected loved one was apparently a lethal savage, who wouldn't necessarily remember him. The emotional confusion was impossible to process. If he were to meet Brandon again, his instinct would be to embrace him, but the reality dictated he would have to flee from him. It was utterly bizarre.

He was barely aware of the shower running until it stopped. After a few minutes, he was startled out of his reverie by Jed Crane coming out of the bathroom with a towel around his waist.

"Hey, Tyler," Crane said. "You OK?"

"Of course not. If anyone could have granted me one wish, it would've been to see my brother alive again. But not like this."

"Yeah, well, I can understand that. But I can't tell you how much I appreciate this."

Tyler turned to him, confused. "Appreciate what?"

"The chance to shower and shave. You've got no idea how much I needed that."

Tyler got off the bed and came toward him. "Jed, come on. After all you've done for us?"

"There's more to it than that. By letting me come in here and use the facilities, you're harboring a fugitive."

"It's not the first time either, and just like the first time, I wouldn't have it any other way."

Jed smiled. "You've got a good heart, you know that?"

"I'll do what's right, even if it means disagreeing with the law. The two don't always go hand in hand."

"You got that right."

There was a knock at the door. "I'll get it," Tyler said.

He opened the door. Emily stood before him with concern in her eyes. "Hi," she said.

"Hi, Em. Come on in. There's someone I want you to meet."

She followed him inside and paused. Tyler looked back at her, and then realized she was apprehensive at the sight of his handsome, bare-chested guest.

"Oh, I apologize," Crane said, and hurriedly collected his clothes from the floor.

"No, no, it's fine," Emily said. "I'm sorry to intrude."

"Hey, you're not intruding, Em," Tyler said. "I wanted you to meet Jed. He helped Brandon and me when we rescued you in Los Angeles."

She looked back at Jed. "I . . . I had no idea. Thank you so much."

She held out her hand and Jed took it with a gracious smile. "It was an honor, Emily. Just give me a minute."

As Jed returned to the bathroom, Emily turned back to Tyler. "Is it true? Is Brandon alive and trying to kill us?"

"We can't be sure of anything right now, Em, but it sure looks that way. Dad ruled out the Tongs as being responsible for what happened at the ranch. We have no explanation for who else it could have been. Jed has proof that Brandon is alive. Brandon tried to kill him in Brazil."

Emily looked away shaking her head. "It can't be true. I saw Brandon. I saw his eyes. There was compassion in them. Love."

"If he's been brainwashed again, he won't be that person anymore. He'll be whoever they turned him into."

"But why would anybody do that?"

"I have no idea. It's a sick world."

After a few moments, Jed came out of the bathroom wearing his worn clothing, and his damp hair neatly combed back.

"Are you all set, Jed?" Tyler said.

"As set as I'm gonna be."

"Do you have to go?" Emily said.

"I'm afraid I do. I have to turn myself in. It's the only way I stand a chance of putting a stop to what's been going on. These are evil people we're dealing with. I'm doing this for all of us."

She moved closer to Jed and gently kissed him on the cheek. "You truly are one of the bravest men I've ever met. I can't thank you enough for what you did for me."

"Thank you, Emily. Just hearing that from you makes me feel better."

"Hey."

They all turned to see Belinda and Charlton in the doorway.

"The door was open," Belinda said.

Tyler waved them inside. "It's OK. Come on in."

Charlton approached Jed and offered his hand. "Mr. Crane?"

"Jed, please."

"OK, Jed. What do you suggest we do about the situation?"

"I think you should split up. Go away. Far away."

Charlton shook his head. "I can't. I have a corporation to oversee."

"You can't go back to the ranch yet, Mr. Faraday. Give me some time. Please. Wilmot and Brandon have to be stopped."

"All right, I'll stay at the hotel. For now." Charlton turned to Tyler. "I think you should go to Los Angeles and work with Nikki for awhile."

"Good idea."

"Belinda, do you have any plans?" Charlton said.

"I have somewhere in mind."

"Not the cabin, surely," Tyler said.

"No, but I need to pick up a few things from the ranch first. Would the police allow that?"

"How about it, Jed?" Charlton said. "I can get Belinda and Emily a police escort to the front door of the guest house. It would be a fleeting visit."

"I can't say I don't have concerns about that, but make absolutely certain the grounds and the guest house are clear before you do."

"I'll need a car," Belinda said with an assertive tone.

Tyler frowned. "You're not flying?"

"I have my reasons."

"OK, when you leave, you can take my Porsche. It's still in the parking lot at the corporation."

Belinda's eyebrows rose. "Are you serious?"

"No question about it."

"Well . . . what are *you* going to drive?"

"There's the Ferrari, among a few others, but it's irrelevant. I'll fly."

"OK, that's settled," Charlton said. "Can't say I'm happy about all this, but what else can we do?" He looked across at Emily. "Do you have plans, Emily?"

Belinda interrupted before Emily could respond. "I'd like her to come with me."

"Really?" Emily said. "Where are we going?"

"I'll tell you later."

The room was uncomfortably quiet for a few moments.

Finally, Tyler drew out a wad of bills and handed it to Crane. "Well, Jed. There's two thousand dollars there to tide you over."

"Oh, no, Tyler, I can't take this."

"I insist, and that's all there is to it."

"OK. Thank you, Tyler."

"No, Jed. Thank *you*."

Jed picked up his backpack. "Good luck, you guys," he said sadly, and exited the room.

"You think we'll ever see him again?" Belinda said.

Tyler looked at her uncertainly. "I sure hope so."

***

"I understand your predicament, Emily," Glen Eisley said sorrowfully. "What happened at the ranch was

196

horrible beyond words. You have to do what's in the best interests of your safety."

"Thank you for your understanding, Glen. I have no idea when I'll be able to come back."

"We'll miss you, there's no doubt about that. And we'll be thinking about you."

"Thank you."

"Come back whenever you're ready."

"I will." She moved toward Eisley's office door, but paused in mid-stride. "If you see Jake at the shelter, would you say goodbye to him for me, please?"

"Of course I will, Emily." Eisley had long-since noticed the attraction between Emily and Jake, and felt sad for her. She was just getting her life in order, with so many possibilities. Now, tragedy had struck, and she found herself running again. He questioned when she was ever going to get the break she deserved.

"Thank you," she said, and left the office.

Outside on the steps, Belinda and three police officers waited for Emily. Two police cars were parked ahead of the steps.

"Are you OK?" Belinda said.

Emily wiped away tears. "I guess so."

Belinda placed her arm around Emily's shoulder. "Come on, Em. Let's get our stuff."

They climbed into the back of the rear police car.

Within thirty minutes, they arrived at the ranch. It was still surrounded by yellow tape, a section of which had been taken down at the entrance to provide temporary access.

The two police cars followed the entrance road to the front of the house past four more police cars in the yard.

They pulled up at the door of the guest house and parked so close Emily questioned whether Belinda would be able to open her door. However, Belinda exited the car first with relative ease. Emily moved across the seat and found herself virtually inside the guest house.

Belinda paused for a moment and gazed at the circular scorch mark where the lock had been.

"What is it?" Emily said.

"It's nothing."

Emily could see she wasn't telling the truth. She knew from the look in her eyes, Belinda was aware of what had made the bizarre entry damage.

Charlton waited inside with the sheriff beside him. "Hi, ladies."

"Hi," Belinda said. "This shouldn't take long."

"You go on ahead."

Belinda made her way into her bedroom.

Emily entered her room, took a suitcase from the closet, and set about packing her essentials. Charlton and the sheriff were outside her door, and she couldn't help overhearing their conversation.

"So, have forensics found anything?" Charlton said.

"Nothing that makes much sense?"

"What's that supposed to mean?"

"We dusted every inch of the place and eliminated your fingerprints, Tyler's, Belinda's, Emily's, and the staff's. But there were a few prints we found in various parts of the house that didn't match any of you."

"Oh?"

"We sent them down the line until we came up with an ID."

"And?"

"Well, it's real weird. According to the database, they were the fingerprints of Brandon Drake. Did he ever come here before he died?"

"No, he didn't."

There was a moment of silence before the sheriff responded. "Why don't you seem surprised by this, Charlton?"

"Just keep me posted, Al. I don't have any answers for you at the moment."

Emily realized she'd been leaning close to the door and decided to make haste.

After filling her suitcase, she carried it into Belinda's room. Belinda seemed busy collecting her belongings. "Would you like some help?"

"No, Em, I'm fine. Almost done."

Emily turned and looked out the window with the sheriff's words echoing in her ears.

"Hey?" Belinda said. "You OK?"

Awkwardly, Emily turned to her. "We're . . . doing the right thing, you know."

"What makes you so sure?"

Emily slowly came toward her. The pain she felt for her friend tore away at her, and it clearly showed in her eyes.

"What's wrong?"

"Jed was right," Emily said. "It was Brandon. I'm so sorry, Belinda."

"How do you know?"

"I overheard Charlton talking to the sheriff. They found Brandon's fingerprints in the house."

Belinda began to tremble. Her lower lip quivered, and she quickly succumbed to tears. "I . . . I didn't want to believe it, Em. Oh . . . God. I knew as soon as I saw the damage to the door. He used a laser torch to get in. I saw him use one on the night I first met him."

Emily held her, unable to hold back her own tears.

"This . . . can't be real?" Belinda wept.

"We'll get through this together. Are you going to tell me where we're going?"

Belinda broke the embrace and wiped her eyes. "To the only place I can think to go."

"Where's that?"

"Boston. I have no choice but to go to my mother's place. Damn, I need you, Em. I can't face her alone."

"I'll be right beside you, all right?"

"I don't know what I'd do without you."

"Let's just finish packing and go."

"OK."

***

Drake lay on a motel bed with a half-consumed bottle of whiskey in his hand. Having driven aimlessly for the last five days, his latest stop was Little Rock, Arkansas. The transmission receiver for the bug he'd planted in Belinda's room had been switched on constantly. He'd kept it on the seat beside him in the Chevy, in his pocket at every filling station, and in every motel room. There had been nothing but silence. Now, finally, he had an answer.

He picked up the receiver and stared at it as the voices of his sister and The Interceptor's lover came through. Intoxicated, he was barely concerned that he'd left evidence of himself at the ranch.

He smiled at the invincibility of his position. Wilmot had brought him back. How would they explain him still being alive? Could they really do anything other than conceal his actions in order to cover their own asses?

And who'd ever guess Boston, Massachusetts would be his next destination?

Twenty-Seven

Capitol Hill

Wilmot pulled up in the parking lot at CIA headquarters, his tension persistent and debilitating. Something was going down. He could feel it. The news that Drake's fingerprints had been discovered at Faraday Ranch had reached him the night before. The matter was now more desperate than ever.

He took his cell phone out and selected Slamer's contact. Talking to him in the car eliminated the risk of interruptions and potential discovery, which was always a possibility in the office.

The call was answered quickly. "Slamer? What the hell is going on?"

"I'm in Dallas."

"Yeah, well they know Drake did Faraday Ranch over. It's got a lot of people scratching their heads, obviously. This is not good, Slamer. How much closer are you to pinning him down?"

"I told you it would go like this, Wilmot," Slamer shot back defensively. "I'm getting a clearer picture of what he's doing, but it's been like trying to track a housefly. The son of a bitch is zigzagging all across the goddamn country."

"And what have you figured out?"

"It seems, after he took off from Mojave, he traveled to his foster parent's place. He killed his foster father, and it's a certainty Drake rolled Mach Industries."

"So, what does all this add up to? I know Brenham still has Jacobson under detention, but they're not allowing any of us access to the details."

"Now that Drake's hit the ranch, it's pretty clear he's on some kind of vengeance trip against anybody from his past."

Wilmot shook his head. "No, that can't be. He wouldn't know the Faradays or Belinda Reese. The last four years of his life were wiped."

"Ever hear of the internet, Wilmot? Not to mention what Cassidy might have told him."

Wilmot gave a sigh of concession. "Yeah, you're right."

"He's obviously learned a few things along the way, and he's got them in his sights. None of them were home when he attacked the ranch, so my guess is he's still after them."

"But where the hell are they?"

"That's what I'm trying to find out. I'm going to the Faraday Corporation today to see what I can come up with. If I know Drake, I'd put money on it that the girl is his prime target."

"Why?"

"He's a predator. If there was ever a type he made a beeline for, it was a gorgeous woman. To him, she'd be the broad he never knew he had."

"Let's hope you're right, because it's a lot more than money you're putting on it." Wilmot ended the call and stepped out of the car.

***

Senatorial assistant Tom Bolton turned with a start to see his petite, blonde secretary standing in his office doorway. "Yes, Jill."

"There's a call for Senator Adams, sir."

"Who is it?"

"He wouldn't say, but he said it was extremely important that he speak with the senator."

Bolton pursed his lips. As the personal assistant of Senator Robert Adams, he was wary of wasting his superior's time with nonsense. On the other hand, he had to be certain what it was about before dismissing it. "I'll take it. Patch him through, would you?"

Jill returned to her desk, and Bolton picked up his phone. "This is Senator Adams' office. Can I help?"

A male voice came through the receiver. "It's extremely important that I speak with the senator."

"I'm Tom Bolton, Senator Adams' special assistant. I screen all of his calls. Can you tell me what this is all about?"

"It concerns the late Senator Garrison Treadwell, and a crisis the CIA is unaware of. I have evidence of this, and I need to get it to the senator. I don't trust anyone else."

"Can you give me your name?" Bolton said.

"You'll get that when I see the senator."

"That's not going to be possible. I need more than you've told me before I can take this further." There was a silence on the line. "Hello?"

"I'm still here. Would you be willing to meet with me? I'll show you what I have, and I can assure you, it will be worth yours and the senator's time."

"Where do you have in mind?"

"I'll let you choose. Preferably, somewhere public, out in the open."

"How about the public park in front of the Treasury Building?" Bolton said.

"When?"

"When can you be there? And how will I know you?"

"Ten minutes. And I'll know *you*." The call ended.

Bolton placed the phone back on the cradle and headed out the door.

With his binoculars, Jed Crane spied Bolton exiting the Capitol Building a short distance from Capitol Hill. Bolton had come out remarkably quickly—too quickly for him to have prepared an ambush. That might have been reckless on Bolton's part, but extremely helpful to Jed. He'd met both Senator Adams and Tom Bolton at CIA headquarters a couple of years earlier, and had been an admirer of Adams' political position and legislative proposals for years. Adams had never been partial to Garrison Treadwell. With those factors in place, Jed knew he was the perfect man to listen to him.

After a brief scan of the area to ensure there were no security personnel in waiting, he lowered the binoculars and made his way toward the park.

So much was riding on this succeeding. He was already exhausted after a three day bus ride from Dallas.

He entered the busy park and came up behind Bolton. The senator's aide looked around aimlessly. It was clear he was trying to gauge a clue as to who'd called him.

"Mr. Bolton?" Jed said with his head lowered.

Bolton turned with a start. "Yes. And who would you be?"

Jed raised his head, revealing his face from underneath a baseball cap. He immediately noticed a glint of recognition in Bolton's eyes.

"Don't I know you from somewhere?" Bolton said.

"I think you do."

And then realization dawned on Bolton. "Oh, my God. You're Jed Crane."

"Yes."

"You're currently listed as missing."

"Is that all?"

"I'm not overly-familiar with the details, Mr. Crane."

"Well, I'm hoping I can change all that." Jed gestured to one of the park benches. "Let's take a seat."

"Suppose you take it from the start and tell me what you've got."

"OK," Jed began. "Five months ago, I was assigned to Nevada to pick up Brandon Drake. I was working with Agents Wilmot, Kerwin, and Rhodes. I'd long suspected them of being involved with Garrison Treadwell. Then I received the news that SDT Director Elias Wolfe had committed suicide, leaving a note confessing to being a traitor. I didn't buy it. There's no way Wolfe was dirty. I took it upon myself to liberate Brandon Drake because I feared for his life."

"Go on."

"A couple of nights later, I stopped over in Utah. It was the most remote spot you could imagine, and yet I woke up to find a bomb under my bed."

"A bomb?"

"They'd tracked me that quickly. From there, I went to L.A. and helped Drake in the rescue of his sister from a human trafficking ring."

"I read about that, but I had no idea you were involved."

"You wouldn't have. I stowed away on a ship and found myself in Brazil. I lived there until nine days ago."

"Why did you come back?"

Jed took his cell phone out and scanned through the photos. "I spent a lot of time trying to figure out a way to expose Wilmot, but it was impossible. He'd been appointed to take Wolfe's place, and I'd most likely been pegged as a traitor too."

Bolton shook his head. "Not that I'm aware of. You're simply listed as missing."

Jed looked into the ether with the humiliating realization he hadn't considered the obvious all this time. "My God. Of course. Wilmot would've kept my name out of it. If they'd searched for me and brought me in, he'd have risked me telling them what I'm telling you now."

"But . . . you said you had evidence."

"I do." He handed the phone to Bolton and pointed to the first image. "I took these just over two weeks ago in Brazil. That's Brandon Drake in the flesh. He arrived with that other guy at the favela I was staying in. They came to kill me."

Bolton went through the images with a bemused expression. "But Brandon Drake is dead. He was killed months ago in Los Angeles."

"Exactly."

"I don't understand. And why would a man you'd helped be trying to kill you? "

"When I first met Drake, he told me his personality and memories were the result of a mind control experiment Treadwell had subjected him to. He'd learned he used to be a psychopath they called The Scorpion. Now, think about it. A faked death and an assassination attempt by a man who used to be my friend." He gestured to the phone. "Those photographs were taken with *that* phone. They're timed and dated."

"You're saying they turned Drake back into a psychopath and sent him out to kill you?"

"I'm convinced of it. What you're seeing there are photographs of a dead man taken three months after he supposedly died. I'm also convinced Drake was responsible for the massacre at Faraday Ranch in Dallas. I need you to get that phone to Senator Adams."

Bolton stared at the phone in silence.

"A homicidal maniac is on the loose right now, and Wilmot is responsible. He's now running SDT *and* Treadwell's faction, which is still active within the CIA. I don't know how far it extends. I can't trust anyone."

After a few moments, Bolton conceded. "I'll get the phone to the senator and tell him what you've told me."

Jed sank back on the bench with relief. "Thank you."

"I appreciate you coming to the senator with this. I can't imagine what you've been through, Mr. Crane. But I can assure you, I know of no warrant out for your arrest. You can take it easy."

"No, I can't. If anyone in the CIA or SDT learns of my whereabouts, it'll reach Wilmot's goons. Once that happens, I'm a dead man."

"I understand. So, where can we reach you?"

Jed stood and shook Bolton's hand. "I'll get hold of *you*." He turned away, his mission accomplished, and disappeared into the crowd.

Twenty-Six

Home, Sweet Home

With Emily by her side, Belinda drove Tyler's Porsche out of a hotel parking lot on the outskirts of Philadelphia. It was the third day of their eighteen-hundred-mile journey from Fort Worth to Boston, and they had another six hour drive ahead of them.

They'd stayed in the hotel until after lunch and didn't depart until 2:30 p.m. Belinda was subconsciously procrastinating. Her sense of dread made the laborious trip all the more harrowing. It had been over six years since she'd seen her mother, and another seven years the time before that. She'd come to believe she would never have to see her again. The pain and rage she felt toward her was deep, and she knew there would be no resolution of the issues. She was forced to acknowledge the fact that she hated her mother. *Needing* her at this time was emotionally excruciating.

"You're awfully quiet," Emily said.

"I'm awfully upset, that's why."

"About seeing your mother again?"

"She was cold toward me all through my childhood, and all because she got pregnant out of wedlock by a guy she didn't even know. Like that was *my* fault."

"Do you believe her church was responsible for making her feel that way?"

"No doubt about it, but she was old enough to think for herself. When I told her a priest had molested me, she called me a liar and a whore. She didn't think there was any way *they* could do any wrong. She allowed herself to be completely brainwashed by them, and I hate her for it."

Emily placed her hand on her shoulder. "I'm so sorry for everything you've been through. You didn't deserve that."

Belinda threw her an appreciative-but-sad smile. She turned her gaze back to the road, her mind awash with what she would say when her mother opened the door to them. Or would it depend on what her mother said to her?

At just past 8:00 p.m., Belinda pulled the Porsche up outside a residential home in the Boston suburb of Dorchester. She held her gaze upon a modest, two-story house amidst a row of similarly-designed homes. Her heart pounded with so many painful memories. *Why must I do this?*

Slowly, she opened the car door and stepped out.

Emily followed and came around the car to join her. "I'm here. You can do this."

Belinda shuddered and apprehensively stepped forward. Within a few seconds, they were standing in front of the door. There was another tense pause before Belinda rang the doorbell.

They waited for over a minute before the door opened. Belinda's body became rigid at the sight of the forty-six-year-old woman in the doorway. Her short, brunette hair and hardened features gave her face a pointed appearance. Her remarkably slender frame suggested a strict diet, which aroused Belinda's curiosity. Her mother had never been particularly body conscious.

"To what do I owe this honor?" the woman said with sardonic iciness.

"I had no choice, Mom," Belinda said. "We need a place to stay."

The woman glanced at Emily. "And who would 'we' be?"

"Ma'am, my name is Emily Drake. I'm Belinda's friend." Emily extended her hand, but the woman didn't take it.

"Drake? Any relation to that soldier she was playing around with?"

Belinda's lips screwed up with seething anger.

"He was my brother," Emily said.

The woman looked at them both derisively for a moment. "Well, I suppose you'd better come in."

Emily quietly said, "Thank you, Mrs . . . ?"

"Oh, it's still Reese. Monica Reese. At least for the next three weeks." She held up her right hand to show a generous, diamond engagement ring.

"Congratulations," Belinda said coldly, although it explained her mother's new appearance. She was obviously trying to impress her new man.

"It's a pleasure to meet you," Emily said.

Uncomfortably, they followed Monica inside.

"So, who's the lucky guy?" Belinda said.

"A very good man I met at church a year ago. He's a successful real estate developer, which means I'll finally be able to get out of this dump."

Belinda grimaced. "How nice for you."

"Yes, Belinda. You're lucky. A month later, and I wouldn't have even been here." She gestured to her daughter's protruding abdomen. "I assume you're married in *that* condition?"

"Yes, I was. Just not in the way you think."

"What's that supposed to mean?"

"Brandon and I married one another with our hearts. Legally, I'm Belinda Reese, but as far as I'm concerned, I'm Mrs. Brandon Drake."

"So, you're pregnant out of wedlock. What a surprise." Monica shot her a venomous smile.

"I don't consider I need the permission of a pedophile to be with the man I love."

"Don't start with that again, Belinda. What are you doing here, anyway?"

"Our . . . lives are in danger. We were advised to leave Dallas."

Monica scowled. "Your lives are in danger? Dallas? What are you talking about?"

"It's Brandon."

"Brandon? I watch the news, Belinda. Your boyfriend is dead."

"So, we all thought. He's alive, and they've turned him into a killer. He murdered all of the security men where we were living."

"You never stop, do you? You should become a writer with your imagination."

"Look, Mom, do you honestly think I would have come here out of choice?"

"She's telling you the truth, Ms. Reese," Emily said. "Check the news. Look up Faraday Ranch. That's where we've been living."

Monica was quiet for a moment. "That does sound familiar. Something about a massacre, if I recall."

"Yes," Belinda said. "That's what we're trying to tell you."

Monica's gaze lingered over Belinda's shoulder at Emily. "So, what's your story, Miss Drake? Or is it *Ms*?"

"Emily, please. Do you recall the story about the Hamlin factory on L.A. Harbor, where my brother was supposedly killed?"

"Of course."

"I'd been kidnapped by a human trafficking organization. Belinda and Brandon came to rescue me."

Monica smirked. "How convenient. And how on earth did you find yourself in the clutches of human traffickers, my dear?"

Emily took a deep breath. "If you must know, I used to be a nun. I was very unhappy and I left the convent. I was kidnapped when I was on the road."

"Oh, I see. You abandoned your calling. You're an apostate. Don't expect any sympathy from me."

Belinda stepped between them, incensed beyond her endurance. "Don't speak to her like that! You have no idea what Emily has been through. What turned you into someone like this, Mom?"

Emily placed her hand on Belinda's shoulder. "It's all right, Belinda." She turned back to Monica. "It wasn't my *calling*. I had no say in it. They took me in when I was a baby."

"So," Monica said, "you abandoned those who gave you care and shelter. It doesn't surprise me that Belinda would make a friend of someone so immoral."

"You might be right. I might be immoral."

"No, you're not!" Belinda yelled.

"Have you ever considered becoming a nun, Ms. Reese?" Emily said. "You seem particularly fond of the idea."

"What?"

"*Do unto others as you would have them do unto you.* Matthew, seven-twelve."

Monica was suddenly silent. Emily came forward and stopped close to her, a rare hint of anger appearing in her eyes. "Your daughter personally delivered me out of the hands of my captive. She befriended me, loved me, and helped me to find my place in society. She is kind, warm, and has a generosity of spirit like no other."

Belinda's lower lip quivered and tears came to her eyes. To have such a calm and loving person as Emily defend her to her mother was such a unique experience, and it overwhelmed her.

"I feel for you, Ms. Reese," Emily said. "You have denied yourself something extremely precious by rejecting Belinda. It's so sad that you've never really known her."

Overcome with emotion, Belinda turned and ran up the stairs. She came to her old bedroom, closed the door, and wept. *Why does she have to be like that? God, I love you, Em.*

She buried her head in her pillow, oblivious to what might be being said downstairs. The agony of knowing her existence came from a monster was unbearable.

After a few minutes, she dried her eyes and sat up. She looked around the room and saw everything was in the same place. The bed, wardrobe, and dressing table were exactly as they always had been. However, the photographs of her as a child, teddy bears, or any possessions that belonged to her, were nowhere to be seen. Even her CD player was gone. Her mother had erased all trace of her from her life. The question that assaulted her mind persisted: *Why?*

Finally, she stood and made her way over to the window. She opened the drapes and looked out over the neon-lit street. Memories of her childhood flashed before her, filling her with sadness and rage. She'd been abused in so many ways.

She lowered her head and rubbed her eyes. Opening them again, her vision focused back onto the street. Someone was standing in the middle of the road. She couldn't make out his face. It was concealed underneath a dark hood. Even from a distance, she could see the hooded top was torn in several places, as though it was riddled with holes. It was probably just a bum.

And then he looked up at her, his face illuminated by the street lighting. Her heart pounded with an amalgam of elation and terror. *Oh, my God. He's found me.*

Twenty-Nine

Dark Eyes

Emily and Monica sat opposite one another in two living room's armchairs. Emily looked at her with sadness and compassion. Monica's expression appeared to be one of bewilderment.

"Family is so precious, Ms. Reese," Emily said. "I am very fortunate to have found mine. I have a brother. His name is Tyler. He's very wealthy, but he's also very kind. He has a terrific sense of humor. Being around him brings a ray of sunshine into my life."

Monica looked away, but Emily persisted. "Tyler's father is a very powerful man, but he took me into his home, supported me, cared for me, and treated me like his own daughter. They've done so much to give me hope. They've shown me that there is tremendous good in the world. Because of them and Belinda, I'm finally beginning to understand who *I* am."

Monica turned back to her with a look that suggested Emily was finally getting through to her. She hadn't said a word since Emily quoted *The Golden Rule*.

"Why do you think you feel so angry toward Belinda?" Emily said. "I hope you don't mind me asking."

Tears came to Monica's eyes. "I . . . I don't know. I'm so confused."

"I'd helped people in crisis when I was a nun, but I'd never felt the warmth I've come to know. I took the love Tyler, his father, and Belinda showed me, and I used it to help others. I now work for The Samaritans. Being there for people is what life is all about to me."

Monica finally opened her mouth to speak. "I think—"

"Oh, my God!" Belinda's voice boomed to the accompaniment of stampeding feet down the stairwell.

Emily and Monica turned sharply as she burst into the living room.

"What's wrong?" Emily said.

"It's Brandon. He's here."

"But how can that be?"

"I have no idea, but I've just seen him in the street outside."

"You're sure it was him?"

"Positive." Belinda looked over at to her mother. "We have to lock every door in the house. Now!"

Her face ashen, Monica stood, ran to the front door, and bolted it.

"Come on. We have to lock every door and window." Belinda ran out of the room.

Emily followed, hurried up the stairs, and then into all three bedrooms. Once she'd locked all the windows, she headed into the bathroom.

Belinda and Monica darted around the rooms of the ground floor, locking every door and window. They didn't say a word to one another.

Belinda finally entered the kitchen and froze. The back door was swinging open. Her heart stopped and she couldn't swallow.

Cautiously, she moved forward. Her hand reached out, her fingers shaking as she came closer to the door. The refrigerator was to her left and a whimper escaped her throat as she came past it. Was someone on the other side?

Almost too afraid to look, she took a brief glimpse before she'd completely cleared the fridge. It was enough for her to know there was nobody there. Brandon was a large guy. There was no way he'd be able to conceal all of himself from that angle.

She looked up again. The back door was inches from her reach. She held her breath and inched forward slightly, still too terrified to touch it. Her right leg shot out to collide with the edge of the door. It closed with a loud slam, causing the key to fall from the lock. She reached down and picked it up with panic speed. Her hands shook, impairing her ability to insert the key back into the lock. *Please, please, please.*

The key slipped into the lock and she twisted it. Moving away, she slumped back into the side wall beside the refrigerator, finally giving a sigh of relief.

Footsteps came closer from the right. Every muscle in her body tensed. She held her breath once again. The steps came closer . . .

Monica eased her face around the side of the fridge. Belinda exhaled again. She never thought she'd welcome the sight of her mother.

"Are you all right?" Monica said.

"I never knew you cared."

They stared at one another for a moment, and then Monica held her hand out for her. "Come on."

Uneasily, Belinda took her mother's hand, pulled herself up, and walked past the storage cupboard toward the hallway.

The cupboard door burst open. Belinda spun around and gasped. He raised his head, and she saw his face underneath the hood. His dark eyes met hers.

His hand seemed to be shaking as he reached over his shoulder to unsheathe the sword.

"No!" Monica said from behind.

He turned around as she ran toward him, unable to stop in time. The sword ran through Monica's solar plexus, exiting through the middle of her back. Her legs instantly failed her, but he held her steady with the sword.

"Mom!" Belinda cried.

Monica choked, clearly attempting to speak. Her gaze turned toward Belinda, and a single word emerged from her throat: "R-run." Her eyes rolled back, her arms became limp, and her body slipped from the blade onto the floor.

He slowly turned around again, and Belinda found herself face to face with the one she once loved with all her heart. "Brandon, don't do this," she said, the distinct undertones of terror in her voice.

He moved toward her and suddenly stopped. His free hand gripped his head and he staggered into the wall.

Belinda noticed the struggle within him. "Brandon, I know you're in there. You can beat this. Fight it!"

He fell to his knees and screamed an anguished bellow the likes of which she had never heard.

She heard Emily run to the end of the stairs and suddenly stop. "Open the door. Hurry!" Belinda said.

Drake gripped the sword handle with his right hand, and drove his fist into the floor with his left. He pushed himself up with perspiration falling from his brow. Belinda noticed the pain in his eyes.

"W-what . . . are you?" he said with a guttural growl.

She stepped back slightly, knowing, at all costs, she had to get through to him. "It's me, Brandon. It's Belinda. I love you. You love me, remember? Can you remember the cabin?"

He fell to the floor again and tried to stab the sword toward her, but she was out of reach.

"You really want to kill me, don't you?" She heard the click of the lock behind her. "You can't kill me, Brandon. I know you can't." She placed her hand on her abdomen. "If you kill me, you'll also be killing your own child."

"No. That's not possible. You're lying . . . bitch!"

"No, I'm not, Brandon. You know I'm not."

"You . . . can't run from me."

"And you can't run from *you*, Brandon." She glanced over at her mother's corpse. There was nothing she could do for her now. *Oh, Mom.*

Emily came up beside her. Drake looked up and tilted his head, as though intrigued by the sight of his sister.

"We have to get out of here," Emily said.

Belinda's eyes blurred with tears and she stumbled backward through the doorway. Emily followed, keeping her gaze on Brandon at all times.

"No!" he roared.

Once they were on the path, they turned and ran toward the Porsche.

Belinda took the keys out of her pocket and unlocked the doors with the remote control. They climbed in and locked the doors immediately. Belinda started the engine.

Emily looked out of the side window and screamed. Brandon was virtually upon them with his sword raised.

Belinda gunned the car forward as the blade came down, barely missing the car. She glanced in the rear view mirror to see him standing in the middle of the street—a hooded specter of death brandishing a scythe. He became smaller by the second as he receded into the distance.

Belinda drove for hours toward the south. Not a word passed between her and Emily. Shock had taken hold of them beyond the point of speech.

At 2:00 a.m. Belinda decided to pull over on a roadside in Pennsylvania. She slumped forward and buried her head in the steering wheel.

Emily put her arm around her shoulder. "Hey. We have to call the police and report what happened to your mom."

"I know." Belinda finally broke down.

Emily reached across and held her tightly. "Oh, Belinda."

"Why did she have . . . to be that way, Em?"

"I spoke to her when you were upstairs. She didn't say much, but I don't think it was *you* she was angry with. It was herself. I could see it in her eyes. She loved you."

Belinda returned Emily's embrace, overcome by the need for comfort. Her sobbing reached a crescendo, until she became exhausted. Half an hour passed before she sat back and dried her face. "He'll find us."

"What are we going to do?"

Belinda looked up and fixed her gaze into the night horizon. "We're heading in the right direction, at least."

"In the right direction for what?"

Strength returned to Belinda as a realization came to her. "There *is* somewhere we can go, Em."

"Where?"

"To the only man I know who can help us."

Thirty

The Operation

Drake wandered through the void. The darkness was quickly becoming his second home. His only companion: his greatest enemy. As with each previous visit, he felt like he'd been walking through it for an eternity.

Finally, he sensed him. "I know you're here."

I'm always here, Scorp. You came pretty close this time, but you're not going to hurt her.

"Somehow, I'll find a way to overcome you, you son of a bitch. She's a vulnerability. An exploitable weaknesses. There's something about her you're using to break me down."

You're the one who's making the vulnerabilities happen.

"What are you talking about?"

The Interceptor appeared before him as though from nowhere. "All you have to do is leave her alone, and I'll leave *you* alone. Haven't you figured that out yet, dipshit?"

Drake lunged at his adversary. The Interceptor sidestepped him with ease and drove his fist into his jaw with inhuman speed. Drake staggered backward, dazed by the blow.

"You think I really did that, Scorp?"

"Who else?"

The Interceptor laughed. "I know you're pretty slow, but I'm sure you'll figure it out sooner or later."

"Take the helmet off!" Drake said. "Face me like a man."

"Oh, I'm happy to take it off, Scorp. You're the one who's stopping me."

"Take it off!"

"It's what's underneath it that you can't face."

"Take. It. Off."

"OK. Let's see how far we get this time." The Interceptor gripped the helmet and slowly pulled it upward. "You don't stand a chance against me until it comes off."

Drake squinted and angled his gaze downward, trying desperately to make out the face under the helmet. He watched as it passed his enemy's mouth and eventually reached his nose—

Drake awoke with a start. The pain in his head the night before had broken him, and he'd fallen asleep in the Chevy.

He looked around as he recovered from his disorientation. It seemed to be an uninhabited forest region where he'd parked under the cover of the trees. He wasn't sure where he'd stopped. Was it somewhere in New York State?

The Interceptor's words rang out in his head: *You don't stand a chance against me until it comes off.* What was it about that damn helmet? Why couldn't he see the face under it?

He waited to recover from hyperventilation, and then grasped a small radio-like device from the passenger's seat. He managed a smile. There was nowhere Belinda Reese could run from him.

***

Senator Michael Adams entered Director Brenham's office at Langley. Brenham stood and offered his hand. "It's good to see you, Mike.

Adams took the director's hand. The lines around his eyes deepened and his complexion appeared slightly redder than usual. Brenham suspected Adams' blood pressure was higher than normal.

"We have some very serious business to discuss, Jack," Adams said.

"Take a seat."

Adams settled into the chair and eased forward. "My assistant, Robert Bolton, had a very interesting meeting yesterday."

"Oh? With whom?"

"An SDT operative who's been listed as missing since the beginning of April."

Brenham's heart pounded and he leaned forward, wide-eyed. "Crane met with your assistant?"

"That's right, and he had a very interesting story to tell."

"Go on."

"He claims the director of SDT, Wilmot, is a traitor, and that he's now leading Treadwell's faction. Apparently,

Wilmot had a very curious duo attempt to take him out in Rio a couple of weeks ago."

"And you believe him?"

Adams took three photographs out of his pocket and placed them on the desk. "I have to believe my eyes, Jack."

Brenham picked up the photographs and sifted through them. "How do you know these weren't faked?"

"Because I have the cell phone they came from. They're timed and dated. I had a specialist examine the data."

"Where is this phone?"

"In a safe place. What's going on, Jack?"

Brenham considered his response, his mind conflicted by personal fears, and also the hope that this might be the break he'd been waiting for.

"Crane claims Elias Wolfe was murdered," Adams said, "and that Wilmot's faction has been out to kill him for months. It seems they're now using a dead man to do their dirty work."

Brenham rubbed his eyes. His immediate reaction was to say, 'That's preposterous', but he knew this was no time for denial. The situation was critical and he needed help. He needed Jed Crane.

"Why don't you seem surprised by all this?" Adams said.

"Because . . . I'm not."

"Well, you'd damn well better start telling me what you know. If there's a chance there's a traitor running SDT and you're doing nothing about it, I'll have the matter brought before the Senate Select Committee before you can blink."

Brenham waved his hand up and down passively. "All right, calm down. All is not as it seems."

"Tell me something, Jack, because I can assure you, you'll never have a more captive audience."

"In that case, you'd better brace yourself. We've known for a few days Brandon Drake is still alive, and he's running wild." Brenham opened a drawer, took out a report and handed it to Adams. "That came through this morning. It's a report from the Boston Police Department. It was called in by Belinda Reese. Drake killed her mother, and almost killed her and his own sister."

Adams looked up from the paper. "So where are they?"

"We don't know. According to the police, she said she was running for her life. Drake was responsible for the hit on Mach Industries, and we have fingerprint evidence that he was responsible for the massacre at Faraday Ranch. Belinda Reese wasn't exaggerating when she said she was in fear for her life."

"Where does Wilmot fit into all this?"

"Drake told Professor Jacobson from Mach Industries that he couldn't remember anything after twenty-twelve. According to Jacobson, Drake said he'd woken up in a facility in Mojave, which is exactly where Wilmot had spent a lot of his time allegedly looking into an ISIS cell."

"The facility that was destroyed in an explosion?"

"The same one."

"Where's the professor now?" Adams said.

"We let him go. He's a material witness, and he's agreed to assist us with the case. We believe Wilmot faked

Brandon Drake's death, and used the same mind control techniques Treadwell used in order to give him a new persona. Possibly his original one."

"What are you doing about it?" Adams said with a demanding tone.

"Treadwell used a memory revision specialist in New Hampshire, a Doctor Frederick DeSouza. We've tried to contact the man, but it seems he's disappeared."

"So, why aren't you going after Wilmot?"

Brenham stood and walked over to the far window. "Going after Wilmot right now could be lethal. We have no idea how far this goes, or who's involved. We need to take them all down in one move, Mike. We can't afford for any of them to know we're on to them." He turned back to the senator. "We've been waiting for hard evidence. If you have it, you have to give it to me. Let me talk with Jed Crane."

"We have no idea where Mr. Crane is. He's an extremely cautious man. He doesn't even know if you're a part of this. All he said to Bolton was that he'd contact us, and not the other way around."

Brenham came closer to Adams. "Do you think I'm a part of this?"

"I don't know what to think. I never liked Treadwell, but I'd never have imagined he'd do the things he did. When Crane contacts us again, I will be personally securing his protection, just as I've secured the information he gave us."

Brenham shook his head at the thought of the senate even contemplating he was dirty. "I don't believe this."

"Put yourself in my place, Jack. You've just virtually told me that half the damn intelligence community is corrupted."

"I need Crane, dammit! I need to talk to him. This is gonna be the most serious operation any of us have ever known."

"And that's exactly why I'm being cautious. We need to work together on this, and I need you to cooperate."

Brenham sighed and looked away again.

"Somehow, I'll get you talking to Crane," Adams said. "We have to take this faction and Brandon Drake down."

"I couldn't agree more."

"Wait for my call."

"You can count on it."

Adams made his way toward the door and paused. "How the hell did it come to this, Jack?"

"I've been asking myself that question every day since this started."

They looked at one another ominously for a moment before Adams opened the door and exited the room.

Thirty-One

Bragg

It was almost 4:00 p.m. when Fort Bragg came into sight. Belinda slowed the Porsche and glanced at Emily. "This is it."

"I have to say, I'm relieved. There can't be anywhere safer for us than this. How can you be sure he'll be here?"

"I can't."

The tension in Belinda was palpable. She could only imagine Emily was going through the same ordeal. Neither of them had slept for almost two days. They dared not risk it until they were safe. Had they slept, there was every chance they'd never have woken up. Brandon would have killed them without hesitation. Exhaustion had begun to affect Belinda's vision, often compelling her to snap herself awake at the wheel.

She pulled up to the base's front gate. A young soldier dressed in the customary tan, gray, and green uniform of the Eighty-Second Airborne Division approached. She lowered the electric side window to greet him.

"Good afternoon, ma'am," he said. "How can I help?"

"Hi," she replied. "It's extremely important that we speak to Sergeant Major David Spicer."

The young man frowned. "Is Sergeant Major Spicer expecting you?"

"No, but he knows us. Do you know if he's on site?"

"I'm not sure, ma'am, but I'll be happy to call it in and check, if you don't mind waiting."

Belinda managed a slight smile. "That'd be great. Thank you very much."

"Who should I say wants to talk with him?"

"Belinda Reese and Emily Drake."

"OK, just give me a few minutes." He smiled at her warmly.

Her gaze followed the soldier as he headed toward the guard room.

"Do you think he'll be here?" Emily said.

"God, I hope so."

The minutes ticked by painfully. Belinda and Emily watched the soldier through the guardroom window. He seemed to be conferring with a slightly older soldier in between repeated phone calls.

After almost twenty minutes, he came out of the guardroom again. Belinda chewed her hair in anticipation.

"Sorry to keep you waiting, ma'am," he said. "I've had to make a few calls to find the Sergeant Major. The good news is he's on site."

Belinda and Emily glanced at one another and smiled.

"One of my colleagues is trying to find him right now to let him know you're here. Please move your vehicle to the right so you aren't blocking the lane. And please remain inside."

"Sure."

Belinda kept the Porsche's windows down to let in some air. Memories came back to her as she looked through the windshield and beheld the spectacle of Fort Bragg. It was over two years since she'd last set foot on its grounds, when she'd been called in to attend Brandon's trial. She glanced at the gates on the far side. The vision of all his fans holding placards came back to her as clear as if it were yesterday.

She heard the guardroom phone ring and the soldier who'd greeted them answered it. "Guardroom. Yes, sir. Thank you, sir. I'll let them know." The call ended and he called to Belinda and Emily. "That was Sergeant Major Spicer. He's on his way over."

Belinda and Emily sat back in their seats, sensing all of the tension leaving their bodies.

After fifteen minutes, a casually-dressed man, apparently off duty, stepped into the guardroom.

Belinda became emotional at the sight of the man who was quite possibly their only hope. "Oh, thank God. David."

"It's OK. I'll take it from here," she heard David say. He came out of the guardroom and walked toward the Porsche. "Hi. It's good to see you again," he said. "Look, let's go back to my place. It's less than a mile past the base, and then you can tell me why you needed to see me. Is that all right?"

"Absolutely," Belinda said.

Spicer turned his attention to the Porsche with a curious expression. "Is this yours?"

"No, it's Tyler's."

He looked at her with a compassionate stare. He didn't know what the issues were, but his eyes told her everything she needed to know. She and Emily had come to the right man.

Belinda followed David a short distance from Fort Bragg, pulled up outside his apartment, and stepped out of the car with Emily.

David climbed out of his car and gestured to his front door. "Come on in."

"Thank you, David," Belinda said, unable to restrain a hint of emotion in her voice.

They entered his residence, and Belinda immediately noted how spotless it was inside. The carpet was freshly vacuumed, the surfaces were polished, and nothing was out of place. It was quite surprising. Surely, he had more important matters to occupy him than making his home meticulous. Perhaps there was more to the lavish interior than met the eye. She couldn't fail to notice a female touch to the ambiance.

He turned to them and tilted his head warmly. "It's great to see you guys again. But are you gonna tell me what this is all about?"

"Oh, David," Belinda said, "I don't know how I'm gonna say this."

"What?"

"Brandon . . . is alive."

His expression darkened. "That's not possible."

"You've got to believe us, David. He's trying to kill us."

"But how?"

"The night before last, we were standing as close to him as we're standing to you right now. He killed my mother right in front of us."

"It's true," Emily said.

David sat down on his couch, his chin falling into his hand in a contemplative manner.

Belinda and Emily sat opposite him. He looked at them attentively while Belinda relayed the story Jed Crane had told her about Wilmot faking Brandon's death and, most likely, restoring his original personality. She explained the massacre at Faraday Ranch had been Brandon's handiwork, and implored him to understand the danger they were in.

"We had nowhere else to turn, David," Belinda said. "You're the only one I know who can help us."

Finally, his expression brightened. "You did the right thing. I can't tell you how sorry I am for the loss of your mother and what you've been through. But there isn't anywhere on earth you could be safer than right where you are."

A warm sense of security filled Belinda's heart, but questions plagued her. "David, I believe they've turned Brandon into The Scorpion again. I just didn't know him. He was crazed, like he wanted to kill me, but couldn't."

"What do you mean?"

"I could see it in his eyes. He hated me, and yet every time he made a move toward me, he fell down. There was a terrible pain in his eyes. Do you think there's some of the Brandon I knew still in him?"

David raised his hands in surrender. "I have no idea. All I can tell you is what I know, and I sure as hell knew The Scorpion."

"Would you tell us? What was he like back then? There's no way he could've known where we were heading, but he was already there when we arrived. What are we up against?"

He looked at them reservedly, and was to reply when there was a knock at his door. "Would you excuse me for a moment?"

"Sure."

David walked out of the living room and opened the front door. A petite blonde woman, wearing Eighty-Second Airborne Division fatigues, stood on the other side. She saluted. "Sir."

"At ease, Sergeant," he said. "Come in."

She stepped inside and fixed her gaze upon him, adoringly. "God, I've missed you." She reached her arms up, placed them around his neck, and kissed him deeply.

He broke away reluctantly. "I have guests, babe. Actually . . . I really need your help."

"With what?"

"Follow me."

He led the woman into the living room and turned to Belinda and Emily. "Belinda, you asked me what Drake was like when he was with us. The lady by my side knows more about Brandon Drake than probably anyone else. I would like you to meet Sergeant Rachel Martoni."

Thirty-Two

Yesterday's Prey

Belinda and Emily sat before David and Rachel in anticipation.

"I'm not sure I follow you," Rachel said. "Why do you want to know about Brandon Drake?"

"I'm sorry, Rachel, I forgot," David said. "You guys have never met before. This is Belinda Reese, Brandon Drake's girlfriend, and his sister, Emily."

Rachel lightly slapped her forehead. "Oh, my God. I'm so sorry, I didn't realize. David has spoken of you both. I just . . . don't know what to say to you. I know you knew a completely different Brandon Drake to the one I served with."

"Believe me," Belinda said, "we've seen The Scorpion. He killed my mother and the security personnel at the ranch where we live."

Bewilderment came across Rachel's face. "What?"

"He's alive," Emily said.

"But how is that possible? He died in an explosion in L.A. David gave the eulogy at his funeral."

Belinda shook her head. "No. We were made to think he died. A brainwashing experiment turned him from The Scorpion into the man I loved. They then faked his death and turned him back into who he was before. Emily and I are here because he's hunting us. We need to know what we're dealing with."

"Oh, God." Rachel paced the room pensively.

"He found us in a place he couldn't possibly have known," Belinda said.

"That doesn't surprise me at all," Rachel said. "He was brilliant at anything like that. He had it all—the fighting skills, the engineering skills, the fearlessness, and incredible resourcefulness. I remember Colonel Woodroffe not liking him. Drake even got away with punching the colonel out. No soldier gets away with striking his commanding officer, but Drake was released from the brig."

"How come?"

"We never knew, at least not at the time. We've pieced much of it together over the years."

"What did you piece together?"

"In the beginning, Drake seemed like a reluctant soldier. He didn't want to be there, and he didn't want to socialize with the other soldiers. It was like he was just using the battlefield to vent his frustrations. I can assure you, he was extremely useful, but he wasn't popular."

"What happened afterward?" Belinda said.

"During the last two years he was with us, he changed for the worse. He became cocky and more arrogant than ever. After he punched out the colonel and was released from the brig, we knew something was wrong."

Belinda noticed Rachel was becoming emotional. "There's more, isn't there?"

"He became a monster. He was consumed with power. We just didn't know where it was coming from. He . . ."

"He what?"

Rachel raised her head, almost stoically. "He raped me."

Belinda gasped, unable to grasp what she was hearing. How could this have been the man she'd fallen in love with? "He raped you?"

"Many times. He blackmailed me with telling the men that I was lesbian. You have to understand, back then the 'don't ask, don't tell' regulation hadn't been overturned for that long. It would've been hell for me."

Belinda glanced at David, and then back at Rachel. "I'm sorry, I know it's none of my business, but I couldn't help catching a glimpse of the two of you in the doorway. I'm confused. Are you . . . bisexual?"

Rachel gave a light chuckle. "No. I'm straight. What Drake threatened me with was a false accusation. But with the army mentality back then, doubt is all it would've taken. Like I said, he was a monster."

"So, what have you figured out since then?" Belinda said. "What gave him this kind of power?"

David replied through gritted teeth, "Treadwell."

"Treadwell?"

"Yeah. Treadwell recruited him when he was in the army, obviously offering him rewards far beyond what the army could. He was already volatile, but with someone in Congress backing him, he had free rein. He'd get sent to the brig and Treadwell would get him out. As far as he was concerned, he was invincible."

"Of course," Belinda said with dawning realization. "Brandon wouldn't have known about any of this because Treadwell wiped his memories. But Treadwell had to have known him before. Why didn't I think of that?"

"Obviously, he became a problem for Treadwell too, which is why his 'nice guy' personality was created," David said.

"How long have you known about what he did to Rachel?" Belinda said.

"Since soon after he was assigned to Mach Industries."

Rachel said, "It was one of the best days of my life when he got transferred."

Belinda turned back to David. "I remember the day I first met you in North Carolina. You were so cold toward him. This is why, isn't it? It's because of what he did to Rachel."

"Partly. I can't even tell you what kind of a bastard he was. It was relentless."

"If he's on the loose now," Rachel said, "with nobody to answer to, and nobody to offer him anything, you're in serious danger, Belinda." She looked at Emily ominously. "Both of you. This is a man who has no conscience. He's a psychopath. I was yesterday's prey, but you are today's. You can't leave here. You have to stay with David."

David stood and headed for the door. "I have to get back to the base. I'll only be a couple of hours. You guys help yourselves to the kitchen and make yourselves coffees or whatever. I'll be back as soon as I can. Rachel, would you mind staying with them for awhile?"

"Of course not."

"Thank you."

Belinda looked at Emily despairingly. "Oh, God, Em. I can't believe it's come to this. And I am so tired. How about you?"

"Very sleepy."

Emily's sad-but-sweet tone compelled Belinda to throw her arms around her. "Oh, Em. You heard what Rachel said. We're in the safest place possible."

"How long has it been since you two slept?" Rachel said.

"Two days," Belinda replied.

"OK, well I don't think David would have any objection to you crashing on his bed for awhile."

"Are you sure?"

Rachel smiled. "As Sergeant Majors go, he's the coolest of the cool, and I know him as well as anyone. I'll stay here with you while he's out."

"That'd be great, Rachel. Thank you so much. But first I really think we should call Tyler. He won't have a clue what's happening." Belinda reached into her jacket pocket and took out her cell phone."

David walked up to his car beside the Porsche. When Belinda had parked, he'd been walking facing the other way. There was no way he could have seen what was stuck to the back of the Porsche.

He slowed his pace and knelt down to look at a familiar, half-moon shaped device stuck to the metal on the underside of the bumper trim. Brandon had used one just like it over two years earlier at Cherry Mountain Plain. He'd thrown it onto the car of the kidnapper who'd taken Belinda—a magnetic homing device. He instantly knew Drake was tracking her. "Oh, my God."

Thirty-Three

To Snare a Scorpion

You and me, together again, this time we'll make it, this time we'll win, we're gonna blast off, blast off, no way to stop . . .

Tyler sat in the booth at A & Z Records. His mind was on other things as Nikki Hawke sang her lungs out on her most recent album inclusion, *Blast Off*. Under Tyler's recommendation, her newly-founded melodic rock band, *Hawkeye*, had recently decided to adopt a particularly unusual gimmick.

Rob Jacques entered the booth looking bemused. "Ty?"

"Yeah, hi Rob. What do you think?"

"What's with the glockenspiel?" Jacques' expression did not convey approval.

"It's a gimmick," Tyler said. "We needed something that'd stand out. The ice effect on the keyboard does the job, but who else is ditching it in place of the real thing?"

"Yeah, but . . . an actual glockenspiel?"

Tyler stood, anxious over the issue with his brother, and it came out in his voice. "Look, I've taken advice on this and researched the hell out of promo gimmicks. There was a band in Canada who gained some notoriety simply by replacing an electric guitar with an electric mandolin. It still sounded like a prog-rock band. I've run this by Alex Dalton, my dad's marketing whiz. He says I have my finger on the button. Now, do you want this to succeed or not, *partner*?"

Jacques raised his hands calmly. "Hey, Ty. I appreciate you explaining. Come to think of it, it may be a stroke of genius. But what's wrong, buddy? You seem as tight as a knot."

Tyler gave Jacques an apologetic tap on the shoulder. "I'm sorry, Rob. I have a lot on my mind."

"I can see that."

Tyler pointed through the booth window. "That's Kyle, our glockenspiel player. It's an entirely new creation in rock. You're familiar with the term 'lead guitar'?"

"Of course."

"Well, I give you . . . lead glock." Tyler relaxed and winked at Jacques, who responded with an amused chuckle.

Tyler's cell phone rang. He took it out and checked the caller ID to see it was Belinda. "I need to take this."

"Sure."

Tyler walked out of the booth, into the corridor, and answered the call. "Belinda? Where are you?"

Her voice came through the receiver sounding emotional and shaken. "I'm with David Spicer, not far from Fort Bragg. Tyler, I've seen Brandon."

He felt as though his heart had stopped beating. "You've seen him?"

"Oh, God, Ty. You wouldn't know him. He killed my mother right in front of me and Emily."

He fell against the corridor wall and slid down onto the floor, devastated.

"Tyler? You still there."

"Yeah . . . I'm here," he said weakly. "What are you doing at Bragg?"

"It was the safest place I could think of."

"Do you have any plans?"

"Not yet. David just left. He'll be back later."

"OK, thanks for letting me know. Keep me posted, all right? I'm so sorry about your mom."

"Sure. Thank you, Ty."

Tyler ended the call, sat back against the wall, and wept.

***

Belinda put her cell phone down and looked up sharply.

David burst into the room and reached his hand out to her. "I need the keys to the Porsche."

She stood slowly and looked him in the eye with knowingness. "He's found us again, hasn't he?"

"Not yet, but I don't know how close he is. All I can tell you is, I have to get that car far away from you as quickly as possible. I'll explain everything when I get back."

She took the keys out of her pocket and handed them to him. David hurried out again.

Belinda walked over to Rachel. "How is he finding us?"

"That was one of his specialties. He would use anything he could get his hands on to get done whatever job he had to do."

Belinda sat down on the couch again, shivering.

Spicer ran along the apartments' sidewalk. He came to the last door on his right and knocked urgently.

After a few moments, a tall, dark-haired man in his early thirties opened the door.

"Sergeant Major," Staff Sergeant Barry Stockton said, and saluted.

"I need your help."

"Sure. What's going on?"

"It's not official. It hasn't got that far yet, but we don't have a moment to waste. I need you to follow me in your car."

"I'll get my keys."

"Hurry."

David pinched his knuckles. He knew he wasn't handling this as calmly as he should, but it was as personal as it was essential.

Stockton stepped out of his quarters and closed the door behind him. "Sir, can you give me any indication of what we're gonna be doing?"

David's pace quickened. "I've given shelter to two civilians. They're being hunted, and the tracker has a homing device attached to their car. I have to get it away from here. It's the only way we're gonna catch him. We're close enough to the base, and I don't think he'll be stupid enough to try breaking onto the grounds."

Stockton stopped at his red M5 sedan. "Sir, why aren't you letting the police handle this?"

"Because they can't handle this. I'll explain later. Let's just say, for now . . . we're going to snare a scorpion."

A hint of suspicion crossed Stockton's face. "No way. He's—"

"Not!" David cut him off and pointed just ahead of him. "I'm driving that Porsche over there. I need you to follow me. We're gonna dump the Porsche, and I need you to give me a ride back."

"From where?"

"Get ready for a one-hundred-fifty mile ride."

"You got it." Stockton climbed into his sedan.

David kept his eye on the rear-view mirror for two hours in order to ensure he hadn't lost Stockton. He knew the danger they were in, and hoped he'd got the Porsche away from the Bragg area quickly enough. This was his only chance to guide Drake away from Belinda and his sister, and his one chance to set up The Scorpion's capture.

None of that changed the fact that Drake could've been around every corner tracking the homing beacon magnetized to the Porsche's bumper. David was more conscious of the other cars behind them than he would've been otherwise. Neither he, nor Stockton, stood a chance against Drake in the event of a confrontation. His choice of destination was not only a means of leading Drake away from a populated area. It also had a historical connection for them all.

He finally came upon a rundown shack on the roadside and spun the Porsche into an inlet, just ahead of the shack. Stockton pulled up behind him.

As David climbed out of the Porsche, memories came back to him. Beyond the shack, on the other side of the shallow hill, was a vast plain of desert land. It was the site of their last official training exercise with Drake—the place where Drake had punched out Colonel Woodroffe for ordering him to do something he didn't want to do.

David ran to Stockton's sedan and noticed the road ahead of him, heading west. The day he first met the Brandon Drake who'd been a stranger to him came back with such sadness. In his mind's eye, he could see the look of anguish in the eyes of a man of courage and honor when a kidnapper took his woman. He recalled the explosions as the kidnapper hurled grenades out of the window at them. He remembered jumping out of Brandon's SUV to avoid the explosion, and Brandon pulling him up the side of the canyon with a spider cable. He hadn't known at the time that the Brandon Drake he'd met that day was the man the world would come to know as The Interceptor—a pop-culture legend.

Nothing made any sense. Drake had become the perfect hero. The Interceptor worked. Why would the government turn him back into a psychopath? They had the ultimate soldier in their grasp.

In a strange turn, Woodroffe always seemed to have the same opinion as Wilmot. The colonel saw the wartime virtues in Drake's psychopathy, but David never could.

He opened the passenger door to the sedan and climbed in. "Get us out of here, Stockton. I've got to call this in." David took out his cell phone and made a call, which was answered almost immediately. "General, this is Sergeant Major David Spicer."

"Yes, Spicer," General Thaddeus Grant said.

"Sir, we have an extremely delicate situation on our hands. I'm currently providing safe harbor for two civilians. I have reason to believe their lives are in serious danger."

"Please explain, Spicer."

"Well, sir, this is going to sound very strange, but it seems Brandon Drake is still alive."

There was a tense silence on the line.

"Sir?"

"I'm here. As I recall, you gave a eulogy at Drake's funeral a few months ago, over my personal objections. He was no friend of the Eighty-Second Airborne Division, Spicer."

"Your objection was duly noted, sir. We believe his death was faked as part of a covert intelligence operation, and now he's on the rampage."

"Tell me everything you know, Spicer."

"The two people I'm sheltering are Belinda Reese and Drake's sister, Emily. Apparently, Drake killed Reese's mother two nights ago, and it's believed he was responsible for slaying a team of security guards at Faraday Ranch in Dallas. These killings can be verified via the media."

"I'm aware of the Faraday Ranch incident. How do you know it was Drake?"

"Belinda Reese and Emily Drake told me they were face to face with him in Boston. They believe he's tracking them." David paused for a moment as he contemplated how he was going to explain the tracking device. He'd known what it was only because he'd seen an identical model over two years earlier during an unlawful meeting with Brandon. According to the rules of conduct, he'd been duty bound to turn Drake in at the time. It was all a matter of how he worded it. "I then discovered *what appeared to be* a homing device on the back of their Porsche. I had to get it away from the area without delay. This may be our only chance of stopping him, sir."

"Where's the car now?"

"I felt the most responsible move was to take it to some place away from a civilian population. Staff Sergeant Barry Stockton and I delivered it to an inlet on the south side of Cherry Mountain Plain. If Drake's following the homing device, that's where he'll show up."

"You did the right thing, Spicer. Come on back, and I'll handle it from here."

"Thank you, sir." The call ended.

David glanced at Stockton anxiously as the sedan sped along the dusty road.

Thirty-Four

Trusted

Wilmot paced his office in Langley. Whenever he was alone, his mind was in turmoil. Not only was Drake still out there wreaking havoc, but he couldn't shake the feeling that something was going down internally. *Firestorm. It's going to come to that. I can feel it.*

His cell phone ran and he answered it. "Wilmot."

"This is General Thaddeus Grant at Bragg."

"Yes, General, what can I do for you?"

"You asked me to send a unit to L.A. three months ago, and I agreed, despite my own personal reservations."

"Indeed you did, General. It was a splendid job."

"Except for the fact that I had no idea what the hell you were doing."

"What do you mean, General?"

"You faked Brandon Drake's death!"

Wilmot shuddered. *How the hell could Grant possibly know?* "General . . . what are you talking about?"

"Don't play games with me, Wilmot. One of your covert operations blew a gasket, didn't it?"

Wilmot was silent. No matter what he said, he knew it would be incriminating.

"Now listen to me," Grant said. "Brandon Drake is tracking his girlfriend and his sister. That's now been mediated. He's currently tracking a homing device to the south side of Cherry Mountain Plain in North Carolina. I suggest you contact the FBI or the National Guard to clean up this mess."

"General—"

The line went dead.

Wilmot felt the blood drain from his face, and urgently took out his other cell phone. His call was answered after four rings. "Slamer? Where the hell are you?"

"Heading south," Slamer said. "Look, I'm driving. It's been a heavy few days. I'm on my way back from Boston where Drake killed Reese's mother."

"How far are you from North Carolina?"

"Just comin' up to it now."

"I just spoke to General Grant at Bragg. He knows Drake is alive, and that he's gonna be showing up at the south side of some place called Cherry Mountain Plain. Look it up. We can't afford for the FBI to pick him up."

"I know where Cherry Mountain Plain is. I'm right on it."

"Take him out, Slamer. You can't afford to fail."

General Grant gazed at his phone in a state of dilemma. Something was very wrong. Wilmot was not someone he could trust. Drake had always been a hazard and a stain on the name of the Eighty-Second Airborne Division. He was an arrogant, disobedient maniac, who always managed to evade sanction. There had never been any justice where his behavior was concerned. He'd escaped from Leavenworth, he'd cheated death, and now he was on a killing spree, which would likely continue. Grant knew that as a matter of conscience, he couldn't leave the matter in Wilmot's hands. Drake was too dangerous.

Despite the unlawfulness of what he had to do, he picked up the phone and punched in an extension number. "Colonel Woodroffe, this is General Grant."

"Yes, General. What can I do for you?"

"I need to see you right away."

***

Senator Michael Adams was startled by the sudden entrance of Robert Bolton into his office. "What's going on, Bolton?"

"Sir, Jed Crane is on the line, and he wants to talk to you."

Adams stood rapidly. "Patch him through right away. And get Brenham on the line."

"Yes, sir."

Bolton stepped out of the room as Adams sat down again. He was quickly alerted by a red flashing light on his phone, and switched on the speaker. "Adams speaking."

"Senator? This is Jed Crane."

"Mr. Crane, I can't even begin to tell you how glad I am that you've called. I can assure you, you have nothing to worry about."

"Have you spoken to Director Brenham?"

"Yes, I had a meeting with him yesterday. I'm pleased to say he's of the same mind as you. He's already on to Director Wilmot."

"Are you sure?"

"Yes, and he's eager to speak to you. All of this is being kept under wraps because he has no idea how far it extends. He's extremely cautious about making a move that might alert any of Wilmot's operatives."

"That makes sense, but I'm still not ready to come in until I have something concrete."

"What do you have in mind, Mr. Crane?"

"I don't know yet."

"Would you be willing to talk to Director Brenham?"

"Can you get him on the line?"

"I'm arranging it as we speak." Adams glanced at the phone cradle and another flashing light appeared. "In fact, I think we have him here. Stand by and I'll connect you."

Jack Brenham sat in his office in Langley holding the phone to his ear, his heart pounding with anticipation.

A familiar voice came on the line. "Director?"

"Jed," Brenham said, beaming. "You have no idea how relieved I am to be speaking with you."

"I know, sir. The senator told me."

"I can't imagine what you've been through, but maybe you can help bring an end to this goddamn nightmare."

"I hope so too."

"Tell me what you know. Do you have anything at all on this faction? Any names other than Wilmot's?"

"I don't have much, but it may be enough for you to get the ball rolling. I have four names, *including* Wilmot's."

Brenham sank back with relief. His greatest fear was that Crane knew no more than Wilmot was involved. Even if it was only one more name, it might have been enough to bring them down. "Who are the other three besides Wilmot?"

"OK, are you ready for this?"

Brenham picked up a pen and held it against a pad with the phone braced under his chin. "Go ahead."

"All right. Wilmot is the leader, and I know Kerwin and Rhodes are in on it too."

Brenham scribbled down the names and stared at them, aghast. "Are you sure?"

"Very."

The director listened as Crane disclosed the only other conspiracy member he knew. As much as Brenham needed the information, it was heartbreaking to hear, nonetheless. "Thank you, Jed. Can I talk you into coming in?"

"I want to, believe me. I'll just feel a hell of a lot safer when I know these bastards are in custody."

"I understand. Where can I reach you?"

"I'll contact you tomorrow. Is that enough time?"

"I'll do my best. Because of the necessity of secrecy, I'm working on much of this alone."

"All right, sir. I'll be in touch. You have my word."

Brenham placed the phone back on the cradle and studied the three names on the pad.

After tearing the paper off, he got out of his chair, exited the office, and walked briskly along the corridor. He arrived at April Hayes' door and entered without knocking.

Sitting behind her desk, Hayes looked up with a start. "Jack."

"We need to talk. I've just spoken to Jed Crane."

"You have? Where is he?"

"I don't know. Mike Adams put me through to him. Crane gave me three new names of personnel he believes are connected to the conspiracy with Wilmot."

"Who?"

He took out the slip of paper and handed it to her, studying her eyes for a reaction. It took moments for him to detect her concern.

"Are you sure this is for real?" she said.

"As sure as I can be. I need your help." He pulled out the chair opposite her and sat down. "I trusted these people. I didn't like Wilmot, but I trusted him. Hell, I even trusted Treadwell and Payne. Now I can't trust anyone. I need to put someone on this."

"What do you have planned?"

"I need an operative to put Kerwin and Rhodes under surveillance."

"Cullen," she said without hesitation.

"I need you to be sure about this, April. I have no way of knowing who's connected with them, and no way of finding out without potentially alerting them."

"Cullen's the one who came to me with it as soon as Jacobson told him about Mojave. I could tell he was genuinely concerned. He can be trusted. I'd bet my life on him."

"You may be doing just that."

She looked at the paper again. "What are you doing about the other one?"

"I can't afford for anyone here to get involved," Brenham said. "I'm bringing the FBI into it. This needs to take place away from CIA headquarters until we know more."

"All right. I'll get hold of Cullen."

Brenham stood. "When you do, tell him I want to see him right away. He's not to say a word to anyone. Now, I've got to get over to the Federal Building."

Thirty-Five

Surveillance

Spicer walked into his apartment to find it was strangely quiet given that he had guests.

Rachel stepped out of the kitchen.

"Where are they?" he said.

She gestured to his bedroom door. "They're asleep. They hadn't slept in two days. I didn't think you'd mind them crashing on your bed."

"You're right, I don't. It's the best thing for them at the moment." He looked away sadly. "If only this could be all over for them."

"What happened?"

David sighed. "Stockton and I took the Porsche out to Cherry Mountain Plain and left it there. General Grant's dealing with it."

Rachel gave him a puzzled look. "Why would you take the car all the way out there?"

He was about to answer when he was halted by the sound of a door clicking. He looked to his right and saw Belinda coming out of the bedroom.

"David, you're back. What happened?" Belinda said.

"He was tracking you. You had a homing device attached to the rear of the car. He must've put it on when you were in Boston. I've taken the car far away from here. When he reaches its location, he'll be one-hundred-fifty miles away from you."

"Oh, my God," she said with barely more than a whisper. "I can't believe it. He was tracking us all the way from Boston?"

"I'm afraid so. But you don't have to worry any more. The car is nowhere near here, and plans are already in motion to intercept him."

She shook her head, clearly torn by ambivalence. "Will they kill him?"

"Nobody can say. I suppose it depends on him."

With a vacant look in her eyes, she returned to the bedroom.

David turned back to Rachel. "Thank you for staying with them."

"Oh, believe me, it was no trouble. They're good people."

"Yeah, they are. I don't even know them that well, but we've been through so much together, it's almost like we're family."

"I can understand that."

"God help me," he said. "I actually hope Drake gets taken out today."

***

Agent Wentworth Cullen sat before Director Brenham in the director's office. He'd never seen Brenham appear so anxious before. "Deputy Director Hayes said you have an assignment for me, sir."

Brenham loosened his tie. "Yeah, I do. Hayes trusts you. That's all I have to go on."

"I don't follow you, sir. Why did I have to undergo a polygraph? I was screened only a couple of months ago."

"There are traitors within the intelligence community, Cullen. We can't even polygraph these guys without alerting whoever else might be involved. They would've passed their routine polygraphs because the questions weren't specific to this case. You should take the fact that you were polygraphed again as a sign that you're trusted more than anyone else right now."

Cullen suddenly realized. "Wilmot."

"He's the leader, and I have two more I want you to check out."

"Who?"

"Kerwin and Rhodes."

Cullen nodded.

"You look like you expected their names to come up. Want to tell me why?"

"They work closely with Director Wilmot, and both are arrogant and power-hungry. It doesn't surprise me in the least."

"We don't know how far this goes, or who else is involved, so I don't need to tell you how sensitive this is."

"Of course. But sir, shouldn't the NSA be looking into this?"

"Ideally, yes. The problem is I don't know if even *they* are infected. I know this isn't in your official job description, but it's the most important assignment I'm ever likely to give anyone. The future of intelligence is on the line, and you are the only living soul I can trust with this right now. We have no choice."

Cullen became pensive as he processed the sinister nature of the circumstances.

"Please know that this is strictly off the record," Brenham said. "You can't say a word about this to anyone. Not a word, you understand?"

"You can rest assured."

"All right. I need you to put Kerwin and Rhodes under surveillance. Bug them, track their every move, do whatever you have to. But I want to know every word they say, and every name they mention. This supersedes any of your current assignments right now. Whether anyone even has a next assignment is down to this investigation succeeding."

"Understood, sir, but I won't be able to monitor them in their homes if I'm working alone."

"Just do whatever you can."

Brenham's tone had risen with a hint of aggression, but Cullen understood perfectly. It was a high-priority crisis. He couldn't deny his own sense of pride that Deputy Director Hayes had named him as the only operative she trusted enough for the task. Finally, he stood. "I'll get right on it, sir."

"Thank you, Agent Cullen. Now, I have another operation to oversee, if you'll excuse me."

Cullen stood and exited the office with the director.

Within an hour, Cullen had prepared himself for his vital mission. He felt no remorse over Kerwin and Rhodes. Despite the requirement for professional conduct between operatives and inter-departmental relations, he'd always despised them as individuals. Of all agents to be traitors, those two caused him the least disappointment.

He approached Rhodes' office with a folder under his arm and knocked on the door. Seconds later, it was opened. Despite Rhodes' conservative, clean-cut appearance, Cullen knew the shark behind the demeanour.

"So, Boy Scout," Rhodes said, "what can I do for you?"

"Mind if I come in?"

"Sure. What've you got?"

"The director had to go out on an operation, and he gave me copies of a file he wanted me to hand to a couple of you." Cullen opened the folder, took out one of the files, and handed it to Rhodes. "There's a suspected al-Qaeda cell living as a family in Michigan. Brenham wants you to look into it."

Rhodes turned away and perused the file. "Why hasn't Director Wilmot come to me with this?"

Cullen eased himself across to the desk while Rhodes' back was turned. He'd needed a reason to get into the office, and handing a bogus, time-wasting assignment to Rhodes seemed to have a note of poetic irony. With a subtle backhand move, he pressed an adhesive bug onto the underside of the desk. "Director Wilmot is being made aware of it as we speak. I guess Brenham thought it was time you got off your ass and did some work for once."

"Very funny."

"I'm CIA. You're SDT. Home turf assignments aren't our place. It's why we keep you guys around."

"I'll check it out."

Cullen smiled, inwardly gloating. "I'd better get going. I have a hell of a lot to do." *A lot to do completely screwing you over, you prick.*

"Yeah. Always a pleasure, Cullen."

Cullen exited the office with a smug grin. He couldn't shake off the rush of having just been placed solely in charge of a major intelligence crackdown—and one he'd been personally responsible for instigating.

He moved along the corridor, down the steps to the lower floor, and headed toward Kerwin's office. Coincidentally, he spotted Kerwin about to enter the room. "Hey, Kerwin, glad I caught you," he said with a false smile.

Kerwin turned his shaven head toward him with a typically hostile stare. "What's up, Boy Scout?"

"Nice to see you haven't lost your charm, Kerwin. The director has a job he wanted me to give you. Can I come in?"

Kerwin invited him into the room, his expression persistently cold and contemptuous.

Cullen followed him into the office. *Damn, I hate you, asshole.*

***

Brenham parked his BMW at a distance from a residential street in Georgetown. Positioned behind a park, the car was concealed by the trees where he could see a particular house clearly.

He lowered his electric window as a team of five FBI agents arrived. He watched while they approached the front door of the house. One of them rang the doorbell.

A minute later, the door opened, the occupant obscured by the agents. They wasted no time storming the property.

Satisfied, Brenham smiled.

Thirty-Six

Showdown

Colonel Darren Woodroffe stood in General Thaddeus Grant's office, bewildered. "Drake's alive?"

"So it seems." Grant awkwardly pinched his thick, gray moustache. He picked up a strip of paper from his desk and handed it to Woodroffe. "Spicer did the right thing taking that Porsche to a remote spot. The location is on there."

Woodroffe looked at the paper. "Very ironic. The place where I had my last altercation with Drake."

"I've informed SDT, but I want a unit dispatched to monitor what goes on. I don't trust Wilmot."

"Sir, that isn't our responsibility. Shouldn't the FBI handle this?"

"There's more to it than that. Drake is a lethal public hazard and an escaped military prisoner. *We* recruited and trained him, and I need to know he's been contained."

"All right, sir. Do you want me to take Spicer?"

"No. He's off duty, and although I could put him back on at a moment's notice, he's not an effective option for this. For some reason, he has regard for Drake."

"I'll take eight men. That should be enough."

"Keep a distance. Only go in if it looks like everything is going down. I know this is technically unlawful, but something is very wrong here. It's a desperate situation."

"Yes, sir." Woodroffe saluted and exited the office.

***

Drake followed the tracker sitting on the passenger's seat of the Chevy. It confused him as to why it was indicating a westerly direction. The blinking location light pointed to fifty miles away and he couldn't make sense of it. *Cherry Mountain Plain? Why in the hell would she go there?*

He continued along a series of long, dusty roads, impatiently glancing at the tracker every five seconds. They weren't moving. The signal was static. *What the hell are they doing? Having a picnic?* He pressed his foot on the gas and glanced at the speedometer: 82 m.p.h.

During the last mile, the location light flashed frantically, indicating he was on top of them.

He sped past the Porsche and hit the brakes as he noticed it. After checking the rear view mirror, he backed the Chevy up and reversed into the inlet. He then gunned the car forward and spun it around, pulling it up parallel to the Porsche. He looked around, but there was nobody in sight.

He climbed out of the Chevy with a sudden suspicion coming over him. He listened for any sound around him. Anything that would indicate a human presence: the sound of footsteps, the crack of bramble, or rustling of any kind. But there was nothing.

He turned his attention to the shack but wasn't about to take any chances before going in. Returning to the Chevy, he opened the trunk, grasped the samurai sword, and strapped it across his back. He opened the attaché case, took out two of the thermo-neutron detonators he'd stolen from Mach Industries, and put them in the pockets of his tattered hoodie.

He picked up the MZ-507 rifle from beside the case, and then turned back to the shack.

As he came closer to it, he began to tremble, and it wasn't the fear that the FBI might be waiting for him inside. It was something else. Something he couldn't identify. *What is it about this run down shack?*

And then it struck him. *The Interceptor has been here.*

Before entering, he stopped. His gaze lingered on the side of the shack and a sense of anguish came over him. But why? It was something about Spicer. Why would Spicer have been here with The Interceptor? Were they looking at something?

Yes.

He could remember the incident on the small iPhone screen. Spicer had been showing him footage of him torturing Nabi in Afghanistan. *So, the backstabbing pricks filmed it when I wasn't looking.*

He knew the torment he was feeling wasn't his own. It was The Interceptor's, and he had to overcome it. *The Interceptor is weak at his core. He's a pussy.*

He gingerly pushed the door to the shack and discovered it wasn't locked. It was barely even attached to the hinges. The shack was empty. *Where the fuck are they?*

He stepped out again and noticed a gaping hole in the wood beside the door frame. He knew the hole something to do with The Interceptor and Spicer. Looking up, he gazed beyond the Chevy and the Porsche. Seeing the inlet from this angle seemed so familiar. It was more of The Interceptor's memories, no doubt—something about a Mustang parked just ahead before the patch of trees by the roadside. He was running toward it and throwing something at the Mustang.

He grasped his head as the pain started up, brought about by his instinctive curiosity and the unremitting attacks of déjà vu. *No. I've got to forget about this. It doesn't matter what happened back then. It was his fight, not mine.*

But it was too late. The view of the location brought flashes to his mind. He didn't know the story behind them, but he couldn't stop the feeling of urgency and desperation from taking him over. He needed to catch the Mustang. But why?

It was *her*. He was trying to save her. She'd been taken. He glanced at the road and somehow knew that if he continued after the inlet, he'd come to a canyon with a deadly drop on the right side of the road. There were bombs exploding. Grenades. He could feel himself jumping out of the vehicle, followed by the impact of his body crashing into the hillside on the left.

It was always about her. She was the source of his weakness and vulnerability. Everywhere he found himself, The Interceptor used her to break him down. He had to find her, and she had to die. There was no other way.

He walked past the cars and headed toward the trees. Perhaps she was hiding among them. He cocked the rifle and continued forward.

He slowed his pace, focusing on what he could see between the branches. Nobody was there. He took another step forward . . .

A series of stabbing impacts struck him in the back, hurling him forward and knocking him off his feet. He fell to the ground, striking his forehead on the gravel. Shaking his head, he forced himself up and turned around to see Slamer standing by the shack holding an automatic rifle. The expression on Slamer's face showed confusion and fear.

Drake chuckled. "You just hit me with a few rounds from an M-16, asshole, and I just got up again. How did I do it? I know what you're thinking, buddy." He moved toward Slamer, removed the sword from his back, and cast it onto the ground. Next, he threw down the MZ-507 rifle and took off the hooded top containing the detonators.

"Are you out of your mind?" Slamer said.

Drake opened the first few buttons of the checked shirt to reveal the advanced armored vest piece. "You really think you have artillery that can get through this, you fuckin' dinosaur?"

Slamer placed his M-16 on the ground. "If you want to test your metal against me, kid, just bring it on."

Overpowering hatred gripped Drake's heart. He wanted to kill Slamer so badly he could feel the fury almost choking him. Nevertheless, he wanted his showdown to be hand-to-hand. No weaponry. "I'm gonna fucking kill you, Slamer!" he yelled, feeling the blood flushing his face.

"Come and get it."

Drake sprinted toward Slamer, leaped into the air, fist poised, and roared.

Thirty-Seven

Mortal Combat

Slamer instinctively backed away as Drake hurled himself upon him. Their fists collided with one another's heads simultaneously, knocking each other to the ground. Both stunned, they shook themselves off and got back on their feet.

Drake assumed a martial arts stance. Slamer raised his fists with his body angled in a boxing style.

Slamer lunged at Drake, aiming his right fist at his opponent's nose. Drake sidestepped the blow knocking it out of the way with a forearm block. In continuation of the same move, he snapped his fist backward, his knuckles shattering Slamer's nose.

With blood splattered across his face, Slamer resumed the fight and swept his right leg round in a low arc, taking Drake off his feet. He came upon Drake and attempted to drive his fist toward his jaw. Drake rolled out of the way, causing Slamer's fist to strike the stony ground. He howled with the pain, giving Drake the opportunity to get back on his feet.

Slamer rose as Drake assumed a stance. Without giving Slamer time to get his bearing, Drake issued a series of kicks to his foe's head. Slamer became notably senseless. The assault was punctuated as Drake leaped into the air and spun around, throwing the heel of his right foot into Slamer's jaw.

Slamer fell and Drake leaped upon him. Slamer turned over and punched upward into Drake's jaw, knocking him three feet across the ground.

Drake struggled to get to his feet. Where he had power, skill, and extraordinary agility, Slamer had devastating strength. Slamer only had to catch him once to seriously impair him.

Drake finally got back on his feet and tried to focus. Despite his blurred vision and his jaw feeling as though it had been torn off, he could make out Slamer coming toward him.

"You're good, junior. I'll give you that," Slamer said. "But I *am* going to kill you."

The comment brought the rage back to Drake's heart, and with the rage, his vision cleared. "Bring it on!"

Slamer charged toward him, but Drake spun around, throwing his heel into Slamer's stomach. The crippling pain caused Slamer to buckle over, giving Drake the opportunity to move in for the kill. "You really think you're gonna kill me, Slamer?"

Slamer shot his fist up into Drake's solar plexus but struck the armor, almost breaking his knuckles. Roaring with pain, he reached out desperately, grasped Drake's legs in a bear hug, and pulled his feet out from under him. Drake struck the back of his head on the ground as he fell beside his opponent. With Drake disoriented, and Slamer gasping for air, they looked at one another, each unable to move.

***

Colonel Darren Woodroffe sat with eight of his subordinates in a Black Hawk helicopter headed for Cherry Mountain Plain. His mind became awash with thoughts as he recalled the times he'd accepted Drake's violent nature as a battlefield advantage. He'd defended him at his court-martial, constantly torn between what was best for the team, and the danger The Scorpion presented to society. There was no easy answer to the dilemma.

Now, it turned out Drake was still alive. Some of Woodroffe's own men had borne witness to the explosion that had supposedly killed him. Woodroffe questioned how Drake could still be alive. The descriptions he'd heard of the explosion were that it was catastrophic. Nobody could have survived it. Then Drake had been buried, and Spicer had given the eulogy. Nobody knew what he'd said, and Spicer wouldn't discuss it with anyone.

So what was Drake? Was he more than a man? The fact that he was still out there hunting and killing civilians was a terrifying concept. Woodroffe questioned if he'd been partly responsible for what was happening. He'd contributed to Drake's training and advocated Drake as an asset in war. His sense of personal conflict wouldn't leave him.

"We're approaching Cherry Mountain Plain, Colonel," the pilot said.

"Land a couple of miles from the south side, Sergeant. We'll make our way over on foot. With any luck, he won't see us coming."

"Sir, I've got visual of the south side from here. It looks like something's going on down there."

271

Woodroffe hurried over to the controls where he could see ahead of him. It was clear enough to make out two men engaged in a violent altercation. "That's Drake. We've got no time. Get us on top of them right away."

"Yes, sir."

Woodroffe turned back to the men. "We're going in. The objective is to take him alive. This won't be easy, gentlemen. Drake is a formidable soldier, the best you're ever likely to see, so don't underestimate him."

Having recovered, Drake and Slamer resumed their fight. They attempted to exchange blows to the head, but only Drake was successful in landing them. While Slamer was astonishingly powerful, his size made him the slower combatant. His punches were far easier to evade than Drake's, although Drake was constantly aware of what could happen if Slamer caught him again. He was strong enough to punch out a brick wall.

Slamer lunged forward and grasped Drake's throat. His fingers tightened and Drake was certain his windpipe was being crushed. He stepped back and ground his feet into the earth with a powerful grip stance, forcing Slamer to stretch out his arm. He began to black out. His vision faded and he couldn't breathe. He gripped Slamer's arm, but couldn't budge it. Getting out of the titanic grip was impossible. He knew he had only one chance before he lost consciousness. Raising his right knee, he twisted his ankle slightly and snapped the blade of his foot down into Slamer's leg, just above the kneecap. The bone shattered, inverting Slamer's knee joint. Slamer fell to the ground, screaming in agony.

Drake staggered backward and gripped his own thighs, barely conscious. He waited for his vision to return and after a few moments, he looked up again.

His face contorted with pain, Slamer looked at Drake— and then over his shoulder. He pointed at something, but Drake wasn't interested.

"So, you were gonna kill me, eh, Slamer?" Drake managed a chuckle.

"T-they're . . . comin' for you . . . asshole."

"Oh, are they? And I'm comin' for *you*, you son of a bitch!" He knelt down and grasped Slamer's head, burying his fingers deep into his left cheek. "Say goodnight, *buddy*."

"B-Black . . . Hawk," Slamer muttered.

 Drake rapidly snapped his hands around in a clockwise motion, breaking his former colleague's neck in one swift move. He let go, and the lifeless body of Kane Slamer fell onto the dust. Only then did Slamer's last words register. *Black Hawk?*

He became vaguely aware of the sound of rotor blades behind him, turned, and looked up. A Black Hawk helicopter was closing in.

He got to his feet and tried to run across to where he'd dropped the saber, the hoodie, and the MZ-507, but he was still disoriented. Between blows to the head from Slamer, and coming within a hair's breadth of having the life choked out him, he knew he wasn't faring well.

He reached the hooded top, put it on as fast as he could, and touched the side pockets to ensure the detonators were still inside. Then he collected the saber, strapped it to his back, and picked up the MZ-507.

The helicopter was almost on top of him.

Woodroffe turned to a Sergeant First Class at his side. "It looks like there's been a fatality, and Drake's loaded. Take a few shots and drive him back."

"Yes, sir."

The young SFC aimed his rifle out of the helicopter and fired repeatedly at the ground.

Geysers of earth and dust sprang up in front of Drake as the bullets struck just ahead of him. He scrambled backward, unable to get his bearings. With one hand on the rifle, he scurried toward the shack. He could feel the shock of the bullets striking the ground at his heels. His adrenaline surging, he couldn't gain the leverage necessary to counter attack.

Finally, he got to his feet and reached the shack. He braced himself behind the far side and caught his breath.

The sound of the helicopter seemed to indicate it was landing. Drake eased himself around the side of the shack and saw the helicopter wasn't on the ground of the inlet. He suspected they'd landed on the plain just above the verge, but couldn't figure out how he was going to get out of there. If he made a run for the Chevy, they would simply track him from the air. Somehow, he had to disappear on foot.

Ahead were the trees. They would provide him with temporary cover, but they were at least a hundred yards away.

Gingerly, he made his way forward and around to the other side of the shack. He came to the shallow verge and braced himself against it, shielded by the Porsche and the Chevy.

His heart raced. For the first time since his escape from Mojave, he wasn't in control. The US Army—his own former division—was upon him. His sense of invincibility was now compromised. They could open fire on him and strike the armored vest piece. However, it would only take a shot to his head, or even a leg, to take him down. He could return their fire, but at that moment, he couldn't even see them.

He cleared the Porsche and kept his eyes fixed on the trees. With no sign of anyone, he ran.

As he sprinted forward, the trees grew closer with each fleeting instant. He was so close.

He came within ten feet of the trees, and five soldiers emerged from them, halting him in his tracks. They trained their firearms on him and he stepped back.

"It's over, Drake," a familiar voice came from behind him.

Drake turned to see Woodroffe and two more soldiers.

"Drop the rifle, Drake!"

The two groups of soldiers closed in on him. *I can't let them take me.* He turned back to the first five and raised the MZ-507.

"Drake, no!" Woodroffe said.

At that moment, the Black Hawk ascended from over the verge and hovered over them. Drake looked up, trying the gauge their plan.

"Now!" Woodroffe bellowed to the helicopter.

The Black Hawk came in lower and the rotor blades created a dust storm. Drake couldn't see anything on the ground, but he could barely make out something falling from the helicopter. By the time he realized what it was, it was too late. A thick rope net fell upon him, casting him to the ground.

The soldiers rushed in and hurled themselves upon him.

"Secure him, gentlemen," Woodroffe said, keeping his gaze on the pile of men. He took out his cell phone, made a call, and pressed his thumb to his free ear to block the thunderous sound of the Black Hawk. "General? This is Woodroffe. The mission was a success, sir. We have Drake."

"Good work, Colonel. Bring him in. I'll have the FBI collect him. We'll hold him at the base until they arrive."

"Yes, sir." Woodroffe ended the call, silently praying this would bring an end to the nightmare of Brandon Drake.

Thirty-Eight

This Time

General Thaddeus Grant sat in his office pondering his strategy. Drake was being flown back to Bragg to be held until the authorities came to collect him. Woodroffe informed him that Drake had killed the individual Wilmot had sent to intercept him. Sending just one man was ridiculous. Wilmot either wasn't taking the situation seriously, or he wasn't aware of what he was dealing with. It was more likely he was dirty and didn't want anyone in the intelligence community to know of his underhanded scheming. That would suggest the CIA and Congress were unaware of his involvement in Drake's 'resurrection'.

After much consideration, Grant made his decision. He had to go over Wilmot's head. He picked up his desk phone and dialed out. After two rings it was answered. "This is General Grant at Fort Bragg. I'd like to speak to Director Jack Brenham." He waited for a few moments while the call was transferred.

The response came through within moments. "Brenham here. How are you, General?"

"Not good, Director. I don't know how much you know, but Brandon Drake is still alive, and he's being flown back to Bragg as we speak. Now, what's going on?"

"I need you to listen to me, General. We are currently investigating the greatest threat to national security this country has ever known. Everything is on the line, which is why I need you to keep this under wraps."

"Does this have something to do with that weasel Wilmot?"

There was a brief pause on the line, and then Brenham said, "Yes, General, as a matter of fact it does. What do you know about him? Has he been in contact with you?"

"No, I called him when we learned of Drake's whereabouts. It seems Wilmot's idea of dealing with him was less than adequate."

"All right, General. We're working with the FBI on the case. I'll arrange to have them pick Drake up and bring him back to D.C. He is absolutely vital to the investigation."

Grant's anger came to the fore in a heartbeat. "You knew about this, and you let that goddamn maniac run loose throughout the country?"

"No, General, I didn't. This all came to light a couple of days ago. We have enough information now to put a stop to it."

"Good. Because this is the purview of the FBI, not the military, as you well know. The Eighty-Second shouldn't have been involved. I did what I had to before any more innocents died. By the way, you should know Drake's girlfriend and sister are also near to the base."

"What?"

"It seems Belinda Reese has a personal friendship with one of our Sergeant Majors. Drake was pursuing them and they sought sanctuary with him. I want them, *and* Drake, away from Fort Bragg as soon as possible. Are we clear?"

"Everything is in hand, General. I'll have an FBI unit dispatched to you immediately."

"I may be guilty of authorizing an unlawful operation with this, but it seems to me that both of our asses are on the line. I'll trust you to keep the Eighty-Second out of it. If there's any delay, I will personally go over your head, regardless of the consequences."

"Understood."

Grant hung up the phone, dialed out again, and waited for an answer. "Spicer? This is General Grant."

"Yes, sir . . . I'll let them know. Thank you, sir." David Spicer hurried out of his kitchen and into his living room.

Belinda, Emily, and Rachel turned to him, eagerly.

"What happened?" Belinda said.

"That was General Grant," David replied. "Drake's been captured and they're bringing him here to await collection by the FBI. They'll be back any time now."

Belinda stood, her expression riddled with concern. "Is he all right?"

"As far as I know. The general didn't go into details."

"Is it really over?"

David walked over and embraced her. "He can't hurt you anymore, Belinda. If you'd like, I'll take you to where you can see him being taken to the brig. That way you'll know he's contained."

She looked away as Emily came up behind her and held her.

Thirty minutes later, Belinda, Emily, David, and Rachel stood at a two hundred yard distance watching Brandon being guided, shackled, out of the Black Hawk. Eight soldiers, led by the colonel, almost obscured him from view. However, it was clear he was incapacitated and totally outnumbered. They led him onto the landing pad and across the grounds toward the location of the brig.

Belinda's eyes filled with tears. As dangerous as he was, she still loved him. Her feelings wouldn't leave her heart, regardless of what he'd become. She couldn't cope with the thought of harm coming to him. A part of her still believed he was the man who had held her in his arms two years earlier in the cabin. None of what was happening seemed real. It had to be a nightmare.

"Now you've seen it," David said. "He can't hurt you or Emily any longer. He's not your problem anymore. The FBI will pick him up, and then he'll be their problem."

"They'll kill him, won't they?" Belinda said. "He'll be executed."

"He'll get a fair trial. You have to understand, he's killed many people. He's extremely dangerous, Belinda. You have to get it out of your head that he's the man you once knew. The Scorpion is evil. There is no similarity between the man you just saw and the one you once loved. That guy's gone, and he's not coming back."

She shook her head in denial. "Don't be so sure of that. I saw the pain in his eyes back in Boston. Brandon is still in there, struggling to get out. I just know it."

"I'll get you and Emily back to your car," David said. "The authorities will contact you during the investigation. As of now, you can go home and get back to living your lives."

Belinda looked at him and managed a smile. "Thank you, David. For everything."

He placed his hand on her shoulder. Emily and Rachel followed them and they made their way back to David's apartment.

***

Jack Brenham walked hurriedly through the corridors of the J. Edgar Hoover Building until he came to the door of FBI director, Jim Connor. Without knocking, he opened the door and stepped inside.

A distinguished, middle-aged man attired in a blue suit and contrasting red tie, stood up abruptly from behind his desk. "Jack?"

"Jim, we need to talk," Brenham said urgently.

"Take a seat. What's happened?"

"Brandon Drake has been captured."

"When?"

"Just a few hours ago. He's being held at Fort Bragg. I need you to arrange for a unit to be dispatched there and bring him to Langley."

"Langley? That's not really procedure, Jack."

"Dammit, I know that! This is the most serious national security problem we've probably ever had. How's the interrogation going with our other detainee?"

"Nothing yet, I'm afraid," Connor said. "You certainly know how to train them to resist, don't you?"

Brenham stood again, despair consuming him. "You've got to help us, Jim. Let us take care of the interrogation. It'll be off the record. The CIA is the most effective intelligence organization in the free world, and it's been infected by traitors. These aren't just regular scumbags.

We have a national crisis on our hands that we can't reveal to anyone."

Connor looked downward in contemplation. Finally, he agreed. "All right, Jack. Off the record, I'll have Drake picked up and both detainees sent over to you." He stood and offered his hand to Brenham. "I'm with you on this."

"Thank you, Jim. The one you're holding right now has all the answers. We can't afford to waste any more time."

"I'll arrange for the transfer immediately."

Brenham entered his office in Langley feeling slightly easier. The net was closing in on Wilmot and his faction with each passing moment. They could be taken down within a mere forty-eight hours.

He was startled by his office phone and answered it. "Brenham."

"Director, this is Jed Crane."

"Jed? You couldn't have called at a better time."

"Why? What's going on?"

Brenham took a deep breath. "Drake has been captured, and they're bringing him back to Langley. We're also on top of the other three individuals you mentioned. We have one under interrogation, and the other two under constant observation. We're so close, Jed."

"Drake's been captured?"

"Yes, they're holding him at Fort Bragg. The FBI are on their way to pick him up."

"Oh, my God. I can't believe it."

"Believe it, Jed. It's safe for you to come in now. Besides, I have a job for you."

"A job?"

"I'll explain it to you when you get here. I also need your testimony about what happened in Rio. Don't worry about anything. I'll meet you personally at the security entrance."

"All right, sir. You've convinced me. I'm about an hour away."

"It'll be good to see you again, Jed. Bye."

Brenham placed the phone on the receiver and glanced out his window. An FBI prisoner transport was pulling up at the main gate. *This time it ends, Treadwell. This time.*

Thirty-Nine

The Prisoner

SDT Agent Pete Kerwin came toward the front entrance of CIA headquarters. Slowing his pace, he tilted his head inquisitively at the sight of an FBI prisoner transport heading toward the side of the building.

Curiosity prompted him to head outside. Making a left turn, his pace quickened until he came to the end of the building. He spotted the prisoner transport turning toward the rear of the complex and frowned. Why would the FBI bring a prisoner to CIA headquarters? And why were they taking such an unorthodox route? None of what he was seeing seemed to fit with official procedure. *Who the hell is it?*

He briskly walked back into the building, pondering which entrance the van would've delivered the prisoner to. He instinctively knew something was wrong. Paranoia came over him as he took the elevator to the lower floors.

He stepped out into the lower ground corridor. After walking toward the rear, he turned left, immediately stopping in his tracks. In the distance he could see a squad of FBI agents and Agent Cullen leading *someone* toward one the interview rooms. But who was it? The prisoner was obscured by the other personnel. And why had Brenham placed an underling like Cullen in charge?

Kerwin turned back, determined not to be seen.

He took the elevator to the upper floors and headed toward the offices of SDT, swiftly arriving at the door of

Wilmot's secretary, Deborah Beaumont. He knocked the door and waited for a moment.

Deborah opened the door with a typically stern expression. "Agent Kerwin. What can I do for you?"

Kerwin knew she didn't like him, but he had to know if Wilmot was alone. "Is he in?"

"Yes."

"Is he in a meeting? I'd hate to interrupt anything."

"No."

"Thank you." He moved on to the next door ten yards away and knocked.

"Come in."

Kerwin anxiously stepped inside.

"What's going on?" Wilmot said.

"I don't know. The FBI just delivered someone to the back entrance. Everything about it looked suspicious."

"Do you have any idea who it was?"

"No. I tried, but the detainee was completely surrounded. Cullen was the one leading the entourage."

Wilmot looked at him bemused. "Wentworth Cullen?"

"Yeah."

Wilmot gestured to his desk chair. "Take a seat. Something *is* going on. I can feel it."

"Any word from Slamer?"

"No, and I haven't been able to reach him. I'm worried. All I was trying to do was make Operation: Nemesis official. Nobody would've known it was Treadwell's brain child. But if they find out we were involved back then, every one of us will be finished."

"Do you think they're onto us?"

"It's looking increasingly like they are. Garrett's coming back tomorrow."

"How's her face?"

"Much better, apparently. It was a mild fracture. She told me the swelling had gone down considerably. She's lucky. A blow from Drake could've taken her head off."

Kerwin leaned forward. "What do you suggest we do if Brenham is on to us?"

"Nemesis has one-hundred-fifty-seven operatives still active within Langley. Their covers are protected, and most of them don't even know the other is a part of it."

"Do you know who they are?"

"I'm the only one who does. I helped Treadwell recruit them all, including you and Rhodes. If this goes down, we're going to need them. It's all of our asses on the line."

Kerwin shivered. "You're thinking of activating *Firestorm*?"

"Only as a last resort. Believe me, I don't want it to come to that." Wilmot's gaze burned into Kerwin's. "Do a little investigative work. Find out who they're holding down there. It might have nothing to do with us."

"I'll do whatever I can."

"Keep it low key. We don't want any of them to be alerted to you."

"You got it." Kerwin stood and exited the office.

***

Jed Crane hid beneath a baseball cap and sunglasses and strolled along the sidewalk approach to CIA headquarters. Wearing a worn-out jacket, jeans, t-shirt and sneakers, he felt a little uneasy about his imminent reunion with the director. His current financial status didn't allow for extravagant attire.

The glass-and-mortar half dome of the New Headquarters Building's main entrance came into view. It was a place of hope to him—of national security and the protection of democracy. But it had been infected by persons who threatened everything for which it stood.

He came closer and noticed the neatly-groomed gardens on either side of the entrance path. It seemed like a lifetime ago since he last saw it. It was such a simple, commonly-seen side of nature. Yet, it filled Jed with a feeling of warmth. The contrast it presented to the hell from which he'd returned was considerable. *Could this be the day I get my life back?*

A black BMW slowed down beside him. Jed kept his eyes forward, and then glanced to the left underneath his sunglasses. It was Brenham at the wheel. With a sigh of relief, he edged toward the car.

Brenham lowered the passenger's side window. "Get in."

Jed opened the door and climbed in.

"This has been an unusual experience for me," Brenham said. "I've been circling around here for the past half hour looking out for you. I didn't know if you'd be driving or not."

"I took the bus. I'm extremely low on funds."

"Not for much longer. I'll see to it that you get three months back pay, up front."

"Thank you, sir. That's very generous of you." Jed's thoughts went out to Juanita. There was no way he could've survived without her. He made a decision to arrange for a percentage of his pay to be sent to her. It would help her to at least get out of that pitiful apartment.

"That's just the beginning," Brenham said. "I have to say though, that get-up you're wearing sure brings back memories of when I was your age." He glanced over at Jed and winked in an obvious move to make him feel at ease.

Jed chuckled. "Unfortunately, we beggars can't be choosers. Do you have any word on Drake's status?"

"The FBI is flying him back as we speak. He should be in our hands later this afternoon."

They continued past the parking lot and headed around the side of the building.

"I'm getting us in through the back," Brenham said. "The fewer people who see you, the better. It's been a nightmare, Jed. I can't trust anyone. Every time I walk past one of our personnel, I wonder if they're one of them."

"Believe me, I understand, sir."

They arrived at an entrance at the rear of the complex. Brenham and Jed exited the car and stepped through a doorway. Two security guards came forward.

Brenham raised his hand. "It's all right."

"Yes, sir."

Jed kept his head low. "Where are we going?"

"To one of the interview rooms on the lower level."

Jed followed the director toward an elevator. The area was deserted, indicating the location was not in active use. It was an ideal set-up for a secret interrogation, but the chilling nature of the situation struck Jed again. They were involved in an investigation to protect the intelligence community—from the intelligence community.

They exited the elevator and walked along a seemingly-endless corridor, eventually arriving at an observation room door. Brenham took out a key card and opened the door.

Jed followed him into a bare room with a two-way mirror. Jed came closer to it and looked down. A young agent was interviewing a prisoner approximately ten feet below them.

"That young man down there is Agent Wentworth Cullen," Brenham said. "I'm very proud of him. I want you to help him in an advisory capacity. He needs your guidance."

"Yes, sir. I'll do whatever I can. Is this the job you were telling me about on the phone?"

"No."

Jed turned to Brenham, confused. "So, what is?"

"If all of this pans out, Wilmot will be in DC Central Detention Facility by tomorrow. I've pondered closing down SDT for some time. It was Treadwell's idea, and it's always left a bitter taste in my mouth."

"But?"

"But . . . it's unique. It gives its personnel the ability to perform investigations in a conventional manner. It allows us to perform tasks that, formerly, we had to call upon the FBI for. The only disadvantage is that once an agent has been assigned to SDT, their cover is blown and they can never return to the CIA, as you know."

"It was a career risk from the start. But I always knew I'd be able to find work in law enforcement if SDT came to an end, sir."

Brenham waved his hand dismissively. "Don't worry about that, Jed. Now you're back, I see the future of SDT."

"The future of SDT? Surely you're not thinking of keeping it. It's been responsible for this whole mess."

"Yes it has, but I had to make a choice. I could petition for it to be closed down, or I could turn it into a force for good. It'd be like spitting on Treadwell's grave."

"OK. So what is it you want me to do?"

Brenham stepped forward with his hand outstretched and a proud glint in his eyes. "SDT may operate independently, but it's still under my jurisdiction. I want to propose *you* as the new director of SDT."

Speechless, Jed placed his shaking hand in Brenham's. "Yes, sir. I accept."

"Good. After everything you've been through to bring these bastards down, I trust you more than I've ever trusted anyone."

They were interrupted by the entrance of Wentworth Cullen. Jed suddenly felt vulnerable and it clearly showed in his body language.

"It's all right, Jed. I told him we'd be in here." Brenham turned to Cullen. "Any luck?"

"Nothing, sir. Even the polygraph showed innocence. I suggest we go to enhanced interrogation."

Jed moved toward the young agent assertively. "No. You're wasting time. That monster is as tough as Teflon and knows every polygraph trick in the book. If you try torture, you'll be at it 'till Thanksgiving."

"So, what do you suggest?"

"Sodium pentothal. No messing around."

"He's right," Brenham said. "We need answers and we need 'em yesterday."

"Get what you need ready," Jed said. "Then I have to talk to you, Agent Cullen. There are a number of other questions we need answers to in addition to the ones you already have."

"I'll get right on it." With that, Cullen left the room.

One hour later, after a thorough debriefing by Jed, Cullen stepped into the interrogation room with a small, silver case. He placed it on the desk before the prisoner and opened it to reveal a clear vial of liquid and a hypodermic syringe. "I tried to be reasonable with you. I gave you every chance to cooperate. We know you're a part of this conspiracy, and we know you have all the answers we need. Now we have to resort to this."

Cynthia Garrett's left jaw retained a yellow bruise from her encounter with Drake. She'd been arrested wearing no makeup, and the turn of events had begun to take their toll on her. Her complexion was pallid, her features were drawn, and her hair was unkempt as she sat shackled to the interview room chair.

Nevertheless, resistance was still apparent in her eyes. She looked up at Cullen with pure hatred.

Forty

Inside the Gate

Garrett's eyes rolled under the effects of sodium pentothal, her venomous, resistant demeanor having disappeared five minutes previously.

Cullen looked at his watch and decided she was in the zone for optimum resistance impairment. His brow dampened with the vital importance of his mission. There was no time for introductory dialogue. He knew he had to get straight to the point. "Agent Garrett, you are a senior member of a conspiracy. An unofficial cell within intelligence, correct?"

With the whites of her eyes showing, she nodded.

"That's a positive response." He ticked a box on an A4 pad. "Agent Garrett, what is the name of this faction?"

Her head rolled deliriously and then dropped to her chest. "O-Oper-ation: N-Nem–e–sis."

"Operation: Nemesis?" He wrote the words down. "And who is the leader of Operation: Nemesis, Agent Garrett?"

"An-drew W-Wilmot."

Cullen smiled and braced himself for the vital question. "How many members are there in your organization?"

Her head rolled again as the words came out. "One hun-dred-fifty-sev-en."

"And do you know who these one-hundred-fifty-seven are?"

She slowly shook her head.

"Does Agent Wilmot know?"

"Y-yes."

"Does a list of these operatives exist?"

Garrett groaned, but it was enough to indicate an affirmative response.

"And where can this list be found?"

"An-drews's ap-artment."

Cullen leaned forward eagerly. "Where in Director Wilmot's apartment can this list be found?"

"F-flash drive . . . behind safe . . . behind painting . . . bedroom . . . in the wall."

"How do you know this?"

"Andy and I . . . are lovers."

In the observation room, Jed shot Brenham a satisfied smile. "There you have it, sir. We have to move."

Brenham took out his cell phone and made a call. "Jim? Jack Brenham. We have it. Fourteen-eighty-seven, Westmont. There's a flash drive in a compartment in the wall behind a safe in the bedroom. The safe is behind a painting of some kind. The list of conspirators is on the flash drive."

"I'll get a squad out there right away, Jack," Jim Connor said. "Just hang in there."

Brenham exhaled. "Thank you, Jim. There's no time to waste. You have to get that flash drive here so we can get it decoded before that son of a bitch leaves. One way or another, this all goes down today. We're gonna need a heavy FBI presence ready to take them in."

"You got it."

Brenham smiled, ended the call, and turned back to the two-way mirror with Jed.

Cullen continued with Garrett's interrogation. "Do you know who killed Director Elias Wolfe?"

Garrett's head rolled again, as though she was trying to resist a most damning question.

Cullen forced the issue. "Who killed Elias Wolfe?"

"I did."

"Did you forge Director Wolfe's suicide note?"

"Yes."

Cullen glanced at the notes he'd taken from Agent Crane. "On April fourth, Agent Jedediah, also known as 'Jed' Crane, woke up in a motel in Stanton, Utah, to find an incendiary under his motel bed. Do you know who planted that incendiary?"

"I did."

Cullen looked up at the two-way mirror with a smile.

Garrett surfed the line between consciousness and delirium, revealing everything through slurred speech.

Cullen learned the origins of Operation: Nemesis and that it was a name known only to those involved. The CIA would find no file or document containing those two words. He prized out of her Wilmot's intention of transforming Treadwell's former home-grown terrorist cell into an official, elite task force, which would've included Brandon Drake. She revealed how Wilmot had faked Drake's death and restored his original persona using Dr. DeSouza at the Mojave Desert facility. Drake's escape, the slaughter of the guards, DeSouza's death, the deployment of Kane Slamer, and the true nature of her own injuries, poured from her soporific throat.

"Why did Director Wilmot want to do all this?" Cullen said.

"Pow-er."

Brenham shook Jed's hand and gripped his free arm in a gesture of jubilation. "We got, 'em, Jed. Goddamn it, we got 'em."

"Yes, sir, we did."

Brenham's gleeful expression faded as he turned to the back wall and hammered his first against it. "Goddammit! First Treadwell created this rogue faction to attack US facilities for the sake of creating an illusory threat. Now, Wilmot is trying to bring it into the mainstream intelligence community, like trying to hide it in plain sight."

"But we're onto him, sir. He isn't going to succeed."

"I know. That's not what's bugging me."

"I don't understand."

Brenham turned back to him with shame in his eyes. "He . . . probably would've succeeded. In my ignorance of its true origins and nature, it's likely I would have proposed it to Congress. I'd have been unaware that I'd sanctioned an operation that had arisen from one of our greatest threats."

"But isn't that what you're doing with SDT?"

"What?"

"You said Treadwell instigated SDT, and now you want to spit on his grave by making it work for *us*."

"This isn't the same, Jed. Wilmot would've been running this goddamn Operation: Nemesis under my watch. All the time, it would've been nothing more than a ruse for him to rise through the ranks of power. I could have inadvertently enabled the most dangerous threat to democracy this country has ever known. We're supposed to be committed to protecting American soil from all threats, both foreign and domestic. The most dangerous enemy is the one inside the gate."

"But you're not enabling it, sir. You're doing everything you can to put an end to this. Let's just stop them. OK?"

The door opened again and Cullen stepped in. "I got as much out of her as I could."

"You did great, Cullen," Brenham said. "We've got everything we need."

Jed shook his head. "Not quite."

"What?"

"We need to know if Wilmot has a contingency plan for when we take them in."

Cullen cringed. "I'm sorry. She passed out. I can't get anything out of her at the moment."

"All right," Brenham said. "When the FBI comes back with that flash drive, we go for Wilmot first and cut off the head before it can alert the tentacles."

"I agree," Jed said.

"For now, I have to get you out of here."

Jed shook his head. "No, I'll stay here and see this through."

"Well, you can't stay in this bare room for hours. You'll go crazy."

"I'll be fine."

Finally, Brenham agreed. "I'll bring some refreshments and a portable television down for you, and then I'll sort out a room with bathroom facilities."

"Thank you, sir."

Cullen turned to Brenham. "What would you like me to do now, sir?"

"Check the surveillance tapes on Kerwin and Rhodes and see if anything's been said in the last two hours. We've got to keep on top of those two."

"Yes, sir."

Cullen and Brenham stepped out of the room and closed the door.

Jed moved across to the two-way mirror and stared at the unconscious form of Cynthia Garrett slumped across the interview room desk. Bitterness rose in his chest at the thought of what she and her cohorts had done to him. They'd tried to kill him twice, forced him into hiding, and his fiancée had no idea what had become of him. They had to be brought to justice, and he was determined to see it happen.

In a locked, isolated monitoring suite, Cullen sat at a computer terminal, wearing headphones. He gazed at an audio bar on the screen before him and moved the slider forward from where he'd set the marker earlier.

For the first ninety minutes, the sound bar was static, with only sporadic blips indicating mere ambient noise. From that, he was able to ascertain Agent Rhodes' office was unoccupied.

At ninety-two minutes, there was a notable spike followed by continuous activity. *Door closing, two men, and a conversation.* Cullen moved the slider back to the beginning of the activity and clicked 'play'. The echoed sound of Rhodes' office door closing came through the headphones, and then the voice of Agent Pete Kerwin. Cullen smiled at the convenience. He'd got both of them in the same room. Sitting back, he listened to the discussion with keen interest:

"I'm telling you, Karl, something's going on," Kerwin said. "Wilmot thinks it might be nothing to do with us, but he wants me to keep an eye on what's going on down on the sub-level."

"Kerwin, you're being paranoid."

"No. What I saw wasn't normal. The FBI doesn't deliver people here. It was like they wanted nobody to know what was going on."

"Except for Cullen, right?"

"Yes. Why the hell would Brenham put someone like Boy Scout in charge of something so top secret?"

Cullen froze. *They're on to us.* With desperate concern, he listened to the conversation as it continued. After several minutes, Kerwin dropped his bombshell:

"I've got to get back down there and see what I can find out."

"All right, you do what you have to do," Rhodes said. "But in my opinion you're worrying over nothing."

"Let's hope you're right."

Moments later, there was the sound of the door closing.

Cullen checked the time of the sound bar spike as the door closed: 12:58. He checked his wristwatch: 13:12. *Oh, shit.*

With frantic speed, he shut down the monitoring equipment, bolted out the door, and ran in the direction of the elevator.

***

Kerwin gingerly approached the interrogation room he'd seen the prisoner being escorted toward, and stopped to look around.

He came to the door and tried the handle. Predictably, it was locked, but he knew the layout. There were observation rooms along the corridor to the right.

He continued along until he reached the door he suspected would be the right observation room. Carefully, he approached it and gripped the handle. Turning it slowly, he pushed it open and peered inside. The room appeared to be empty. He stepped toward the two way mirror and suddenly halted. Someone *was* in the room.

Kerwin looked to his left and saw a look of horror in the eyes of a man in a baseball cap. Only then did he realize who it was. "No. It can't be."

He turned to run, but suddenly felt his throat being constricted by Jed Crane's forearm.

"You son of a bitch!" Crane pulled Kerwin back inside and kicked the door shut.

Jed gasped for breath as Kerwin jabbed an elbow into his solar plexus. The pain was crippling, forcing him to crawl to the back of the room. He looked up to see Kerwin's six-foot-four, shaven-headed form coming closer. Within seconds, he felt himself being lifted up by the lapels under the force of two sixteen-inch biceps. In desperation, he ignored the debilitating pain in his stomach and wrapped his hands around Kerwin's throat. Kerwin pressed his right palm into Jed's face, causing Crane to lose his balance.

The door burst open, and Jed felt the pressure leaving him. He looked up. Cullen was wrestling his opponent away from him, but knew the young agent was no match for a behemoth like Kerwin.

Shaken, Jed hurled himself at Kerwin and drove his fist into his jaw with every ounce of energy remaining in him. However, his adversary remained conscious.

Cullen grasped Kerwin's left arm and held it in a lock.

"Hold him, Cullen. We've got to restrain him," Jed said.

"I'm tryin'."

Jed realized there was no way Cullen could hold Kerwin indefinitely and took over with the arm lock. "Get out of here and lock us in. Get the director!"

Cullen nodded and ran out the door. The click of the lock ensured Kerwin was trapped.

Jed momentarily released the rogue agent and pulled him up by the lapels. "Goddamn traitor." With a carefully planted punch to Kerwin's chin, he finally succeeded in knocking him out.

Exhausted, he sat back against the wall gazing at the limp figure of his former colleague. *Hurry, Cullen. Please, hurry.*

Forty-One

Firestorm

Brenham waited while Cullen unlocked the observation room door.

Crane looked up, startled, and then relaxed. He gestured to Kerwin on the floor. "Not a minute too soon. He's starting to stir."

Brenham glanced at Cullen. "Cuff that son of a bitch. We're gonna have to work together and get him secured in one of the interrogation rooms for now."

Jed assisted Cullen by holding Kerwin's hands behind his back. Once Kerwin was incapacitated, Brenham stepped over and helped them to pull him off the floor.

"Cullen." Brenham gestured to the door.

Cullen ran out of the room and returned a few seconds later. "It's all clear. Let's go."

The three men held a tight grip on their senseless captive and ushered him out of the room.

Cullen slid a card key into another interrogation room's key reader. Crane and Brenham wasted no time dragging Kerwin into the room. With an unceremonious shove to Kerwin's back, Jed pushed him onto the desk.

Urgently, Cullen closed the door and locked it. The three men stood for a moment to catch their breath.

"If that clown was sniffing around down here, chances are Wilmot suspects we're onto him," Brenham said.

Jed nodded. "I agree."

The director's cell phone rang, and he answered it. "Brenham . . . Yes . . . Yes, of course. I'll be right there." He ended the call and turned back to Jed and Cullen. "Crane, you've got to get back to that observation room for now."

"Yes, sir."

"Cullen, go get coffees for the two of you. You're gonna need 'em."

"What's going on?"

"You've got the toughest interrogation of your career to conduct. The FBI just arrived at the front gate with Brandon Drake."

Brenham entered his office with Jim Connor by his side.

Connor took a flash drive out of his pocket and handed it to him. "This is it. It was exactly where she said it was."

Brenham stared at the flash drive with hope tempered by bitter disappointment. The end of Treadwell's faction was now in the palm of his hand—along with the names of men and women he'd trusted. While it represented the end of a terrible evil, it came at the cost of trusting his own judgment.

"I know, Jack," Connor said, as though reading Brenham's thoughts. "But the flash drive is encrypted. You have access to tech that'll crack it far quicker than we could."

"I'll get it to Carrie Wilson immediately."

"Do you trust her?"

"I don't know. I won't know anything until this thing is opened, and we're running out of time. There's no time to polygraph her."

"I'll have a unit on hand in case of an incident."

"Did you manage to get any information out of Drake?"

Connor shook his head. "Just a mouthful of attitude. The army gave us all the artillery he took from Mach Industries. We passed it on to Agent Cullen. The Chevy he'd been driving around in was registered to a young man named Luke Smith, a computer repair technician from Flagstaff, Arizona. He'd been listed as missing for three weeks. The kid was only twenty-six years old. The Flagstaff Highway Patrol have alerted Mr. Smith's family"

"Oh, dear God." Brenham closed his eyes with the devastating thought of the grief Luke's family would have to endure. Surely there could be no news more heinous for a mother and father. "Thank you, Jim. For everything."

The two directors exited the office and headed for the lower floors.

Five FBI task force officers accompanied Brenham and Connor into one of the CIA's numerous operations labs. A young woman with blonde hair, sparsely adorned with black streaks, faced them with an understandably concerned expression.

Brenham handed her the flash drive. "Carrie, this has been encrypted. We need you to find out what's on it."

"I'll do my best," Carrie Wilson said, and inserted the flash drive into a laptop USB port. After accessing the drive, she smiled confidently and began a hacking procedure.

Before many minutes, she came to the first stumbling block. "I can already see it's riddled with firewalls, and that's just for the first encryption."

Brenham leaned forward. "First?"

"That's right. Once I've cracked it, a second encryption will appear. Whoever secured this sure as hell didn't want anybody finding out what's on it."

"Do you think you can crack it?"

"A month ago, it would've taken considerable time, but since we had the *Zenith Decrypt Fourteen* installed, it'll be a lot faster. A single decryption will take me around five minutes. A double will be ten."

"Thank you, Carrie." Brenham turned to Connor. "In ten minutes, we'll have the answers we've been waiting for." He looked over Carrie's shoulder as page after page of computer codes scrolled along the screen.

***

Wentworth Cullen sat opposite Drake in an interrogation room. A squad of armed FBI agents waited outside the door.

Secured to the chair with steel wrist and ankle chains, Drake's chilling, granite-like glare was unremitting. His attaché case of stolen artillery sat alongside the MZ-507 rifle, the samurai sword, and a backpack filled with cash on the desk.

"Had yourself quite a field day, didn't you?" Cullen gestured to the equipment, his cavalier approach barely concealed his unease. "I mean just look at this stuff. It's incredible. Since you won't tell us the location of the electron key that unlocks that armor you've attached to yourself, we have a team over at Mach Industries picking one up as we speak. You'll be flesh and blood like the rest of us soon enough."

Drake's hateful gaze beamed through his eyes, and then he lowered his head. It was clear he had no intention of cooperating.

"What did you hope to accomplish with all this?"

Drake raised his head again. "War!"

"War? War against whom?"

"You bastards who took my identity from me, my freedom, and gave me nothing but lies."

"That's what I want to talk to you about. I had nothing to do with any of that. I'm under orders to gain as much information as possible about the traitors who did this to you."

Drake chuckled. "Do you really think I'm dumb enough to buy that?"

"You're facing charges ranging from breaking out of Leavenworth to mass murder, Drake. Right now, I'm all that stands between you and a goddamn lethal injection."

Drake's expression darkened again. "That's not gonna happen."

"Oh? What makes you so sure?"

"Nobody takes me down but *me*."

Cullen swallowed hard. Drake had just made a statement implying he was prepared to take himself out before letting anyone else do it. If that was his mentality, he was virtually invulnerable to questioning. "Look, it doesn't have to be this way. My department can pull all kinds of strings. We've been infiltrated by a rogue faction that we have to take down. Your testimony could help us considerably. This is a golden opportunity for you, soldier, so don't throw it away."

Drake sat back and looked at Cullen as though studying him in an attempt to assess his truthfulness. Finally, he spoke. "Wilmot."

Cullen leaned forward eagerly. "Tell me what you know, and I mean everything, Drake. I want it all. From the beginning."

"Then if I were you, I'd get ready for one hell of a long story."

Cullen took out a Dictaphone and pressed record. "Go for it."

***

Brenham and Connor stared over Carrie Wilson's shoulder while she entered a final bypass code. A window opened displaying a three page list of names and access codes.

"Save that to a flash drive, Carrie, and then delete all the data from the mainframe," Brenham said. "We can't afford for anyone else to find it."

"Yes, sir."

Brenham studied the list on the screen hungrily, his heart racing with despair at the sight of names of people he would have trusted with his life. Fortunately, Carrie's name wasn't among them. The list showed *Nemesis* was spread throughout both the CIA and SDT. "Oh, my God," he said. "This is every bit as painful as I thought it would be."

There were no unfamiliar names, which suggested the FBI and NSA were clear of *Nemesis*.

"I recognize some of the people on this file, sir," Carrie said. "May I ask—?"

"Carrie!" Brenham cut her off.

She transferred the file to another flash drive, and then immediately deleted the original from the mainframe.

Brenham continued with a calmer tone. "Carrie, I want you to keep quiet and follow me. It's for your own safety."

"Safety?"

"Just do it."

"Yes, sir."

Brenham turned back to Connor. "Get your men ready. All of these clowns have to be taken in, but first we take Wilmot."

Connor followed Brenham out of the lab with Carrie in tow.

Thirty minutes later, three FBI agents accompanied Brenham and Connor along the corridor to Wilmot's office.

Deborah Beaumont stood in apparent alarm as they came past her open door.

"It's all right, Deborah," Brenham said, secure in the knowledge her name hadn't appeared on the list. "I want you to go up to Assistant Director Hayes' office. Carrie Wilson is there with her, and I want you to stay put."

"Yes, sir," she said, clearly puzzled.

They moved farther along until they reached Wilmot's door. Connor gave his agents an instructive nod. He then stepped back while the officers opened the door and stormed into the office.

Startled, Wilmot stood, his face ashen.

Brenham stepped forward. "Take him in."

"On what charge?" Wilmot said.

"Treason."

As the agents moved in, Wilmot drew a cell phone from his pocket and held it up. "I wouldn't do that, if I were you."

"Wait!" Brenham halted the agents in their tracks and noticed Wilmot typing something into the keypad. "We can add smuggling an unauthorized cell phone in here to your list of charges."

"You wouldn't believe what I've managed to have smuggled into this place," Wilmot said. "If you don't back off right now, Brenham, I'm going to destroy you."

"Why, Wilmot? What do you hope to accomplish?"

"I'm trying to make America an invincible force that nobody can make war with."

"With *you* at the helm?"

"Something like that."

Brenham gestured to the agents again. "Take the son of the bitch."

Wilmot pushed another button on the cell phone a split second before the operatives grasped him. The phone fell from his hand.

Brenham picked it up and read the screen—Sent: Firestorm. "What does this mean, Wilmot? What the hell is *Firestorm*?"

The building suddenly shook. The unmistakable sound of gunfire rang through the floor from below, accompanied by a cacophony of screams.

Wilmot grinned vengefully. "That is."

Forty-Two

The Torch

Drake concluded his account of events, and Wentworth Cullen shook his head in astonishment. "It's an extraordinary story, Drake, I'll say that much. In summary, you were a part of *Operation: Nemesis* from the beginning. Recently, you learned that, after you were injured in Afghanistan, Treadwell gave you a new set of memories that led to you becoming this *Interceptor*. Under this identity, you assisted in the rescue of your sister, where Wilmot faked your death. Afterward, he kept you in a CIA facility in Mojave where he restored your true identity. It was in this facility that Agent Garrett tried to seduce and kill you, and from where Wilmot sent you on a mission to kill Agent Crane, with a mercenary named Kane Slamer . . . whom you killed a couple of days ago." He tapped the backpack. "And this is the money you say Director Wilmot paid you to kill Agent Crane?"

"Pretty cool, eh?" Drake said glibly. "Make a terrific TV series, wouldn't it?"

"Don't get smart with me, Drake. Your ass is still on the line. If it wasn't for the fact that all of this fit so perfectly with what we already know, you'd be facing the death penalty. And you still are unless you cooperate. You could get away with the state pen if you stop screwing around."

Drake laughed. "Oh, you're such a fuckin' amateur. Or have you forgotten Leavenworth?"

"According to you, you can't even remember that, so don't be a wise guy. You are not The Interceptor."

Drake lurched forward and Cullen recoiled, despite Drake being held fast by shackles. "You're fucking right I'm not, and I'm gonna destroy him!"

"Killing Belinda Reese won't destroy that part of you."

"Like hell, it won't. She's who he cares about the most, and he's in my head. If I kill her, I take him down."

They were both startled by the sound of gunfire coming from above.

Cullen glanced at the door and then back at Drake. Satisfied the prisoner was secured, he picked up the MZ-507 from the desk and approached the door. Apprehensively, he slipped the key card into the reader and opened it ajar. He peered to the left and then to the right but saw nothing. The FBI agents were gone. Bracing the rifle, he stepped out of the room and closed the door behind him. It locked automatically.

Drake gazed at the attaché case Cullen had left on the desk and smiled at his good fortune. Having no idea what the gunfire was all about, he seized it as his opportunity for escape.

Gripping the armrests to which his wrists were shackled, he shuffled forward, dragging the heavy iron chair with him. With so little leverage, it became an arduous task, despite having to move only a few inches.

His abdomen pressed against the desk giving him the opportunity to reach as much of himself forward as possible. His chin was still out of reach of the open case. Raising himself as far out of the chair as the few chain links would allow, he lurched forward again. The strain caused blood to pound in his head, and he could feel his face becoming flushed.

Holding his breath, he positioned his chin inside the rim of the open case and drew himself back.

With the case finally positioned on the edge of the desk, he looked inside and quickly saw the laser torch. He perched himself up again, and moved the other items away with his nose. The torch tipped onto its side on top of one of the thermal neutron incendiaries.

He lowered his head into the case and gripped the torch between his teeth, careful not to come into contact with the activation switch. Leaning back, he shuffled the chair back a few inches.

He lowered his head again and brought his mouth to his shackled right hand. His fingers grasped the torch enabling him to adjust its position, and aimed it at the floor. He felt around the device for the switch and quickly located it. With one touch, the beam shot out, boring a slender hole in the flooring.

Intensely focused, he used his fingers to twist the torch upward. The laser cut through a section of one of the desk legs.

Slowly, and with desperate precision, he brought the beam up farther, cutting it through the armrest of the chair and up to the lock casing of the shackle.

The beam reached the cuff, but the heat rapidly transferred to the surrounding metal. His wrist burned unbearably, causing him to suck in air through his teeth. Perspiration fell from his brow, but he persisted. There were only a couple of millimeters remaining.

The laser finally severed the lock and the serrated clasp fell from the casing. Drake shook his hand, reeling from the burns on his wrist.

With his left hand free, he repeated the procedure with the right shackle, occasionally stopping momentarily for the metal to cool. He resumed, and after a few moments, the shackle opened.

He looked down and saw the ankle cuffs were connected to chain links welded into the legs of the heavy chair. Regardless, he knew he had to cut them off at the locks. Simply severing the chains would mean he'd have the cuffs attached to his ankles. He braced himself for the burning temperature transference, aimed the laser torch at the left ankle cuff, and touched the switch. The shackle was clasped around his jeans, which presented the additional danger of them catching fire.

Slowly stopping and starting, he succeeded in freeing his left leg before repeating the procedure on the right shackle.

Finally, he stood free and placed the torch on the desk. He then took out four thermo-neutron incendiaries from the attaché case and put them in the side pockets of the hoodie. He took the Samurai sword and hooked the holding strap across his back, followed by the backpack filled with cash.

Picking up the attaché case with his left hand, he grasped the laser torch with his right and headed for the door.

Smiling gloatingly, he pointed the torch in the direction of the door lock and activated it. After he'd cut the beam around the lock, he stepped back and kicked it in. A gaping hole appeared and the door swung wide open.

He looked at the laser torch for a moment and realized what a formidable weapon it would make. Cullen had taken the MZ-507, but what he had in his pockets would exceed any damage the rifle could cause, by far.

***

Operatives in all departments of the CIA had been sitting at their terminals, or flitting from office to office attending to their various assignments. It had been a typical working day.

In the blink of an eye, reality exploded. A strange chorus of beeping, encrypted cell phones preceded approximately every fourth agent producing firearms and opening fire on their colleagues. At computer terminals, *Nemesis* agents stood up from their screens and took pistols secretly fixed under their desks. Rapidly, CIA headquarters became a bloodbath.

Jim Connor urgently took out his cell phone and opened a line. "This is Director Connor at CIA headquarters. We have a code red. Reinforcements required immediately. I repeat—code red!" He looked across at his men. "Get down there, now."

The entourage of FBI agents raced out of Wilmot's office.

Brenham gripped Wilmot by the lapels. "What have you done, you son of a bitch!"

"You forced my hand. I fought back. If I'm going down, I'm taking you with me. The CIA is . . . no longer."

Overcome with rage, Brenham swung at Wilmot, knocking him out with one blow.

"Jack," Connor said, "I have reinforcements on the way."

"I heard. Jim, we have to get to April's office. Deborah and Carrie are in there."

"All right." Connor gestured to Wilmot. "What about him?"

"You're right. We need to contain him."

"Let's drag him out of here. I'll help."

"Thank you, Jack."

***

Drake stepped into a bare, sterile corridor. The sound of gunfire continued to echo through the building. To get out, he knew he'd have to get past some kind of war that was raging.

A man in a suit came to the end of a stairwell ahead of him. The man was obviously an operative running from the carnage, as evidenced by his breathlessness. He ran along the corridor and froze at the sight of Drake. Their eyes locked.

"Who are you?" the man said.

Drake aimed the laser torch toward him. "This just ain't your day, is it?" He activated the beam, aimed at the man's midsection, and moved his hand across, effectively slicing the man in two. The laser seemed to have halved and cauterized him at the same time, leaving little blood.

There was a momentary look of shock and bewilderment in the man's eyes in the instant before he collapsed in two parts.

Drake glanced at the laser torch again and grinned before moving toward the stairwell.

Forty-Three

Battleground: Langley

Brenham and Connor dragged Wilmot into an elevator with his arms gripped across their respective shoulders. Brenham selected the destination floor.

"I think he's coming round," Connor said.

Brenham's glanced at the elevator floor panel. "Just one more floor and we're there."

The doors opened, and the two directors pulled their captive into a corridor.

Wilmot suddenly lurched forward bringing his fists back and hammering the stomachs of his captors. Brenham and Connor fell to the floor, gasping. Connor reached out in a vain attempt to grasp Wilmot, but he was out of reach. He could do no more than watch as their enemy ran back in the direction of the elevator. Brenham winced as he attempted to stand.

"The rest of my boys should be here imminently," Connor said. "With any luck, they'll grab the bastard."

"I hope you're right."

***

Wentworth Cullen braced himself behind a wall, briefly catching a glimpse of what was ahead of him. Smoke filled the complex and was drifting closer. The roar of gunfire continued, but it was impossible for him to ascertain who was an ally and who the enemy was.

318

A familiar operative appeared through the smoke, and he seemed to be running in his direction. Cullen knew him as Robert Catley, a twenty-nine year old analyst. He didn't know him well, but he knew he was committed and conscientious. The terror in Catley's eyes was clear. However, their horrified glare instantly vanished to the accompaniment of a gunshot. He fell onto the floor to reveal his killer behind him. It was Rhodes.

Rage swelled in Cullen's heart. Catley was approximately the same age as him, and he'd just witnessed the scum of the earth gun him down without mercy. Fury overrode his own fear. He looked vengefully at the MZ-507 rifle in his hand. The basic mechanisms seemed to be the same as any standard rifle, although he suspected it had features that exceeded those of an M-16. But it didn't matter. His only concern was the moment. Karl Rhodes had to die for what he'd done.

Cullen emerged from behind the wall. "Rhodes!"

Rhodes looked up and raised his pistol again at the moment Cullen discharged the MZ-507. A strange hum arose from the rifle and a titanium bullet shot through Rhodes' body, causing his torso to explode. A pair of legs and his head and shoulders sank into a crimson lake on the gleaming floor.

Cullen trembled with the shock of what he'd just seen. It was ghastly—and yet so just. He struggled momentarily with the ambivalence of rejoicing in something so terrible.

He jolted back behind the wall and tried to focus on the sadistic, murderous evil he'd just vanquished. But it wasn't working. The horror of what he'd just done wouldn't leave him. He knew he had to put it into perspective. He'd just slain a brutal monster and most likely saved others in the process. *Yes, that's my duty. To protect the innocent and the helpless from all threats, both foreign and domestic. This is what I signed up for. This is why I was born. This is who I am. I am a defender of my country. Pull it together, Wentworth. Pull it together.*

He stepped out into the carnage with the rifle poised. Squinting through the smoke, he tried to make out the good guys. FBI agents fired in the direction of the aggressors. It took Cullen a few seconds to assess who the enemy was. The legitimate agents were fearful and trying to find shelter. The Nemesis agents were firing *at* them. Cullen made the decision to follow the FBI's line of fire. Fueled by adrenaline, he charged forward and opened fire. Nemesis operatives fell to a barrage of FBI bullets and the MZ-507.

Cullen ran across to an FBI agent he believed was leading the retaliation and crouched behind a counter with him.

"What the hell is that?" the agent shouted across the noise.

"It's an experimental rifle."

"Damn handy, if you ask me. We're outnumbered right now, but reinforcements are on the way."

Cullen noticed the agent's Kevlar attire and shuddered. "I have no protection."

"I can see that. Maybe you should get out of here and live to fight another day."

"I can't do that. My colleagues are dying here."

"And you're gonna be no use to them if you die too. Gimme the rifle."

"What?"

"Gimme the rifle. I have Kevlar, you don't. That weapon is more powerful than mine. I have far more of a chance of driving them back with it *and* staying alive. I'll cover you so you can get the hell out. You're right in the thick of it here."

Cullen felt defiant, but ultimately concurred and handed the MZ-507 to the agent. "You're right. Good luck, my friend."

The officer rested a hand on Cullen's shoulder. "I know what you're thinking, but you're wrong. You're not a coward. You've just proved that. Now, get ready."

Cullen stood with him.

"OK, now run!" the agent said.

Cullen turned and sprinted back down the corridor with the unmistakable, electronic hum of the MZ-507 firing behind him. He quickly came to the turn and ran to the right along the next corridor.

Turning another corner, he froze when an agent came across his path with a pistol. He knew him as Bradley Foster, a longstanding data analyst. Was he with Nemesis? Or was he loyal to the CIA? It was an impossibly uncomfortable moment, and he could see in Foster's eyes that he had the same questions.

Then Foster smiled and raised his pistol. Cullen was unarmed. If Foster was on the level he'd have no cause to raise his firearm to him. Desperately, Cullen backed away, and was startled by the sound of a gunshot. He glanced down but there was no sign of a wound on him. He looked up again and saw Foster's eyes had become vacant. The gun slipped from his grasp and blood dripped from his mouth. Finally, he collapsed. Jed Crane stood behind him holding a .45.

"Come on," Crane said. "We have to get out of here."

Cullen picked up Foster's gun and ran to him. "Where did you get that?" he said, pointing to Jed's pistol.

"I managed to roll one of them and cold cock the son of a bitch. Something real weird is going on."

"Yeah, tell me about it."

"No, I mean *really* weird. When I came out the observation room, I found a guy who'd been cut in half. Both halves of him were cauterized."

"What the—"

"We've got to get to the rear exits. It's our only chance."

Cullen ran with Jed, his heart pounding with more than exertion.

***

 Drake came to the top of a stairwell and confidently headed toward the sound of the gunfire.

He saw a man running toward him through the fog of gun smoke. He couldn't make out his face immediately, but just like the last one, he looked harmless. One of many suits.

As the man came closer, Drake finally recognized him and smiled with rancorous opportunism. The man noticed him and stopped in his tracks. It was Wilmot.

"So, Christmas has come early this year," Drake said.

Wilmot staggered back. "No. It can't be."

"Oh, but it is, ass-wipe."

"Drake, look, we can work this out. We can escape together. I can help you."

"Familiar words. I seem to recall you saying something similar when I woke up in Mojave. You were my new best friend. You were gonna take care of everything and see to it that I had everything I needed. You lied to me about what year it was, Wilmot. You set that bitch, Garrett, on me to seduce and kill me, and then you sent Slamer out to kill me. For your information, his neck snapped a lot easier than you'd think." He put the attaché case down, reached over his shoulder, and drew the Samurai sword.

"Don't!"

"This is the weapon that made me who I am. You brought me back, so I think it's kinda ironic that it'll be *this* sword that ends your lousy life, asshole."

"Drake, please."

He gazed gleefully at Wilmot's perspiring brow and shaking hands before raising the sword. "You reap what you sow, Wilmot." With blinding speed, he drew the sword back and cut it across, severing Wilmot's head in the blink of an eye.

Casually, he returned the sword to the sheath, picked up the attaché case, and continued toward the battleground.

He quickly came to the main arena and grinned. The familiar rush of battle came over him, driving him forward.

A young agent, whom Drake presumed was with the side attacking the CIA, saw him and fired. The bullet bounced off the armor beneath his tattered clothing. As Drake continued toward him, the look of terror on the agent's face became apparent.

Drake took a thermo-neutron detonator out of his pocket and activated it. He looked to his left and noticed an alcove. He then threw the incendiary approximately thirty yards into the battle, and ran into the alcove. Crouching down in the far corner, he heard a deafening blast. The gunfire stopped and the carnage was instantly silenced.

He turned to see the area was thick with smoke. As he stood, he was startled by the deafening rumble of concrete and metal collapsing in the distance.

Slowly, he stepped forward and beheld the devastation. There were no signs of life. He had no idea a thermo-neutron incendiary would cause so much damage. It had taken out at least a quarter of the front of the complex.

Snapping out of his mesmerized state, he planned his strategy. At the end of the corridor was the main reception area with the CIA emblem on the floor. If he could get past the smoke and rubble, he could get out. But he had to look inconspicuous. The sword on his back would not serve him well when stepping out into a Langley street in broad daylight.

Reluctantly, he removed the sword from his back and cast it to the ground. He opened the attaché case and rummaged around for the smallest devices he might have been able to use. The laser torch would make a convenient replacement for the sword, and the sonic force emitter may prove useful. Both were pocket-sized items, and he still had three incendiaries in his pockets.

Taking the sonic force emitter and laser torch, he secured the backpack of cash across his shoulder, and headed for the exit. He glanced behind him briefly, somewhat saddened that he had to abandon such fantastic weaponry. However, he couldn't take the chance. They would've slowed him down and exposed him.

His eyes smarted under the effects of the smoke, and his coughing was debilitating en route to the exit. Fires were spreading and he knew he had very little time before the place was consumed. He heard the faint drone of fire engine sirens in the distance.

After several minutes, he reached the exit and hurried out, gasping for air. The long entrance road was ahead of him, but despite his breathlessness, he knew he had to run as fast as he could. In the distance, he heard another chorus of sirens. This time, there were more than just fire engines coming.

A few yards past the flower gardens, he looked to his left and saw a cluster of trees. They would provide him with temporary cover and invisibility. The death and destruction inside the building would create a moment of disarray, distracting the incoming personnel. He hadn't a moment to waste.

Urgently, he ran toward the trees, just as the first wave of fire trucks and police cars appeared. Once inside the cluster, he succumbed to another bout of coughing, but staggered on to the end.

With a struggle, he made it through the trees and sprinted across the remaining grass. At the end, he discovered a road and a sprawling parking lot on the other side. The cars would provide him with further cover.

He looked up and saw two FBI helicopters heading in the direction of CIA headquarters.

Looking around him, he spotted a man in a suit stepping out of a silver Lotus Exige. *A fast car*. The man seemed to be transfixed by the smoke and flames rising from the New Headquarters Building.

"Hey, buddy," Drake said, feigning fear.

The man rushed toward him. "Are you OK? What happened?"

"I'm a politics student. I was trying to talk to someone in there for help with a research assignment. Before I could even ask, there was some kind of a terrorist attack. They're all dead."

"Oh, my God!"

Drake joined the man, and together they moved toward the Lotus. "You know what?" Drake said.

"What?"

"That's a really nice car."

Forty-Four

Aftermath

Two days had passed since Firestorm. Jack Brenham sat with his chair turned from his desk, deep in thought. Coroners were still collecting the remains of the dead, and a constant FBI presence remained in the building.

The press added further concern. It had been a national crisis event, and 'no comment' simply wasn't acceptable. The public had the right to know. But revelations of a major corruption in the intelligence community, mind control operations, and a faked death, would cause a major panic. The president's advisors were frantically trying to formulate an 'official story.'

Brenham was aware he was sinking into depression, which was something he couldn't allow.

He was drawn out of his thoughts by a knock on his door. "Come in," he said, trying to sound stronger than he felt.

He turned to see the saddened faces of Jed Crane and Wentworth Cullen. "It's good to see you boys. Thanks for coming in."

"Is there anything we can do, sir?" Jed said.

"Not right now. I'm just glad you both made it."

"So are we. How many did we lose?"

"So far, the death toll stands at four-hundred-twenty-six. Only two members of *Nemesis* survived. It's ironic. Garrett and Kerwin are still alive, only because they were contained. That'll soon change. They're both facing the death penalty for treason and murder."

"Did Assistant Director Hayes make it?" Jed asked.

"Yes. Deborah and Carrie were with her. They're fine too."

Jed gave a sigh of relief. "Cullen and I got out through the west entrance. It wasn't easy. They were everywhere we turned. What happened after the FBI got here?"

"It was quick. Strategic, efficient, and well-organized. They swept the complex in units and dispatched all of the hostiles. Unfortunately, Drake escaped."

"Escaped? How?" Jed exclaimed.

"The bulk of the damage downstairs was caused by a thermo-neutron incendiary. Drake did it."

Cullen lowered his head. "Oh, my God."

Brenham noticed his horrified tone. "What is it?"

"I was interrogating him about the equipment he stole from Mach Industries. His weapons were in the interrogation room when the attack happened. I took his rifle and locked him in the room. I thought nothing of it. He was chained to the chair."

"It wasn't your fault, Wentworth," Brenham said. "You did what you had to do."

Jed turned back to the director. "What about Wilmot?"

"He's dead. Decapitated. He must've run into Drake. After Drake got out, we believe he killed an executive in one of the parking lots and took off in the guy's Lotus."

"Well, isn't that a way we can track him?" Jed said. "We know what car he's driving."

Brenham shook his head. "Drake's too smart for that. The car was found abandoned in the same wooded lot where he left the TS-3. No traffic cameras anywhere. He knows what he's doing. He wouldn't have been driving it for more than thirty minutes."

"So, what are you gonna do?"

"I've arranged for a nationwide manhunt with every police department and FBI office in the country. We're trying to avoid public involvement, although the Texas Highway Patrol is alerting Belinda Reese and the Faradays."

Jed rubbed his eyes, clearly fatigued. "Are you sure there's nothing we can do?"

"You can go home, Jed. Take some time to get your life back. I'll call you in when headquarters is back in shape. There'll be a memorial service for the deceased operatives. I have to compose a speech in honor of Elias Wolfe, too. He was a distinguished member of the CIA before he was appointed director of SDT. I'm arranging for a star for him on the Memorial Wall. I'd like you to be there."

"All right. Thank you, sir."

Brenham looked up at Cullen. "You too, Wentworth."

"Yes, sir."

"What are you going to do, Director?" Jed said.

"So much, I don't even know where to begin. I have to contact Dr. Steven McKay, for one."

"Martyn McKay's brother?"

"Yeah. He was the one who instigated the investigation into Treadwell's faction to begin with. Elias Wolfe was working on it when he was murdered."

"All right, sir. If you need us for anything, you know where to find us."

"Thank you, Jed."

Crane and Cullen exited the room, leaving Brenham to his contemplations. He sat back in his chair and his woe returned. *So much death. How could we have screwed up so badly?*

***

Patricia White stepped into her home in McLean, Virginia. At thirty-two, her occupation as a genetics research scientist demanded her working hours were often long, although she rarely noticed. It was more than her profession. It was her passion.

She looked around her comfortable, suburban abode as she had done each day for the last three months. It was so lonely. Her fiancé, Jed Crane, had disappeared eleven weeks earlier. She couldn't understand it. SDT operated from CIA headquarters under the jurisdiction of Jack Brenham, but its personnel were not subject to the same rules of secrecy. If Jed had still been a mainstream CIA agent it would've made more sense, even though she'd have been none the wiser. But as a member of SDT, he was under no obligation to keep his occupation secret from his nearest and dearest.

She'd contacted Jed's director, Wilmot, and he'd promised to look into his disappearance, but nothing had happened. Jed had vanished, and she didn't know if he was dead or alive. The recent news reports and footage of 'an incident for which there was no comment' at CIA headquarters, compounded her disquiet.

She entered the bedroom and discarded her purse on the bed. The sight of the bed had, of late, caused her to become saddened. She'd become aware of how she still slept on her side, even though Jed wasn't with her.

Turning to a mirror on the wall, she noticed the sadness in her eyes. Habits such as makeup and lipstick had fallen by the wayside weeks ago. Her brunette hair was pulled back into bun—the simplest way of not having to concern herself with hairstyling.

She heard a click at the door and turned with a start. "Who's there?"

Footsteps approached from the hallway, and she fearfully backed away.

A tall, scruffy, unshaven man appeared in the bedroom doorway. The fear fell away from her as she processed his face. He looked so different. "Jed?" His name fell from her lips with uncontrollable emotion.

Jed came closer and held her. "Oh, baby. I'm sorry. I'm so sorry." He pulled away slightly and looked into her tear-filled eyes.

"W-what happened? Where have you been?" she said. "I've been going out of my mind. You left one morning in April and just disappeared."

"I had no choice, baby. My life was in danger. I couldn't even contact you because it would have endangered you. But it's all over now. I have so much to tell you, I don't even know where to begin."

"It's all right. You're back, and that's all that matters."

"Look, I really need a shower and a change of clothes. I'm a wreck. After I've got myself cleaned up, I'll tell you the whole story. OK?"

Within an hour, Jed had shaved, showered, and changed. He entered the living room and noticed Patricia's warm eyes gazing at him with undeniable joy. A bottle of champagne and two glasses sat on a glass table before her. Now that he was cleaned up, he knew his appearance would make her feel more at ease. He was himself again.

"I can't tell you how I've longed to see you again," she said. "Just to know you were alive."

"Believe me, babe, you've been in my every thought."

"So, what happened? I need to know, Jed."

"All right. But what I'm about to tell you must go no farther. The president is working on ways of explaining it to the public. I shouldn't even be telling you."

"You have my word."

Jed sat down beside her, opened the champagne, and poured them both a glass. "On the morning I left to go to work, it was just another day at SDT. It had been a long day, and I was working overtime. I had a call from Director Wolfe, and he wanted me to accompany Wilmot, and two others, Kerwin and Rhodes, to Nevada, on an investigation into Brandon Drake."

"Brandon Drake?"

"Yeah. By the next day, I realized something was seriously wrong. Drake and I found ourselves running for our lives."

As Jed continued his extraordinary tale, his mind became filled with thoughts of Drake. He couldn't come to terms with the monster his friend had become. Where was he at that moment? And who would be his next victim?

Forty-Five

The Call

Belinda, Emily, Tyler, Nikki, and Charlton returned to the ranch to discover forensics had left the place in considerable disarray.

"Just great," Charlton said.

"It's not that bad, Dad," Tyler said. "We'll get a cleaning crew in. It shouldn't take more than a couple of days to straighten it out."

"Yeah, you're right." Charlton turned to Belinda and Emily. "How are you ladies coping?"

"Still pretty shaken," Belinda said. "It's good to be home, but it's difficult to get our heads around it all."

"Just take it one day at a time. We're here for you."

She smiled sadly and gave him a hug. "Thank you, Charlton."

"When do you have to talk to the police again?"

"Tomorrow, apparently. It's going to be horrendous. Emily and I have to give detailed statements of what happened to my mom. We may be subpoenaed to give evidence at Brandon's trial. I just don't know how I'm going to cope looking at his face across a courtroom giving evidence against him. I just keep thinking this can't be real."

Charlton looked down thoughtfully. "I'll see if I can pull some strings so you don't have to go through that. Maybe they can set up a live-link in the court, or even take a deposition."

There was a knock at the door. Charlton walked over to answer it. A short, middle-aged woman with a Latin appearance waited in the doorway. "Inez?"

"I came as soon as I heard you were back," she said in a thick, Spanish accent.

"Oh, Inez. I don't expect you to clean all this up by yourself."

"Don't worry, Mr. Faraday. The sooner I get started, the sooner it'll be done."

"Thank you, Inez, but I'm getting a cleaning firm in to help you." Charlton smiled at the loyal, conscientiousness of his cleaning lady of fourteen years. He'd be sure to reward her handsomely.

As she walked past him, he noticed the sheriff's car heading toward the house along the entrance road. *Oh, hell. This is it.* He waited while the sheriff pulled up and climbed out of the car. "Good afternoon, Al."

"Charlton. How's it looking in there?"

"Like we've been robbed."

Al looked at him awkwardly. "I'm sorry about that, Charlton. I really am."

"Don't worry about it. I have everything in order. What can I do for you?"

"Mind if I come in?"

"Sure."

The sheriff followed Charlton inside and closed the door behind him.

Tyler appeared at the end of the corridor. "Hi, Sheriff."

"Hi, Tyler."

"You're not going to interview Belinda and Emily now, are you?" Charlton said. "They're both pretty shaken up."

"No, it's nothing to do with that."

"So what is it?"

The sheriff gestured to the living room. "Can we talk in private?"

Once alone in the living room, Charlton turned to the sheriff with some impatience. "So, what's this all about, Al?"

"Have you seen the news?"

"No, I've been busy moving out of a hotel."

"You haven't heard about the incident at Langley?"

"What incident at Langley?"

"The FBI contacted me. They're on the way over here, and I wanted to give you a heads up. A war broke out at CIA headquarters. I don't know what it was all about, but at the time, Brandon Drake was in custody, and he escaped."

"Are you serious?"

"There's a nationwide APB out on him. They're worried he's going after Ms. Reese after the incident with her mother, and him tracking her to Fort Bragg."

"You're sure about this?"

"I'm only going by what I was told by the FBI. They spoke to the agent who interrogated him, and he was adamant Drake wanted to kill her. They're keeping it out of the press."

Charlton sank onto the couch. "Oh, Jesus. Isn't this ever gonna end?"

Charlton and the sheriff were startled as Tyler walked in with Nikki.

"I'm taking Nikki to the office with me," Tyler said. "I have to finalize the Osborne contract, and then we're going out for dinner tonight."

Concern suddenly came over Charlton at the thought of them going out alone with Drake on the loose. "That's fine, but . . . I was meaning to ask you. I thought you guys were supposed to be recording in L.A."

"We recorded all available tracks, Mr. Faraday," Nikki said. "I need a few weeks to write the rest of the album."

A curious glint appeared in Tyler's eyes. "Why the change of heart, Dad? You weren't exactly a fan of the idea."

"Oh, don't mind me. I was just surprised. I think it's great that you're branching out."

"Good to know, Dad. Catch you later." With that, they left.

"Are you thinking they'll be safer in L.A., Charlton?" Al said.

"Can you blame me?"

"Wait for the FBI to get here. They'll be able to advise you. It'll probably mean you guys have to move out again until they grab him."

"I know."

Belinda walked out of the kitchen as Charlton was showing the sheriff to the door.

"It was good seeing you, Charlton."

"You too, Al."

The sheriff noticed Belinda and shot her a sheepish smile. She didn't reciprocate.

Charlton closed the door and turned to her. "Don't worry. It wasn't about you. I'll be upstairs. I want to see how bad it is up there."

"Sure."

Belinda returned to the kitchen where Emily was making a pot of coffee.

"Is everything OK?" Emily said.

"I'm not sure. The sheriff was just here. Charlton said it wasn't anything to do with us, but I can't get past the funny look the sheriff gave me. Something's wrong. I just know it."

"You've been through hell. We both have. You're probably just a little jittery."

The phone rang in hallway.

"Let Charlton or Inez get it," Emily said.

"You're right. I don't feel like being sociable."

Moments later, the call was answered. Inez's distant response could be heard from the kitchen.

Emily smiled. "See? Want a coffee?"

"Sure."

Inez entered the kitchen. "Ms. Reese?"

"Yes."

"There's a call for you."

"Who is it?"

"He wouldn't say. He just said he wanted to talk to you."

Belinda walked out of the kitchen without a word. *It's got to be the feds.* With trembling fingers, she picked up the phone and put it to her ear. "Hello?"

"I could've killed them all."

Belinda felt her knees buckling and her stomach turned over. *No. It can't be.* "W-why are you doing this?"

"It will all stop if you meet me. If you don't, I'll kill every last damn one of them."

Her mind became numb. He was asking her to sacrifice her own life. It was her life, or the lives of Emily, Tyler, Nikki, Charlton, and whoever might get in his way. She knew it had to end. But it wasn't just her life she'd be sacrificing. It was her baby's life too. *His* baby.

Then she remembered the time he killed her mother. Something happened to him. He'd collapsed and couldn't make a move toward her. She was so certain *her* Brandon was still locked inside him somewhere, and he wouldn't allow The Scorpion to kill her. If she could get him to their special place, perhaps she would have more of a chance of bringing him back. It might cause the memories of their happiness together to return to him. With so many other lives in danger, she had to try. "All right. I know just the place."

"Somewhere remote, where I'll be able to see you haven't come with the police or the FBI. Wherever it is, bitch, I'll be watching it, so don't think you can screw me over."

She shuddered at his words. He sounded nothing like the Brandon Drake she once knew. "You know the place," she said. "*Our* place. It's forty miles from anywhere. You can watch from the ridge and see that I'll be alone in a vast mountain range."

"That cabin place?"

"Yes." She glanced at her watch and calculated the time it would take her to get to Aspen in the Porsche. It would be at least a fifteen hour drive, and it was already 6:00 p.m. "I'll be there by tomorrow morning. I'll drive through the night."

"Done." The call ended.

She touched her jacket pocket and felt for the keys to the Porsche. She hadn't thought to give them back to Tyler.

The front door was ahead of her, and she knew she had to head straight for it. She couldn't even say goodbye to Emily. Nobody could know where she was going. *I have to protect them.*

As quietly as possible, she opened the door and ran to the guest house.

Once inside, she entered her bedroom and rummaged around one of her drawers. Quickly, she found the key to the cabin. Slipping it into her pocket, she ran out again.

She climbed into the Porsche and started the engine. As the tires screeched, she saw Emily running out of the house in the rear view mirror, pleading with her to stop. "I'm so sorry. I love you, Em."

Leaving a cloud of dust across the driveway, she gunned the car forward.

***

Tyler and Nikki arrived home at just past 11:00 p.m. to see the yard filled with FBI vehicles. Tyler's anger rose. "I am so goddamn tired of this. My brother was captured. Isn't that good enough?"

"Just take it easy, baby," Nikki said. "Maybe they just want Belinda and Emily's statements."

"Yeah, maybe." He climbed out of the Ferrari and quickly noticed an empty space. "Where the hell is my Porsche?"

Angrily, he thrust the front door open and saw a crowd of federal agents in the hallway. The incessant mumble of chatter filled the air. Charlton made his way through the crowd to greet them. "What the hell is going on this time, Dad?"

"Tyler, it's serious," Charlton said. "I didn't want to worry you, but yesterday, there was a major incident at Langley. Brandon escaped."

"What?"

"There's more. Belinda had a call earlier this afternoon. She jumped in your Porsche and took off without saying a word to anyone."

Tyler looked at Nikki in horror. "Oh, my God. Do they know who called her?"

"No, but they suspect it was Brandon."

"You think she's gone somewhere to meet him?"

"More than likely."

Tyler made his way through the FBI agents. "Is Emily OK?"

"I'm here," Emily's voice came through the crowd.

He noticed her eyes were swollen, indicating she'd been crying. He quickened his pace toward her and gave her a hug. "Oh, dammit, Sis. Why would she do something like that?"

"We were making coffee and the phone rang. Inez took the call and then came in saying it was someone who wanted to talk to Belinda. She went out to take the call, but I stayed in the kitchen. I thought it might've been private business, and I didn't want to eavesdrop."

"Hey, hey. It's OK. You said Inez took the call initially?"

"Yes. She's over there." Emily pointed across to the corner of the downstairs office through the open door.

Tyler could see Inez was shaken. "Inez? Are you all right?"

"I-I feel so guilty, Mr. Faraday," she said, tearful and quivering.

"But why, Inez?"

"I took the call and passed it on to her. If I hadn't—"

"No, Inez, that's crazy. You haven't done anything wrong. But maybe you can help. What did this person sound like?"

"Like I told the FBI men, he sounded hard. His voice was deep."

Tyler closed his eyes, crushed. *That sounds like Brandon.* "Did you hear anything else? Anything at all?"

"That's what I'm trying to remember. I was cleaning this office when Ms. Reese was on the phone. Her voice was so quiet, I couldn't really make anything out. I wasn't really listening."

"That's all right, Inez. Just keep trying to remember. If there's anything, even a word that comes to mind, you let us know, OK?"

"OK."

It was coming up to midnight. Inez had remained at the ranch, determined to recall anything Belinda might have said. There *was* something, but she couldn't be sure she'd heard it right.

She walked up to the living room and knocked on the open door. Four FBI men sat with Tyler, Nikki, Emily and Charlton.

Charlton looked up as she entered. "Is everything all right, Inez?"

"Mr. Faraday, I think I remember something, but I'm not sure if I heard it right."

Tyler snapped his head toward her. "What, Inez? What did it sound like?"

"Well, what she was saying was very faint, like a distant buzzing sound. But I remember something that sounded like 'rich'."

Tyler looked away, frowning. "Rich? *Rich?* Nah, that can't be right. Anything else, Inez? Any other words with it?"

"Not really. 'From the rich', I think she said."

He shook his head, bewildered. Everybody's eyes were on him. Then he looked up again with sudden realization. "Inez, are you sure the word wasn't *ridge*?"

"It could have been . . . Yes, I think you're right. It could have been *ridge*."

Tyler stood up urgently and turned to the FBI officers. "She's gone to the cabin. Alone."

"What cabin? Can you tell us where it is?" one of the officers said.

"More than that. I can take you there. You're gonna need me."

"Sir, I don't think—"

"I'm going with you. It's not up for debate."

Charlton stepped toward him. "Tyler, just let these men—"

"I'm going with them, Dad."

"So am I," Emily said.

Forty-Six

Redux

Belinda drove at excessive speed through the night, aware she should have been exhausted. But there was no way she could've slept. Her anxiety had reached a pinnacle of intensity, her heart pounded incessantly, and she was plagued by bouts of shivering. She couldn't even contemplate food.

Her mind had been in turmoil for the duration of the journey. She had a good life now, and people she could call a true family for the first time in her life. She didn't want to die. She certainly didn't want her baby to die.

But what other choice did she have? Brandon couldn't be contained. He'd escaped from Leavenworth, the army had captured him again, and the FBI had collected him from Bragg. He still escaped. There was no stopping him. Unless she could bring him back to his former self, he would kill her and her baby, the Faradays, and countless others. It was a no-win situation. If she failed and lost her life, at the very least, he might spare the others. However, the terror wouldn't leave her. She'd sobbed at the wheel until she had no more tears.

At 8:00 a.m. she arrived in Aspen. Having spent so much time living in the cabin, she was relatively familiar with the town and knew where she could rent a snowmobile.

344

She pulled up outside the store of a snowmobile rental place. Her body felt stiff as she climbed out of the Porsche, and it took a few moments for her to adjust.

The transaction was completed within thirty minutes. There was no warmth or levity about her, and she was aware of it. The employee persistently looked at her with concern, but once her identification and credit information had been verified, he provided her with a snowmobile. She suspected it was going to be a freezing ride and bought the necessary protective headwear and insulated clothing.

By 9:00 a.m. her journey from Aspen to the cabin had begun.

Along the thirty-seven mile distance, her instincts felt as though they were trying to pull her back toward the town. At 65 m.p.h., she would reach her destination—and her fate—within thirty minutes. Every second she felt as though she was walking the scaffold to the gallows.

She came to a vast terrain of pure snow with no trees in sight. When they used to cross it in the Turbo Swan, they knew the cabin was close. Once, it filled her with excitement. This time, only dread. A slight incline was approaching. Beyond it she would see her first view of the cabin in the distance.

A minute later, she could see it ahead of her. *Oh, God.* She swallowed hard, and her hand automatically relaxed its grip on the accelerator. *I can't do this. I just can't.*

But she knew she had to. She had no choice.

Terrified, she pulled up outside the cabin and climbed off the snow mobile. Stepping up onto the porch, her hands trembled. She fumbled around her pockets for the key.

She opened the door, relieved it was locked. There was no way Brandon would still have a key to the front door. He wasn't in the cabin. She was sorely tempted to lock the door again but knew she couldn't. He had to have access to her. There was no other way.

Looking around the living room, memories of such happy times came to her. She recalled the first time she'd stepped into the cabin after he'd saved her life.

She looked to the right and saw the rug beside the fireplace, upon which she'd made love to him for the first time. *Oh, Brandon. How could it have come to this?*

She moved over to the rear window, and cast her gaze onto the forest of Aspen trees just beyond the clearing. In the center was Brandon's grave. She recalled the extraordinary event at his funeral when his full-grown pet, a wild bear, appeared through the trees in anguish. It seemed to know Brandon was dead.

But Brandon wasn't dead. Was it his 'death' the bear was mourning? Or a sixth sense of the knowledge of what he'd become? In a very real way, Brandon *had* died that day in Los Angeles. The monster that now walked around with his face wasn't Brandon. It was a distorted, cruel antithesis of who Brandon had been.

The cabin was freezing. There were logs, kindling, newspapers, and matches still sitting beside the fireplace. She moved over to it and proceeded to light the fire.

Finally, she sat in Brandon's leather recliner and awaited her fate.

An hour passed, and she began to feel strangely relaxed. The serenity of the cabin, the flickering of the flames from the log fire, and the beautiful memories gradually enabled her heavy eyelids to close.

A sudden, violent crashing sound drew her out of the first moments of slumber. Startled, she opened her eyes to see him standing in the doorway. The open door was cracked. He'd clearly kicked it in. His clothing was soiled and tattered, and the hood of what remained of his top was across his head. A few days' growth was visible on his face.

Oh, my God. This is it. Cautiously, she stood. "B-Brandon, we can talk."

"We have nothing to talk about, bitch!"

He took something out of his pocket—a small, silver, cylindrical device. Belinda recognized it immediately. She'd seen him use one just like it to cut through a door lock on the night of the Carringby attack. Caught in the grip of terror, she was paralyzed with fear. *This is how I'm going to die. He's going to cut me to shreds with a laser torch.* "L-look around you, Brandon. Please. I beg you. Don't you remember?"

He glanced around the room, but didn't speak or show any reaction.

"Look at the fireplace. The rug," she said imploringly. "We'd saved lives together with one phone call. Remember, Brandon? They were going to blow up Colton Ranch munitions factory. We stopped it. Right afterwards we made love on that same rug."

He gasped and aimed the laser torch toward her, but she could see his hand was shaking.

"No, Brandon. Don't do this. This isn't who you are." Her mind raced trying to find words that might break him down. "Remember Snooky, the little bear cub who used to come to you? You used to feed him out back." She pointed to the side window. "Look out there. That's where you fed him. Where you loved him. When we thought you were dead, he came to your funeral, Brandon. He came because he loved you. I love you. I. Love. You."

She could see pain registering in his eyes, but he seemed to be fighting it. His shaking hand caused his grip on the laser torch to loosen.

"I . . . have to stop . . . you," he growled. "I have . . . to stop . . . *him*."

"Who, Brandon? Who do you have to stop?"

"The . . . Interceptor."

Belinda smiled briefly, but she quickly succumbed to tears. *Oh, Brandon. You're still in there. You're breaking him down.* "We were happy here, Brandon. I know what you went through as a child. David told us both. You were brutalized. That can't have felt good, can it?"

He staggered toward her, barely able to stand. "W-what does that have to do . . . with anything?"

"Everything. The one you call The Interceptor is trying to show you life doesn't have to be that way. You have become the thing you despise the most. The Interceptor is trying to show you peace and happiness. So am I."

"I . . . hate . . . you."

She touched her abdomen, her voice choked. "Do you hate your baby, too? Do you remember Los Angeles, Brandon? Where you saved little children from the monsters in the night? If you kill me, your only child will die."

Drake screamed, and the laser torch fell from his grip. He collapsed onto the floor, gripping his head. Belinda saw the scar in the middle of his forehead deepen and turn a bright shade of red.

In the darkness, The Scorpion danced a ballet of aerial kicks with The Interceptor, but he couldn't land a blow anywhere. Every time his foot would've connected with the helmet, The Interceptor vanished and reappeared behind him. It was always the same and the frustration was more than he could bear. This time, The Interceptor seemed faster and more powerful than ever.

He turned around to where the black-garbed warrior had reappeared and lunged forward. His fists shot out repeatedly with dazzling speed, but none of his punches touched The Interceptor.

"I told you how to do it, Scorp," The Interceptor said. "Just let me take my helmet off."

Drake's rage became so powerful, it exceeded anything he'd ever felt before. "I hate you! Take it off, you fucking coward. Show yourself. Do it. DO IT!"

The Interceptor gripped his helmet and brought it up until it reached his nose. "It's your anger that's letting me do this, Scorp." Bringing it up farther, it finally cleared his head.

Drake gazed upon him for the first time. It was his own face, albeit with longer hair. It almost touched his shoulders. There was compassion-like softness in his eyes. Immediately, Drake found himself struggling to look at him. It was as repellent as trying to look into a bright light.

"This is how I looked when I died, Scorp."

Drake backed away from him, his heart suddenly gripped by fear. "Stay back!"

The Interceptor came toward him. "What's the matter, Scorp? Too much for you? Or is it the hair?"

Drake raised his arms to his eyes to cover the vision, but somehow, he could see right through them.

"I tricked you, Scorp. I knew if you'd let me take the helmet off, you'd be screwed. You wanna know why?"

"Why?"

"Because you can't face *you*. Sure, you've known I was you for quite awhile. But there's knowing it . . . and then there's *seeing* it. Belinda is amazing. She always was."

"Stay away."

The Interceptor reached out his hand into the void. "Look."

Drake turned to where The Interceptor was indicating and images appeared in the darkness. He saw The Interceptor gliding Belinda Reese from the roof of a burning skyscraper, and his van facing a police blockade before exploding. The flying car emerged from the flames. He saw Belinda caressing his face in the cabin and the two of them feeding the little bear cub outside.

The scene shifted to him saving her from two police officers. Then the two of them were safe inside the flying car facing the army and Treadwell.

They were running together out of a TV studio into the streets. He was then in a speeding SUV with David Spicer, racing along Cherry Mountain Canyon. The scene instantly switched to him running with Belinda Reese along the side of a train as the FBI pursued them.

He saw The Interceptor swinging down into a parking bay with Spicer and a unit of troops by his side. They were dispatching a group of Chinese child slavers.

Finally, he saw himself going down in the flying car and it exploding on impact.

"Now, you remember," The Interceptor said. "You can't fight this. This is the *you* the world loves."

Drake became frantic in his attempt to shield his eyes from the visions, but his transparent arms wouldn't allow it. "No," he cried. "Stop it. Stop it. Stop it!"

"You're going down, Scorp." The Interceptor lunged at The Scorpion and gripped him by the throat, forcing him down through the blackness of the void.

However, The Scorpion reached up between The Interceptor's arms and grasped his throat. Together, they continued to descend through the darkness, locked in a moment of Drake's own inner struggle.

Belinda came steadily toward him as he writhed on the cabin floor. "Fight it, Brandon. I know you can hear me, baby."

His face relaxed and the scar on his forehead faded, although the pain in his eyes was still apparent. "B-baby?"

Belinda beamed with joy. "Brandon?"

"Baby, you have to . . . get out of here," he said. "I'm holding him off . . . but I can feel . . . the rage. It's fighting to break through. I . . . don't think I can hold it."

"No, babe. I'm not gonna leave you. You made it back." She threw her arms around him and he returned her embrace.

"I'm so . . . sorry, baby. So sorry for everything . . ." His tears flowed as he broke down in her arms.

"It's not your fault, Brandon. You didn't do anything, baby. It was *him*."

"But . . . I *am* him."

"No. You're not."

He struggled to get to his feet. "I have to get away from you. I can't hold him off forever." He gripped his head again and screamed.

"Brandon!"

With a roar of agony, he ran out the door and headed around the back of the cabin.

Belinda ran out after him, but by the time she reached the clearing, he'd already reached the trees. "Brandon, stop. Please. We won. You and me, baby. We won!"

But he didn't stop. She continued after him as he disappeared into the trees.

Forty-Seven

Tunnel of Light

Tyler sat with Emily and seven FBI agents in a helicopter, flying over the Aspen Mountains. His tension was palpable, and he couldn't help noticing Emily trembling.

The leader of the operation, Agent Clay Jameson, had worked frantically to enable a speedy operation. Procedure had been a considerable impairment.

"What time is it?" Tyler said.

Jameson glanced at his watch. "Just coming up to ten-thirty."

"Dammit! She left just after six yesterday. It's a fifteen hour drive. With the Porsche, more likely thirteen."

"She'd also have needed time to acquire a transport to this cabin, and then the time it would take to reach it."

"So? Let's say she made it in fourteen and a half hours. She's been gone for almost seventeen. Anything could've happened during the remaining two and a half."

Jameson shot Tyler a sympathetic look. "I know how you must be feeling, Mr. Faraday. But it took time to arrange for the personnel, the helicopter, and to gain authorization for you and your sister."

"You couldn't have found this place without us."

"Actually, we could. Your brother's funeral was covered by the press. The location is a matter of public record."

"No, it isn't. The press reported it from Aspen. No reporters came anywhere near the cabin. I'm not saying you couldn't have found it, but it's a vast, mountainous region with no landmarks. It would've been like trying to find a needle in a haystack."

"True," Jameson said. "Well, we can't be far from it now."

Tyler unbuckled his seat belt and edged over to the cockpit. After glancing out the window, he turned back to Jameson. "We're not. The ridge is right ahead."

***

Belinda came to the end of the trees and discovered a hill ahead of her. Looking up, she spotted Brandon halfway to the top. It appeared to be approximately a mile high, but he seemed to be scaling it like a spider.

She was seized with a moment of dread, uncertain she could endure such a climb, especially in her condition. But she had to reach him. He *needed* her. It had a relatively shallow gradient and wasn't as steep as the ridge.

Through labored breathing, she scaled the snow-coated rock, her hands grasping any protruding edge she could find. She dared not look down.

She was reminded of the glide from Carringby Tower to the adjacent skyscraper. The drop had been about five hundred feet. At the time, she'd kept her eyes tightly closed. Her terror had been so extreme she couldn't bear the sight of the chasm. This time, it was different. Her love for Brandon had made her stronger than she'd ever been. At all costs, she had to get to him.

She'd lost track of time halfway to the top. Exhaustion was overcoming her, and she was tormented by doubts that she'd make it. The stress on her body and her baby's health were serious considerations.

She realized she had to get to the top, but the only way was for her to slow down. That created an additional dilemma. She had to reach Brandon as quickly as possible before The Scorpion regained dominance over him.

With excruciating effort, she finally reached the plateau and sank to her knees. She looked up and saw a snowmobile, and then realized where she was. The plain at the top of the ridge continued into the horizon. The end was too far for the eye to see from that vantage point. This must've been where it led.

When she'd suggested the ridge to The Scorpion on the phone, she thought he must have suspected the authorities would be waiting there for him. She looked back and could clearly see the cabin far below. It made perfect sense. From here, he would've been able to see the FBI should they have arrived at the ridge, and watch for her arrival at the cabin.

Looking to her right, she saw him standing on the edge of a precipice. "Brandon!"

He turned slowly. "Baby, you shouldn't be here."

"I'm not going to abandon you, Brandon. I love you."

"I love you too. More than you know," he said with emotion in his tone. "But this is very dangerous for you."

"Why, Brandon? You're back."

"For the moment, but The Scorpion is inside me. I can feel the conflict. The rage is constantly trying to take me over. He could return at any moment."

"Then fight it, Brandon. Fight *him*. I know you can win. Hold on, baby. *Hold on!"*

He shook his head with a look of hopelessness. "It's taking everything I've got, babe. What if I'm sleeping and I have no conscious control? I could go to sleep as me and wake up as *him*."

"We'll get help for you."

"There is no help, sweetheart. The only man who could've helped me is dead. I—*The Scorpion*—killed him." He turned back to look over the edge.

It suddenly dawned on Belinda what he was planning, and horror filled her heart. "No, Brandon, I'm begging you. Don't do this."

"This isn't a suicide. This is an execution. I'm doing this for you and the countless innocents The Scorpion might kill. I can't control this. You have to believe me, there's no other way."

She came closer to him, unable to stop her tears. "Brandon, there has to be another way."

He looked around again and his gaze shot beyond her. She turned to see what he was looking at. A helicopter was approaching.

"That's the FBI, babe. I'd know it anywhere," he said.

"Oh, my God, no!" Belinda yelled. "Not now. We're so close." She waved her hands for them to back away, but it continued toward them.

She turned back to Brandon. For some reason, he was removing his hooded top and checked shirt. Then she saw the astonishing, futuristic armored vest plate underneath.

He reached into his jeans and took out a small, black, thumb-sized device. "Looks like the son of a bitch picked up the key from somewhere." He attached it to a point at the side of the armor and pressed a sensor on top of the key. The magnetic seal on the armor was cancelled and it fell from his body. He wrapped his arms around his bare chest, warming himself against the freezing cold.

"Please, Brandon," she cried.

"Baby, they're going to kill me anyway for The Scorpion's atrocities. I'll get the death penalty." He looked away and chuckled lightly.

"What's so funny?"

"It's something The Scorpion said once. It's probably the only thing I agree with him on."

"What's that?"

"*Nobody takes me down but me.*"

She quickened her pace toward him in the grip of desperation. "Brandon, please. Don't do this. Don't die."

A look of peace came across his face, and he smiled the most loving smile she'd ever seen. He gestured to her protruding abdomen with an inexplicably confident serenity. "I'm not gonna die."

Reaching out both arms, he closed his eyes, and leaned back over the precipice.

"Brandon, no!" She ran to the edge, but she was too late. She reached out for him hopelessly, keeping her gaze on his as he descended. "No!"

She was startled as a familiar sound filled the air. Once again, the mournful cry of the bear echoed across the canyon.

Tyler looked on through the window horrified as the helicopter landed. "Oh, God, no!"

Emily got out of her seat and moved over to where Tyler was looking. "What happened?"

"He's gone. Brandon jumped." He saw her tears welling up, and a sinking feeling gripped his stomach.

"Is Belinda OK?" Emily said.

"She looks fine to me."

"That means he didn't hurt her. If he took his own life rather than hers, it can only mean his other self returned. I can feel it."

Tyler took Emily in his arms as the helicopter door opened. He glanced behind him to see Jameson and the men preparing to get off.

"We have to go," Emily said. "Belinda needs us."

"You're right."

Tyler and Emily joined the agents and stepped down onto the snow.

***

The Interceptor remained in a mutual throat lock with The Scorpion as they sank through the void.

And then suddenly, The Scorpion vanished. The Interceptor glanced, bewildered, at his empty hands.

He stopped sinking and stood, confused. He looked around the darkness, but there was nothing.

And then, a brilliance filled the void. He turned to it, but despite its brightness, it was easy to gaze upon. It was irresistible. It rapidly took shape and became a tunnel of light. He stepped toward it, drawn to its inimitable magnificence.

Images—scenes from his life—flashed before him at the end of the tunnel. *Both lives*. It seemed so strange to him. He saw his own life, his mother Annabelle, his father, Major Howard Drake, and his malevolent grandfather. He saw Belinda and Tyler and scenes of their countless escapades.

Running simultaneously, he saw The Scorpion's life. He watched, fascinated, as the horror of his natural father stabbing his mother to death before hanging himself, played out before him. He witnessed the cruelty he'd endured at the hands of Joe Cassidy, his arrests, court appearances, and the battles he'd fought with the Eighty-Second Airborne Division.

The visions of his duel lives continued right up to the scene at the mountaintop and him throwing himself off. It all seemed so long ago now.

But the visions didn't stop there . . .

His parallel life scenes merged into one. He saw a young boy with blond hair and kind eyes. Instinctively, he knew it was his son.

He watched as the boy grew into a young man. He seemed to be wearing the armor from the hologram at Mach Industries, and he was helping people. There was a beautiful young blonde woman and an earthquake. The young man was trying to get her to safety while wearing the armor. Then he was flying into what looked like a volcano trying to retrieve something. The technology The Interceptor was seeing seemed so unbelievable it filled him with awe.

Seeing his son's life before him made no sense, and yet it felt so right. He *knew* it. "I love you, Son," he whispered. "I am so proud of you. Be what I never had the chance to be."

The light suddenly disappeared and he found himself inside some kind of a technological complex. Intrigued, he walked toward a window with the stars of the night sky beyond. He braced his palms against the glass and gazed into the cosmos. Looking to his right, he realized it wasn't the night sky he was looking at. The Planet Earth was below him.

Then he understood. He wasn't really there. He was seeing through his son's eyes. This was a scene from *his* life. He couldn't imagine the circumstances under which his son could find himself in such an extraordinary place. Nevertheless, he gazed longingly at the vision of the earth.

He felt a dark veil falling upon him, but it didn't seem to matter. He smiled his last, knowing that somehow, some way—he would find his way home.

Epilogue

Nine years later

May 14th, 2025

Belinda tapped her foot impatiently on a tile while sitting outside the principal's office at the school her son attended in Dallas. What did he want to see her about?

As she waited, she occupied her mind thinking about what had happened through the years to bring her to this point. The memories: the ones she wanted to remember, and the ones she couldn't forget. The friends and enemies.

She smiled when she thought about how important Jed Crane once was in the lives of those she loved, and how he'd virtually saved the CIA.

Sadly, Charlton Faraday passed away in 2023, leaving Tyler in control of the Faraday Corporation. Supported by many company directors, the corporation thrived. However, Tyler's grief over his father's death, and Nikki being on tour much of the time, eventually took its toll on their relationship. After seven years, they finally parted. A year passed before Tyler returned to his former, highly-motivated self. Belinda encouraged B.J., as Brandon, Jr. came to be called, to spend as much time with his uncle as possible. Not only did it help Ty, it gave her son the father-figure he needed.

Emily was in a relationship of sorts with Jake, the guy she'd met at the shelter. He'd gotten a job as a software engineer. They appeared to be in love, but Belinda knew Em wasn't quite ready to make a lasting commitment. For the time being, Emily, Belinda, and B.J. lived at Faraday Ranch. She didn't expect that to change as long as Tyler welcomed them.

A month ago, David Spicer came back into her life. He asked her out and she'd accepted. Her first instinct had been to decline, but eventually she realized she had to get on with her life. She had enormous regard for David. He'd been kind to her in the past, and had participated in rescuing her from a psychopath. His relationship with Rachel ultimately faded after he retired from the service in 2021 to become a semi-pro golfer. He'd chosen the peaceful life after two decades on the battlefield. She almost laughed out loud thinking about the day he'd knocked on the door and handed her five hundred dollars, asking her to give it to her son. "I owed it to Brandon from a poker game, and now I want to pay it back. I want B. J. to have it."

She came back to the present as her name was called and was soon sitting with the principal in his office.

"Well, Ms. Reese. You should be very proud," Principal Doug Hinckley said. "Brandon is top of most of his classes. It's really remarkable, although he struggles with math. But in all other subjects, nobody can touch him. He's extraordinarily creative."

Belinda flicked a strand of her dyed-blonde hair from her eyes. "I sucked at math too. I don't really think it's much of an issue."

"Ms. Reese, we suspect Brandon is a potential genius. Have you ever considered having him tested for his IQ?"

"No, I haven't, and I don't care about that. I just want him to be happy."

"I understand, but he has such potential. I'd like to suggest that you consider allowing him to attend classes that are more challenging."

"That seems reasonable, but I am more interested in how he interacts with the other pupils."

Hinckley smiled with utmost professionalism. "Ms. Reese, Brandon is extremely popular. The other pupils gravitate toward him because of his father. They all read comic books, and to them, he's the son of *The Interceptor*."

Belinda looked away, deep in thought. Brandon, Jr. bore such a striking resemblance to his father. It often crossed her mind that he might have been more than *just* his son. She couldn't forget the look of confidence and peace in Brandon's eyes on the mountaintop. He seemed fearless, as though somehow, he knew he would return. But return as whom, or what?

Or was her mind playing tricks on her? The first time she'd believed Brandon was dead, when the SUV exploded, her belief was based on her own misapprehension. The second time, when the Turbo Swan crashed, it was a faked death set up by Wilmot. She questioned whether something about all of it had affected her perception. Had it led her to think the idea of Brandon dying wasn't possible? *Stop it, Belinda. That's ridiculous.*

***

Heather Addison nervously walked across the school playground with a backpack containing her books and lunch box. Her unkempt, golden blonde hair and pre-used clothing suggested poverty. At eight years old, a wallflower, and not particularly popular, she was terribly shy. Coming from a poor family, she suffered at the hands of bullies with their cruel jibes.

She sat down on a bench and watched as the children played with one another, running and frolicking across the yard. It was the end of the day, and they were all waiting for their parents to collect them. She felt so distant, as though it was a world in which she had no place.

She felt her backpack being snatched from her. "Hey!" She looked up and saw three older boys standing over her. The biggest held her backpack, smiling cruelly. "Give it back," she said.

The boy laughed. "How much will you pay me? Oh, I forgot. Poor little Heather hasn't got any money."

Heather stood, but the boy held her backpack out of her reach. He threw it to one of the other boys. Heather reached for it again, but the boy threw it to the other.

Suddenly, a shadow fell upon them. "Give it back to her."

Heather looked past them to see a familiar eight-year-old boy standing behind them. His blond hair and dazzling green eyes gave him an almost-angelic appearance.

"Beat it, Drake, this don't concern you," the bigger boy said.

The blond boy stepped toward them slowly with an avenging look in his eyes. "I said . . . give it back to her."

Belinda came down the school steps, her mind filled with thoughts. As she came to the bottom, she looked to her left and saw a crowd of children huddled around a spot close to the playground bench. Curiously, she walked forward.

She made her way through the crowd of children and saw three boys on the ground, unconscious. She caught the eye of a little girl. "What happened?"

"They were picking on Heather, Ms. Reese, but B.J. stopped them."

Oh, my God, no. "W-where is he?"

The little girl pointed to the entrance gate with an excited look on her face. "B.J.'s the coolest."

Belinda looked across in the direction the little girl had indicated. Her son was walking hand-in-hand with Heather toward the main gate.

She was instantly reminded of the fateful night eleven years earlier, when his father had rescued her from the roof of a burning skyscraper. Tears rolled down her cheeks as her fear that he may have some of The Scorpion in him instantly vanished. Her son wasn't The Scorpion at all. He was a rescuer.

Her enduring question returned. Who would his father have been had he not been abused as a child, and hadn't been brainwashed with a series of false memories? She'd never known *who* was at his natural core. Nobody had. Perhaps Brandon, Jr. was the answer.

She wanted B.J. to have his own identity, but she couldn't forget Brandon's words to her, moments before he threw himself off the mountaintop: *I'm not gonna die.* It was the reason she'd named her son after him.

But who was her son? Who would he become? So far, he seemed to have much in common with The Interceptor, but he was only eight. His persona would take time to develop.

She knew the answer wouldn't be revealed today. But maybe, just maybe . . . *tomorrow.*

Hold On!

Tomorrow

The year is 2042. Twenty-six-years after the events in the *Hold On! Trilogy*, devastating earthquakes and tsunamis are striking in the most unlikely locations. Scientists have no explanation for the phenomenon.

Brandon Drake, Jr., (B.J.) a rookie, government agent, courageously 'borrows' the INT-Nine, an advanced prototype suit of armor in order to rescue his childhood sweetheart, Heather Addison. Their lives change forever as B.J. becomes the new Interceptor. However, tragedy strikes when the armor fails during a rescue.

While the world adores him, B.J is forced to become a fugitive when Congress orders Project: Interceptor closed down. His life is complicated further by his mother's belief that he isn't just his father's son – but his father *reborn*.

With The Interceptor on the run, new bonds are made and new heroes arise. In order to save the world from annihilation, they must join forces to discover the meaning of the mysterious abbreviation – C.O.T.

A stand-alone *Hold On!* event.

About the Author

Peter Darley (P.D. to his friends) is a British novelist, whose professional history is in showbusiness. He is a graduate of the Birmingham School of Speech and Dramatic Art, and he studied television drama at the Royal Academy of Dramatic Art (RADA.) His television credits include guest-starring roles is UK productions such as BBC's *Crime Ltd, Stanley's Dragon* for ITV*, The Bill*, and Sky One's *Dream Team*, and numerous TV commercials. He has also worked as a model, presenter, and voice-over artiste for ten years, and has acted as an agent for several variety acts.

His lifelong admiration of heroes, and love of roller-coaster-style thrills have been a huge influence on his writings.

He is professional close-up magician, a keen athlete and body builder, and lives with his wife in rural England.

Made in the USA
Charleston, SC
15 December 2016